The Vengeance of The Invisible Man

by
Robin Bailes

The Universal Library Books

1 – The Mummy's Quest

2 – The Werewolf of Priory Grange

3 – The Vengeance of the Invisible Man

4 – The Immortal Dracula

Prologue – One Night in Cambridge

It was late evening, and Pembroke Street was as deserted as a street has a right to be when the weather has all the bite of late November but none of the festive cheer of the following month. The rain, cold as ice and threatening to turn to sleet at any moment, was whipped up by the sharp wind that howled along the avenue of college buildings, streaking the windows and driving residents, students and even the hardiest of drunks indoors.

But Pembroke Street was not completely devoid of life.

A shadow passed through the light of a street lamp that struggled against the sheeting rain. Through the worst that the elements could hurl, a single figure plodded, hunched against the cold, bowed against the gale, hands thrust deep into the warmth of their pockets. The figure wore a long coat that flapped in the wind and slapped wetly against their legs; a woolly hat, pulled down low, soaked and plastered to their scalp; and, behind the coat's raised collar, a thick scarf, wrapped from neck to eyes.

Buried beneath these practical precautions it was impossible to say if the figure was young or old, male or female, fat or thin or something in between. They were simply an anonymous, androgynous figure, tramping through the heart of Cambridge's university district on a night when no one ventured out unless they had a very good reason for doing so.

Turning right onto the narrow, isolated Tennis Court Road, the figure walked a little further then stopped to look up, shivering as freezing rain trickled into previously inaccessible chinks in the armour of their clothing. Above them, a golden light shone from a row of windows in the Hopkins Building. Even through the roar of rain and wind, it was just possible to make out the faint strains of music, the tinkle of polite laughter and the hum of erudite conversation. A party was in progress. Probably a Christmas party. It was early for Christmas parties but Cambridge University believed in making the most of the season, and there were so many parties to get through (faculty parties, college parties, staff parties, departmental parties) that it was important to start early or you

4

wouldn't get them all in. A Cambridge don who reached Christmas without having already eaten his bodyweight in turkey was considered a bit of a social pariah.

The bundled-up figure stood staring up at the windows for a long minute as the wind whirled the rain about them in a tight vortex. Finally, they stepped into the comparative shelter of a doorway, observed only by a sodden pigeon, hunched for shelter in a nearby tree.

Then the figure did something which, considering the weather, was really quite remarkable. They began to take off their clothes.

Professor Herbert Digges had lived in Cambridge since he had been a student at the University. That had been a certain number of years ago, which was ironic as he preferred to be uncertain about how many (a witticism he always rolled out at parties like this one).

He had been to his share of these affairs and he enjoyed them as much as it was possible to enjoy spending the evening in the company of the same people with whom you spent your days. This particular party was, in a sense, his. He hadn't done anything to organise it, but it took place in his department (the Biochemistry Department), which meant that he could make regular forays down the hall and up the stairs to his 'nook', which was how he referred to his office.

The Hopkins Building had only a few characterful rooms like this, tucked away in its architecture like lint in the corner of a pocket, and you had to hang around the upper echelons of Cambridge University scholarship a longish while to wangle yourself one. Herbert Digges was a world class 'hang-arounder', and he had patiently waited for time or career-ending scandal to clear his path. In fact, 'office' was barely the right word for the cosy little room lodged under roof. It was lined with books (some of which, Digges had to confess, had come with the room) and an open fire burnt in the grate, framed by an ornamental surround and boasting a comfy club fender, around which students sat to grill toast when Digges held study groups. That was what his professors had done when he was but a lad at this university, and Cambridge was keen on

5

tradition. The leather swivel chair behind the desk had been there as long as anyone could remember and might as well have grown up from a seed planted in the rug-strewn floor. The rooms of many Cambridge professors gave that impression of having been cultivated rather than decorated, like a jungle that sprouted books instead of fruit, and flourished in a nourishing atmosphere of heady academia and choking pipe smoke.

It was to this womb-like retreat that Herbert Digges now made his way, because while the brandy at the party was excellent, the bottle he kept stashed in a false copy of H. G. Wells' *The Food of the Gods and How It Came to Earth* was exceptional. He nodded to the porter on the door (Peter? Possibly Luke), who was ensuring that inquisitive guests did not leave the function room to peer into the *sanctum sanctorums* beyond. At the end of the corridor he turned left to ascend the wooden staircase which sang a familiar melody of creaks and squeaks beneath his feet. At the top, he paused to catch his breath – not as young as he was – before locating the key hanging from a chain that passed through the button of his waistcoat.

Cambridge University has a certain old-fashioned reputation of insular academic fustiness that does not, in the main, reflect an institution that takes pains to admit students from around the world and from all walks of life, and one that tries hard to be at the cutting edge of research in every area. But it was also University policy (unofficially) to keep a few anachronistic clichés about the place just to lend the right tone, and this was a role that Herbert Digges was happy to fulfil.

Entering the room and closing the door behind him, he stopped, as he usually did, to glance in the mirror and tug at his grey beard. Not bad. A little flushed with drink, but all in all, not bad for a man of his years.

He went to the bookshelf in which the bottle was secreted. This was the room to which he had brought his wife when they were courting; the room in which he had conducted a clandestine affair with one of her friends; and the room in which that affair had become suddenly and expensively a lot less clandestine when his wife walked in.

6

So many memories.

Professor Digges poured a glass of brandy and seated himself in the dented chair. It had taken several years to make the dents fit his own frame as they had been previously moulded to the ample rump of Professor Conrad, who had preceded him. After he was dead, Digges was sure that another pair of buttocks would go about reshaping the contoured leather. He hoped that his imprint would last longer than Conrad's.

The desk was another antique, passed from occupant to occupant, though this one had started to show signs of its age and a professional restorer had been hired. Because the desk was too large to go out the door (Digges sometimes wondered how it had come in, in the first place) the man came during the day, and there were some signs of his presence; sawdust on the rug, the intrusive scent of manual labour in the air, and piles of Digges' papers on the floor, carefully organised there until the desk was again load-bearing.

From one of these piles, Digges picked up a notebook and idly leafed through to where he had left off. He sipped his brandy as he pondered the problem sketched out on the last page. It would be risky, but it might be worth the risk.

He sat up suddenly as he heard a noise. The creaking of his staircase, playing its tune at a reduced volume and tempo that suggested someone creeping. Perhaps a mischievous student, planning some practical jape, had bypassed Peter (or Luke? Perhaps John. It was definitely Biblical).

Tossing the notebook onto his desk, Digges rose and made his way to the door with a speed and fluidity that defied his years (Cambridge professors tend to age well; they stay out of draughts).

"Hah!" He flung the door wide to confront the miscreant.

But the stairway was empty.

Digges hurried down the stairs to scan the corridor.

Nothing but Peter (or Paul?), standing by the door at the far end.

It was not impossible that the owner of the creeping footsteps had ducked into one of the other rooms that lined the corridor, but surely he would have heard that?

7

A mystery. But Herbert Digges had no real inclination to investigate. He made his way back up the stairs to his room, and closed the door behind him before returning to his seat.

"Good evening, Professor Digges."

The voice made Digges jump, spinning his chair around to where it had come from.

But there was no one there. It was not a large room but it was cluttered enough that hiding was possible, and Herbert Digges began to look behind curtains, in corners and under the couch (which had played a prominent role in the end of his marriage).

"You're looking in the wrong place, Professor." The voice came from directly behind him. "I'm right here."

Digges spun around. "Where?"

"Here."

A pair of hands closed around Digges' throat, fingers tightening viciously, digging into the loose skin of his neck. He could feel two thumbs pressing hard into his Adam's apple, crushing his windpipe.

And yet there was still no one in front of him. He was alone in the room.

If he had been able to say anything then he might have asked something cliché like '*Who are you?*', but as the world around him turned red before fading to black, Professor Digges realised that he recognised the voice. And there was, anyway, only one person it could be.

If anyone had asked Professor Herbert Digges where he would like to die, then he would have unhesitatingly picked his nook, that little corner that had, over long years come to resemble the inside of the professor's own head. When his body was found there later that night, some hoped that dying here had provided some small solace in his final moments. But the look on his face suggested otherwise.

Chapter 1 – A Message From Zita

The train from London King's Cross got into Cambridge station, platform 1, in early afternoon and Amelia Evans took a deep breath as she stepped off. Cambridge air tasted different and no one would ever convince her otherwise. It wasn't that she hadn't enjoyed the interesting places in which she had spent the last six months, but coming home was still special. She felt physically lighter, as if she was floating a foot above the ground as she walked.

Amelia had been out of town since summer, popping back from Egypt for a single night to pick up some supplies before heading on to Romania, and to an archaeological dig in the Carpathian mountains. That brief pit-stop didn't really count, and even if it did this remained the longest Amelia had been away from Cambridge since she had moved here.

With a grunt of effort she shouldered the bag that had been growing steadily heavier all the way across Europe, and made her way out of the station and along Station Road. A gap in the traffic allowed her to dart across Hills Road and she turned left onto Bateman Street, noticing as she went that the sign had been vandalised into Batman Street by some student who thought they were a) hilarious, and b) the first to do it (they were wrong on both counts).

A cold November drizzle had sprung up as she walked, but even that and the threatening clouds could not dampen Amelia's affection for this place or the thrill she felt at being back home. Cutting into the labyrinthine mess of streets – as if someone had dropped a small village between Hills Road and Trumpington Road – Amelia let her feet go onto auto-pilot while she marvelled at the familiar. It was all still here. Of course it was; she hadn't really been gone that long. Then again, a lot could happen in a short time; she had done battle with an Ancient Egyptian Queen. But that was another story (literally), and she was finding that coming home could be as exciting as leaving it.

As with everything else, the house in which she occupied the second-floor front flat, was still there, and had not been burnt down or demolished while her back was turned. Her key still fitted in the lock, the stairs behind the door looked and smelled the same, the doormat still needed replacing.

Entering her flat and dumping her bags gratefully to the floor, she took in the old place. It was as she had left it, because, once again, she hadn't been gone that long. The pile of notebooks filled with her messy scrawl still sat beside her chair, as did the library book on which she would now have to pay a pretty hefty fee. There was even food in the cupboards, although it was probably no longer edible.

When the need to go to Egypt had arisen, she had left in a hurry and had never imagined it would be this long before she was back. The place had an oddly *Marie Celeste* vibe to it – abandoned on the instant.

She looked out of the window and smiled on the familiar view, then glanced down at the phone, which was flashing with stored messages, most of which would probably be irrelevant and none of which she could face now.

The second-hand sofa she loved looked very inviting, and she wanted nothing more than to collapse onto it. But once she did that, further activity would cease to be an option for the day, and she had to go shopping if she wanted to eat later.

"Okay…"

A quick shower later (colder than she would have liked) and with fresh clothes on, Amelia headed into town via Trumpington Street. She could not help smiling as she passed the impressive edifice of the Fitzwilliam Museum on her left. That was where all this had started, for better and worse – and there had been plenty of both. That was where her life had changed, perhaps forever.

She turned right onto Bene't Street, grumbling under her breath at the assembled tourists who, even in this cold weather and out of the tourist season, insisted on gathering to gawp at the ridiculous Corpus Clock, blocking the pavement completely. It was the mark of a proper Cambridge resident that you reserved a virulent hatred for these people. She crossed Market Square, enjoying the sights and sounds of another of her favourite places, then on down

Sidney Street to the cramped supermarket that had been forced in to fill a gap in the market whether there was room for it or not. She bought as much as she felt physically capable of carrying back, staples mostly; bread, milk, cheese, fruit, cereal, baked beans, crisps, chocolate – things without which a person cannot survive. Most importantly, she bought tea.

There was, Amelia had discovered, no tradition of tea-drinking in Romania, or at least not tea as an Englishwoman would understand it. The drink had apparently made up some ground in recent years due to tourism, to the extent that in cities you could get hold of it, but in the mountains people just stared at you blank-faced. Amelia had suggested having tea transported in bulk to the archaeological site where she was working from the nearest civilised town ('civilisation' in Amelia's mind was defined by the proximity of a proper cup of tea), but site manager Maggie Moran had in turn suggested transporting Amelia back home. It was possible that no one outside of a desert had missed a beverage as much as Amelia had missed tea.

Back in her kitchen, Amelia placed the kettle on the hob then put her shopping away, dropping a teabag into her Paddington Bear teapot. The kettle whistled, she poured the boiling water into the pot and put a hedgehog-shaped cosy over it. The smell was actually making her tremble with anticipation. Addiction is a terrible thing.

Still, she would not rush things. The pot found its home on the coffee table by the sofa and was quickly joined by a cup and saucer (milk already in – a debate she was not willing to enter into). She went to the phone, scrolled through the options and began to '*Play Messages*' as, with shaking hands, she poured herself a cup. She sipped and sighed. If crack was half this good then no wonder people had trouble quitting.

Lying down full length on the sofa, Amelia sipped her tea, deleting pointless messages as she went.

"Amelia?" A familiar voice snapped down the phone in a staccato style that Amelia had come to know well over the last few months. "Maggie. You back? You back? You back? Pick up if you're back. I guess you're not back. Just called to say; looks like you were right. Things are shutting down here. People heading home. Not sure if it's Christmas or the weather. Probably the weather. Snow over everything. Gotta dig up the dig before we can dig it. So at least you won't miss anything much. Speak soon."

Amelia made a mental note to call the site manager who had shared her Egyptian adventure, and whom she had come to respect and like as they had worked together in the Carpathians.

"Hi Amy." Amelia stiffened. Only one person in the world called her Amy. "Mum said you were back – or possibly that you were coming back (I forget which) but either way give me a call, I'm going to be in your area in a day or so – work thing – and I thought we could catch up on all you've been doing, gallivanting around the world like a bad-ass, I'm so jealous, I haven't had a holiday in forever, not since that guy – you know the one – and that was barely a holiday, we didn't leave the hotel. Call me, call me, call me."

Amelia drained her cup and refilled it, hoping that tea would restore that mellow attitude which messages from her younger sister invariably eroded.

Amelia and Zita had little in common beyond the usual genetic prerequisites. Ancient Egyptian culture, which had for some years been the major part of Amelia's life, bored Zita to tears. Amelia was a gifted linguist, specialising in ancient languages, while Zita's GCSE French teacher had begged her never to visit the country for fear she might unwittingly cause an international incident. Zita was an outgoing, easy-going, party-going social butterfly while her sister preferred to curl up at home with a book, and had on occasion faked illness to avoid the sort of event in which Zita revelled. None of which was to say that Amelia did not love her sister; she loved her very much. It was just that they struggled to find enough crossover to make a conversation last longer than a cup of tea.

It was also important to note that Zita was not a screw-up, just because she had taken a different career path to that of her sister. One thing the pair did share was a love of books, and Zita had gone into publishing as a promoter. She now lived in a minimalist London flat with a fast-moving carousel of men, whom she insisted on referring to as 'lovers' rather than boyfriends.

Amelia finished her second cup of tea and called her sister.

The call went to voicemail. "Hi Zita, it's me. I just got back a few hours ago. If you're in town then definitely give me a shout and we can catch up." She paused. "And obviously if you need somewhere to crash then let me know. Bye."

Truth be told, Amelia had only made that offer because Zita had said this was a work trip and she worked for a successful company that could afford a decent hotel room.

This done, Amelia washed up the tea things and went downstairs to pick up her mail from Dr Bassermann, who had been kind enough to collect it rather than leaving it lying on the hall rug for months.

"Welcome back!" Like so many who lived in this area of town, Dr Bassermann was connected to the University, but Amelia was ashamed to say that she had never grasped in what capacity. Amelia did not really get to know her neighbours, and would not have got to know Dr Bassermann (whose first name was also a matter of mere conjecture), had the Doctor not made the first move.

"Thanks."

"How was the trip?"

"Good," replied Amelia. "The weather turned – we're up in the mountains – so I decided to come home early for Christmas."

"You must tell me about it. Would you like a cup of tea?"

"I just had two."

"Is that a yes or a no?"

Over a cup of herbal tea – not Amelia's preferred drink, but it would do – Dr Bassermann asked a battery of questions about the trip and Amelia did her best to field answers where she could.

"I copied down a lot of the text from the tomb to see if I can make some headway deciphering it before the New Year."

Dr Bassermann tutted. "That's no way to spend Christmas."

"I'll spend Christmas itself with family," Amelia shrugged.

"Still on your own?"

Amelia focussed on her tea. She would have preferred for no one to know of the unpleasant end to her relationship with Frank Jenson, but someone living just downstairs was bound to have heard things.

"I've been busy."

Dr Bassermann nodded, polite enough not to press the point. "Well, the dig sounds exciting."

"Very."

It was. Pictographic writing of this sort had never been found in this part of the world before, which meant that Amelia's skills were valuable in a place where she had never expected to find herself working. Her previous field of research had come to an abrupt end and this new opportunity had been a Godsend as well as a thrilling new chapter.

And yet…

For whatever reason, Amelia was struggling to maintain her enthusiasm. In Egypt her life had taken an exciting and unexpected turn. Also a very dangerous one, and she definitely had not wanted to follow that path any further.

And yet…

She was enjoying herself but she felt as if something was missing, and she wasn't sure if it was something from work or from life or from inside her somehow. The worsening weather in the Carpathians had given her the excuse she needed to bail on the dig and go home for a bit to see how she felt there.

"There's been some excitement here too," Dr Bassermann went on.

"Yes?"

Dr Bassermann reached for a newspaper lying on the sofa. It was just the local paper and headlines were usually along the lines of 'New Road Planned', 'Bike Stolen', or 'Local Dog is Jerk', so when something of genuine interest happened, the paper lapped it up: 'Professor Murdered! Police Baffled!'.

"When did this happen?"

"Just last night."

When she got back to her flat, Amelia found the phone ringing and she answered quickly.

"Hello?"

"Amy!" It wasn't that Zita Evans was loud, but her voice was

14

so filled with energy that it seemed to bounce around inside your head like a squash ball. Long conversations with her sister always left Amelia feeling lightheaded.

"Hi Zi. How you doing?"

"Goodgoodgoodgoodgood. You? How was Egypt?"

"Romania," corrected Amelia.

"Yeah but I haven't spoken to you since Egypt."

"Really?" Amelia felt a pang of guilt. She had dropped the odd email to keep Zita up to date with where she was, but she hadn't realised it had been that long since they had spoken.

"Egypt was amazing." That was true. It skirted around the whole 'walking mummies, resurrected witch Queens and armies of the living dead' aspect of the trip, but no one could dispute amazing. Amelia had been sworn to secrecy by a man named Boris (just Boris), a representative of a shadowy organisation called Universal, whose mandate seemed to have less to do with Egyptology and more to do with keeping the world safe from the dead who refused to stay that way.

"Coolcoolcool. And Romania? I've never been to Romania, never even thought about going there really, not altogether sure I could point to it on a map."

"I'll point it out when you visit."

"But how was it?"

"Good." How would it be if she went back in the New Year? Amelia didn't want to drop out from the dig but that vague sense of dissatisfaction niggled at her. "Not as amazing as Egypt, but some of the stuff we're finding is pretty incredible. Archaeologically speaking. We could rewrite the history of Eastern European civilisation."

"That sounds pretty exciting."

It did, didn't it? Amelia wondered again what the hell her problem was.

"You should write a book," Zita went on. "I could publish it."

Amelia demurred. "I don't think I'm the right person to do that."

"Then who is? You're an expert in your field. Who better?

15

Who else? You're always holding yourself back, putting yourself down when you should be putting yourself out there, and you do it personally as well, Amy."

One of the things that consistently irritated Amelia about her sister was what a good handle Zita had on her. She changed the subject.

"So you're coming to Cambridge?"

"That's the plan, that's the plan, day after tomorrow – work; you know?"

"Well we should definitely catch up."

"For sure, for sure, for sure; let's do lunch, or dinner, or tea. But, Amy, I was wondering if you could do me a favour too?"

Amelia stiffened and wondered if her offer of a place to sleep was about to come back and bite her on the backside. "Of course. If I can."

"If I email you the manuscript of a book, could you give it a read before I arrive? I mean like skim through – it's not long."

"Okay." Amelia was happy enough to read virtually any book, but Zita did not usually involve her sister in her work. "Am I looking for something in particular?"

"Yeah. No. Not particularly. Just give it a read and…" Zita paused (which was a rarity). "We got this book sent in direct – hard copy, no agent. Normally it wouldn't have gotten read but it was lying around and someone had a flick and said, you gotta read this and everyone who read it was like; yeah, want a piece of this. Not that it's particularly well-written, you know, but the idea, the concept, it's original and imaginative, maybe got that X-factor that everyone's always looking for. Anyway, we've been through the edit and we're having the launch event in Cambridge on the 1st (the writer's from Cambridge – did I mention that? That the writer's from Cambridge? Well he's from Cambridge.) so I'm coming in to meet him and co-ordinate this launch at some bookshop and it's just…" She tapered off.

"You don't like him?" suggested Amelia.

"I haven't met him," replied Zita. "I've spoken to him on the phone a couple of times, but he calls us – never the other way around. We've got no number, he doesn't seem to email and all his mail goes via one of the colleges or something. I don't know what he looks like – Amy; I don't even know his name."

"You don't know his name?"

"He uses a pen name. Kind of. You'll get it when you look at the book, it sort of goes with the whole – what's the word – 'concept'. And from my point of view in promotions (did I tell you I've been made head of promotions? No? Well I have. New office, big raise, all good). From my point of view it's all good, gonna make it a lot easier to sell and to market, but at this point I'm going to meet a guy I don't know and I'm a little weirded out and I'd just like your take on the book."

For Zita to ask for Amelia's take on anything was almost unprecedented.

"Of course. Send it over."

"Will do, thanks. We had to digitise it ourselves cos the guy sent hardcopy. I can't tell if he's technophobic or hyper-secretive. Look Amy, I gotta go, but I'll be in town in a couple of days – I'll give you a call when I arrive – and we can catch up properly then, I want to hear all about your world travels. Meet anyone?"

"Lots of people," Amelia hedged.

"Guys, Amy."

"Some of them were male, yes."

Zita sighed. "You need to get back out there. See you soon."

"Bye, Zi."

Amelia hung up and gently rocked her head from side to side, feeling as if its contents had shifted away from the ear to which she had held the phone.

Not long after, as she was starting to make dinner, the email from Zita arrived. Amelia downloaded the manuscript file and put it up on her laptop to read as she cooked a simple dinner.

The title page bore the legend:

The Life of an Invisible Man
By
The Invisible Man

Based on that title, Amelia guessed it was a look at the

diminished role of traditional 'masculinity' in modern society. She quickly discovered that this was not the case.

Chapter 2 –Harrigan

'*Professor Murdered! Police Baffled!*'

Inspector Clive Harrigan stared at the headline. In his view, 'baffled' was a little harsh. That was a little strong. A little unnecessary. Especially this early in an investigation. When you first found a dead body then, unless there was a man standing over it, wearing a mask, holding a bloody knife and asking if you liked scary movies, then not knowing who did it was to be expected. That didn't make you 'baffled', it just meant that you hadn't had a chance to figure it out yet.

"Thoughts, Harrigan?"

Harrigan looked up from the paper at the superior officer who had handed it to him.

"Sir?" It hurt Harrigan to admit it to himself, but having a superior who was younger than him, and by a decent number of years, did rub him up the wrong way. It was not that Chief Inspector Lane (called Growley by those who knew him better, though Harrigan had not the least idea why) was some pimply teenager who had been groomed for the role, but that was actually part of the problem. The fact that his superior was a mature forty five, but still much younger than he was, only highlighted Harrigan's own advancing years.

"The papers are making us look ridiculous." The Chief Inspector pointed an accusatory finger.

Harrigan returned the offending article to his boss's desk. "It's the local rag. Nothing much happens in the city so they're making the most of it. I mean 'baffled'? What does that even mean? It's only been four days. When you first find a dead body…"

"It means," Chief Inspector Lane interrupted, "that not only do we not know *who*, we do not know *how*."

Hangdog Harrigan (a nickname he'd been unable to shift), hung his head. "Right."

He had hoped this would not come up. In fact he had rather hoped that his superior hadn't read the article.

"Is that all you've got to say?"

The murder of Professor Herbert Digges was not exactly a 'locked room' mystery, but it wasn't far off. His office door had been unlocked, but the corridor that led to it had been watched by one of the college porters. If that was not enough, there was also a security camera in the corridor, and while it did track up and down it did not seem possible for someone to steal past it. There had been a roomful of people (attending some party) who should have been witnesses, but no one remembered seeing any strangers – and given how tight-knit these faculties were that probably meant there had not been any. Which theoretically meant that a roomful of witnesses became a roomful of suspects, but everyone seemed to cover everyone else and the porter swore up and down that none of them had left. It was a set-up that would have had Agatha Christie rubbing her hands and seeing big royalty cheques floating in front of her eyes.

"What about the porter?" asked Lane, seeming to read Harrigan's thoughts.

"As far as we can see from the camera, he never moved."

Lane nodded. "So someone doctored the camera."

"The tech boys are looking at it."

"And what are you doing in the meantime?"

Harrigan shifted uncomfortably. "Talking to people. Trying to learn a bit about this Professor Digges. Who he was, whether he had any enemies…"

"Oh for God's sake, Harrigan," Lane didn't shout, he wasn't angry, he just rolled his eyes in exasperation. "How many times? We are trying to solve a murder, not write a biography. We figure out *how* this was done. That'll get the papers off our backs and will lead us to the who. Understand?"

"Sir."

Harrigan left the Chief Inspector's office with his shirt sticking to his back. It was a generational thing. Back in his day the major component of crime-solving was shoe leather. If you walked enough miles and talked to enough people then sooner or later you learnt what you needed.

Or you didn't.

Either way you'd done your best.

There were probably good things about the advances made in modern policing, but Hangdog Harrigan was the old dog to whom new tricks could not be taught. He believed in the value of talking to people but he was surrounded by youngsters who thought the answer always lay in a laptop or an i-phone, and the irritating thing was that they were often right.

Harrigan glanced at the calendar as he went back to his desk. Not long now. Not long until Christmas. Not long until retirement.

It had become a joke about the station; *'Only four weeks left till retirement? You know what that means'*, and they would mime a gun or a noose or a slit across the throat, and everybody would laugh at the old Hollywood cliché. Harrigan weathered the jokes and joined in the laughter, but underneath he was starting to feel nervous. He didn't believe in fate, but that didn't mean he was comfortable when people went about tempting it. Besides, just recently he'd had a… it was too much to call it a premonition – maybe a presentiment? Call a spade a spade; he'd had a *feeling* that he was going to die.

'And I was only four weeks from retirement…'

He'd had that feeling before of course, most people in the police had at one time or another. You got into bad situations with bad people and you thought; yep, this is it. But this was different. There was nothing specifically threatening. This new case was a puzzler but there was no suggestion that it put him in danger – the killer didn't even seem to be armed. But the feeling remained.

Maybe he'd just seen too many movies. Certainly he fitted the type. From his rumpled suit to his rumpled face and from his estranged wife to the awkward relationship he had with his children, Harrigan was a walking cliché of the cop whose time has passed.

'I'm getting too old for this shit.'

He'd been road-testing possible last words, because if you were going to die a cliché then doing so with a pithy one-liner was the only way to go.

Of course, it had all been different in his glory days…

Actually, it hadn't been all that different. And 'glory days' was a pretty grand term for what had presumably been his 'prime'. He'd

21

always done his best, his clearance rate had always been solidly average (or only just below), and he had always thought that his breakthrough would come; that one case that would put him in the first rank of detectives, that one moment of brilliant inspiration that enabled him to crack the case that no one else could. Now he had a month left on the job, and the worst part of realising that your best days were behind you was acknowledging that they hadn't really been anything special.

Not that he hadn't enjoyed them. Harrigan liked his job. It was the only thing he had ever wanted to do. Even as a child he had wanted to be a detective, and finding out that he wasn't as good at it as he might have hoped had only dampened his enthusiasm slightly. It was still a good life. He felt like one of those middling sportsmen, destined to be an also-ran but earning enough to live on while doing something they loved.

But even though he wasn't sure what he would do with his retirement, he did want the chance to find out.

'*I always knew I'd never get out of this job alive.*' That was a good one.

Harrigan walked from the station to the crime scene. Partly because he wanted the time to think, partly because he liked walking, partly because he still hoped that shoe leather would eventually get him the solve on what might wind up being his last case. If he could keep hold of it. The murder of a University professor was pretty high profile and the case would never have landed on Harrigan's plate had some very bad prawns not landed on Inspector Foster's the night before. If Harrigan could solve it, then he could end his career on a high.

'*At least I went down swinging.*'

He showed his ID to the young constable guarding the crime scene – it would have been nice to be recognised, but he wasn't a man who made the big impression – and paced slowly down the corridor towards the staircase which led up to Professor Digges' office.

Four doors led off the corridor (three offices, one fire exit) and Harrigan had methodically tried them all when he arrived on the scene; all locked. They could have been locked after the murder, but everyone was insistent they hadn't been. That said, there were a lot of things that people were insistent about and they couldn't all be true. Someone was lying. Then again, Cambridge University bred insistent people who would argue that the sky was green if someone like Harrigan told them it was blue.

Harrigan went up the creaky staircase and stood in the middle of Professor Digges' room. No sign of a struggle, but the man had been advanced in years so had presumably been overpowered.

"Right." Sometimes talking these things out helped. Harrigan addressed himself to a painting on the wall of one of the room's former residents, who seemed to be glaring either at his painter or at Harrigan himself. "The porter on the gate says no one came in without a pass. But there's so many people who have passes and jumping the fence would be easy enough, so getting into the grounds wasn't a problem."

He looked to the painting for confirmation and got a glaring response.

"Getting into the building wouldn't have been any great challenge either. But the function room had porters on both doors. The one at the entrance was adamant that no one came in who wasn't supposed to. The one at the exit leading to the corridor is equally adamant that no one came through but Digges himself. Security footage backs them both up."

Harrigan paused while the painting continued to glare at him. The problem with Chief Inspector Lane's approach – discover the how and then the who – was that it was impossible. There was no way anyone could have got into this room.

"So they had to have been in here already. Waiting."

That felt like a breakthrough but Harrigan knew he was as far away as ever. They had gone over that possibility. The porter had eventually gone to check on Digges and found him dead. No one in the room, windows locked from the inside, camera footage proving that no one came out.

Harrigan turned to the professor's desk and, for what seemed like the hundredth time, looked at the notebook that had been left

23

open there. Why did no one outside of a crime novel ever use their last moments to scrawl the name of their killer? It would be so helpful. Most of the notes were illegible but one word stood out, circled in red and written more clearly; '*Monocaine???*'. Just outside of the circle, a second word had been added as an afterthought; '*Dangerous*'.

He needed to talk to people, to find out what sort of person Professor Herbert Digges had been; who were his friends, who were his enemies and how far might those enemies go? He'd also like to know what monocaine was.

"Originally it was to be on the Thursday," said Dr Sutherland, a tall, sharp-faced woman, who seemed genuinely moved by the Professor's passing, and who had organised the party. "But the Professor asked for it to be moved and I said yes." She looked up at Harrigan. "Would he still be alive if I'd said no?"

"If someone's out to kill a person," Harrigan replied as comfortingly as he could, "then what day they do it seldom matters."

Sutherland nodded sadly.

"I wonder if you can tell me a bit about the professor? Did he have any enemies?"

Dr Sutherland sighed. "I suppose I can say it now he's dead. No, I don't think he did."

"You say that like it's a bad thing."

Sutherland looked almost shocked. "Well of course. No scientist of any merit would admit to not having enemies. If you don't have enemies then your work is not worth stealing. No one is jealous of you. Don't misunderstand me; Professor Digges certainly had enemies in his prime. I'm sure there were people who hated him." She shook her head. "But not anymore, bless him."

"Well there was his ex-wife." Next in was the Professor's secretary, Curt Howard.

"Go on," encouraged Harrigan, hopefully. A murder taking place in the high-flown world of university politics, or worse still scientific intrigue, left him scrabbling, but the good, old-fashioned bumping-off of a spouse he knew how to handle.

24

"He cheated on her, she found out, ugly divorce." Howard shook his head. "But last I heard she'd remarried quite happily. And God knows she took him for every penny she could."

"Did he have many friends?" Harrigan tried a different tack.

"I don't know about *friends*," Howard hedged. "But a lot of amicable acquaintances. Quite a social butterfly. He liked a party. Or a dinner. Or drinks or whatever really. Didn't do much science anymore."

"What can you tell me about monocaine?"

Dr Carol Griffin, one of the Professor's colleagues in the Biochemistry Department, puffed out her cheeks. "Not something we use if we can help it. But it's a powerful stabilising agent."

"Dangerous?"

"Not deadly," Griffin hastened to explain, "but while it can stabilise a chemical formula, some believe it has a destabilising effect on people's behaviour."

"Some believe?"

"Not enough research has been done," the doctor admitted. "Made a lot of rats crazy, I understand. It's a little hard to come by; extracted from an Indian flower. Most people would just use a different stabilising agent."

"Have you got any idea why the Professor might have been using it?"

Dr Griffin shrugged. "If it was me, and if I'd tried *everything* else to make a chemical formula stable and nothing worked, then monocaine is where I'd turn."

"Inoffensive," shrugged Professor Tottenham, the oldest of Digges' colleagues still at the University. "I guess that would sum the old duffer up. At least these days."

"These days?" Harrigan pressed.

"I don't want to dredge up the past."

"Well I do." These interviews had yielded little else of use.

Tottenham shifted in his seat uncomfortably. "Well of course if you're in science for any length of time you're bound to get involved in something that the public, the press, the 'establishment' doesn't approve of. Herbert – in the sixties I suppose it was – got

25

involved with this project on LSD and mind control."

"LSD can be used to control minds?" Harrigan would have assumed the opposite.

"Depends what you lace it with." Tottenham raised his crazy eyebrows suggestively. "There was a lot of talk back then about the wild younger generation and how do we control them. Herbert floated the idea of releasing a form of LSD into circulation that just… took them down a peg. Made them a bit more respectful of authority."

"Drugging the general public?"

"Well they'd be drugging themselves," pointed out Tottenham. "There was quite a stir at the time and Herbert kept his head down for a while. No idea if he ever did anything with the theory. Doubt it. Funding, you know." He shrugged. "But it was all so long ago."

It was a long day. The interviews painted an interesting picture of the victim, but nothing that gave Harrigan a firm lead, and certainly nothing that brought him closer to knowing *how* the Professor had met his end. The killer was a man who could work miracles, and when Harrigan found him then he was going to shake him by the hand and beg to know how it had been done. It simply wasn't possible.

Chapter 3 – The Book Launch

Zita arrived a few days after her sister's return and the pair met for tea at Amelia's flat. Tea was another thing that they had in common. Tea and books. They were two years apart; near enough to be close as children but far enough apart to drift during the teenage years. No one could fail to spot that they were siblings, but their appearances highlighted both their similarities and their differences. Both were slimly built and on the short side (Zita would have said 'petite'), both had dark hair which they wore long and had similarly shaped faces. In thought, both tilted their heads at the same angle and a dimpled frown furrowed between their eyebrows. The differences were obvious and yet hard to pinpoint; a mutual friend had once described them as looking like 'a before and after poster', though he had not said what the poster might be advertising. They both had dark, soulful eyes but Zita's seemed brighter and more active, always on the move, while Amelia's were slow and introspective. When Zita smiled she showed teeth while Amelia's mouth turned subtly at the corners, as if she was embarrassed to be happy. Zita seemed to radiate something that her sister did not. In addition, Zita wore make-up like most people wore clothes; as a matter of course. On those occasions when Amelia felt obligated to make up, she was always conscious of it, as if she was wearing shoes one size too small.

Amelia blamed her parents for a lot of this. While she had been named after her father's maiden aunt from Abergavenny, Zita had been named after a glamorous actress. Sometimes how you are named can have a surprising impact on how you see yourself, and Amelia was sure that a psychological study of the Evans sisters would have revealed the impact of nominative determinism. (She also had a sneaking suspicion that her Mum had wanted her daughters named from opposite ends of the alphabet because it cut off discussion about a potential third child; *What would we call it?*)

"Hi, hi, hi, hi, hi!" Zita had done the repeating thing for as long as Amelia could remember and she assumed it was her sister's way of holding onto a conversation while she thought of something to

27

say. "So good to see you, been so long, how've you been, tell me everything – like *everything* – this place hasn't changed at all, did you read the book?"

"Nice to see you too" replied Amelia.

Having managed to calm her sister's natural energy with a comfortable chair, a cup of tea and some Hobnobs (taste in biscuits was another check in the similarities' column), Amelia answered her sister's question.

"I read it."

"What do you think? What do you think? I mean it's creative, it's a cool idea, I'm sure it'll sell if it's properly marketed, but doesn't it seem a bit on the creepy side when you put it with everything else? The no emails, phone calls, address, picture, *name*. I mean, maybe I'm reading too much into something that is obviously a work of fiction and when Thomas Harris sent *Silence of the Lambs* along no one was going '*Better keep an eye on this guy*', but he didn't keep his identity secret. At least I don't think he did, I don't know but I don't imagine he did, and if he did then wouldn't people have been freaked? Am I freaking over nothing?"

"I don't think you are."

That actually stopped Zita in her tracks. "Oh. Really?"

It occurred to Amelia that her sister had come in search of reassurance more than advice, but she wasn't sure that it was a reassurance she could offer.

"Look Zi, you're right; this is fiction and you don't judge a writer by what they write."

"Otherwise Agatha Christie would have spent years in jail."

"Exactly," Amelia nodded, cagily. "I'm not worried about what he's writing. I'm worried about how." And as Amelia's eyes met Zita's, she knew that her sister had been thinking the same thing.

"Everyone's been really up on it and I don't want to be the voice of doom, shooting down what I *do* think could be a really successful book, but I just think it's a bit…"

"Creepy." It was the word Zita had used and the one that Amelia had found herself coming back to.

"Yeahyeahyeahyeahyeah." Zita nodded like the Churchill dog.

28

"But I don't know why."

That was a question. A book about an invisible man had *massive* potential to be creepy. Everyone wanted to be invisible for a day, and snooping on the opposite sex was always high on people's wish-list of things to do during that day. But the book contained nothing of that variety. It was almost odd in its asexuality. It was hard to put your finger on what made it feel 'creepy' except to say that the writer had a gift – if that was the right word – for making you feel as if he was there with you, reading over your shoulder.

'*The world had become my Facebook; that artificial intimacy that can make you feel close to a person you have never met. I could be standing near enough to watch the status change in your eyes.*'

And yet it wasn't voyeuristic, almost the exact opposite; this man didn't want to look at you, he wanted you to look at him. He wanted to be part of your life. Not in a sexual way, not as a predator, but as a fixture. He wanted to be there with you, with everyone. And not just wanted; *needed.*

'*In a park I sat with a picnicking family. They had no idea I was there, even when I joined in with their laughter.*'

There was a desperation to the writing that seemed to crawl off the page.

"It's like…" Zita searched for the right description. "You know sometimes in a bar you'll see a guy trying to seal the deal with a girl and he's already got the 'no' but he just keeps going, not in an aggressive way, but almost like 'if she pities me I can still land this' – you know?"

"Yeah," Amelia nodded. "Except he's not trying to get the girl he's trying to get… us."

"Yeah."

"He wants to be liked."

Which didn't seem like such a terrible thing when you said it. But on paper, that desperate need to be liked took on a life of its own. The Invisible Man in the story did not do anything wrong (at least not much; there were a few petty thefts as you would expect from someone getting used to being invisible for the first time) but reading his story made you feel uncomfortable. It made you feel sorry for him too, but still uncomfortable.

"Sort of makes it brilliant," admitted Zita. "I mean, this is one of the things that stands out. Anyone can write a first-hand account of being invisible and play like its real – keep their name secret and all that – but giving it this character is what really brings it off the page and I think people will identify. There's a reality to it."

Amelia nodded. Creepy though she had found it, the book had also been compelling right from the first line, '*My body still shaking, my heart trying to tear itself apart, I broke through the undergrowth and stumbled blindly onto the path, and into the light of a new world.*'.

She had started by just skimming through, knowing that she had to read the whole thing before Zita arrived. But once she had done that, she had gone back to the start and read it properly, in earnest, and had still managed to finish before her sister's arrival. Partly that was because it wasn't a very long book, but it was also because she couldn't put it down. The previous night she had stopped reading at one in the morning and gone to bed, then lain awake thinking about the book for half an hour before getting up to continue reading. It was fascinating. *He* was fascinating.

"So what do you think? About the meeting I mean, about what I should do? I've got to be there, it's important for work, but we never usually do things like this. I've arranged to meet him at this bookshop for coffee half an hour before the launch so we can go over things and he says he'll be there and it's a public place so I don't know what I'm worrying about but I don't know him and I just don't know what I ought to do – I mean I have to go and I'm going to go but… You know?"

Amelia thought for a moment. "How about I come with you?"

Zita beamed her biggest smile. "That would be awesome. Thank you. Now," she added milk from the jug to her empty cup, then filled it up from the pot, "let's talk about you."

"His name's Jack."

The book launch was on the 1st of December, targeting the Christmas market, and Amelia had met up with Zita in the bookshop's café on the second floor, which also housed books on Fashion, Interior Design, Transport, Gardening and other subjects which failed to hold Amelia's interest. The sisters had deliberately arrived an hour before Zita had arranged to meet the writer whom they knew only as The Invisible Man, so they could talk tactics, but the conversation had quickly got off base, returning to a subject Zita had introduced the previous day.

"I don't know why I didn't think of him before," Zita rattled on. "He's based in Cambridge, he's tall – you like tall men, don't you? Or at least don't dislike them. I think everybody likes tall men. He's…"

"I'm really not looking for a guy," Amelia interrupted.

"You don't have to look. I found one. That's what I'm trying to tell you; his name's Jack…"

"You said. I'm just not convinced that…," Amelia tried to be as polite as she could, "that your taste in men synchs with mine."

"That's the great thing," Zita enthused. "We went out once and it was just awful. I mean I had to ask him out – he's just so good looking and I do like tall men even if you don't – but we were such different people and the bar I picked was too loud for him and when I suggested going to a club he looked like I'd put him up against a wall with a cigarette and a blindfold, and I thought; I know someone who hates cool stuff just as much as this guy does; Amy! You have to give him a chance."

"I'm not sure I do," muttered Amelia, although a lot of her refusal was a kneejerk reaction to being set-up by her sister. On the basis of Zita's brief sketch it *did* sound as if she and Jack might be compatible.

"You can't let Frank ruin all other men for you."

Amelia shot her sister a venomous glance. Frank had been her partner for some years. They had been happy together and bought a flat together and planned a life together. Then she had learned that he had had a string of affairs. It had inevitably coloured Amelia's opinions of the male of the species, but she was over it. She was over Frank and she was over her trust issues. She just wasn't interested in being set up.

31

"I've got plenty of stuff going on right now. I don't need a man to make my life complete."

Zita bit into the chocolate brownie she had bought herself because she ate when she was nervous. "I don't need a brownie to make my life complete, but if I see a nice one then you'd better believe I'm going to sink my teeth into it."

"Zita..."

"Amy," Zita cut her sister off, "there's nothing wrong with focusing on work and what you're doing sounds very interesting and important and I'm thrilled that you enjoy it so much but there's a difference between focusing on it because you don't want anything else in your life and focusing on it because you're afraid of allowing anything else into your life. I know *I* brought up Jack and maybe that's my bad because this isn't about sex or even about men (I mean, it could be about men if you wanted it to be and Jack would be a really tall and handsome place to start) but really it's about you and about you having a life outside of your flat or a museum or a hole in the ground in Romania. Don't hide from life, Amelia, don't be afraid to be seen. You're too good for that."

She popped the rest of the brownie into her mouth, leaving Amelia to once again reflect that her sister knew her too damn well.

"Isn't this guy due?"

"Don't change the subject," Zita admonished, "You should be putting yourself out there, Amy. And again that doesn't have to mean like 'on the market' for guys, it could equally mean putting yourself out there as an archaeologist."

"I'm not technically an archaeologist."

"You know what I mean. You never put yourself forward, let people see who you are or how good you are at what you do. I thought Egypt and Romania might change that but here you are hiding away again and – wait up, this guy should be here by now, shouldn't he?"

Amelia nodded, grateful for the change in subject that the Invisible Man's absence had granted her. She looked around. It was mid-morning on a weekday so neither the bookshop nor the obligatory coffee shop squatting within it were packed with people, but there were a few about and more would surely turn up for the launch that was soon to take place. A dais and lectern had been set-up, with rows of chairs and a screen displaying the cover art for *The Life of an Invisible Man*. There was also a table ready for the author to sign copies (prior purchase compulsory). What was missing was the author.

Could one of the men seated in the coffee shop be the Invisible Man? Or one of those who drifted between the shelves, leafing through books about gardening and/or transport? Perhaps he was listening in to their conversation surreptitiously.

There was a man sitting by himself nursing a hot chocolate with whipped cream on top which had slowly slumped into the drink. He looked kind of creepy. Another man was seated in one of the comfortable chairs that bookshops provide, reading a book that he probably had no intention of buying. As Amelia looked at him he happened to glance up at her and she looked away. Had he been spying on them throughout?

Zita checked her phone for messages then looked at her watch. "I don't really have a Plan B for what to do if he doesn't show."

"I guess you'd have to make excuses and do the talk for him."

Zita looked shocked. "I couldn't possibly talk just off the top of my head like that, I wouldn't have a clue what to say."

"Really?" Not knowing what to say had never struck Amelia as a problem from which her sister suffered.

"Maybe he's planning to make an entrance? Then again, he doesn't seem like the type who'd want a lot of fuss and hoopla. Up to this point he seems to have been keeping his head down. I'd say he was more likely not to show up."

Amelia tilted her head to one side uncertainly. All of the Invisible Man's actions seemed to back up what Zita said, but Amelia couldn't help thinking that, actually, keeping your identity secret like this was a form of attention-seeking. Sure, there were people who used a pen name and refused public appearances because they disliked the limelight, but they usually took a practical approach and had an agent to act as a go-between. Not giving public appearances was different to arranging them then not showing up;

one suggested shyness, the other self-aggrandisement.

That was probably simplifying what could be complex psychological issues and Amelia wouldn't have made that sort of sweeping determination had she not read the book. In as much as she could divine his character from that, the Invisible Man didn't seem like someone who wanted to hide away.

"Okay," Zita stood up, "I guess I'd better go and talk to the manager (do you remember her name? Doesn't matter, I've got it written down somewhere) and tell her there's been a change of plan. What do you think? Say he was ill? Unavoidably detained? Probably best to – you know – play up the whole invisible conceit and say he had trouble flagging down a taxi. Something like that? I think he…"

Zita's monologue was cut off by a scream from the alcove in which the Interior Design section was located. Everyone in the coffee shop turned to look. For a moment they saw nothing, and then, from behind the wall of shelving, a single book floated out, crossing the central aisle and finding a gap in the Transport section on the opposite wall.

Amelia could only stare; jaw slack, eyes wide. In the past year she had seen some things – some wonderful, more terrible – things that went against the natural order of the world. But there was something so stunningly simple about a book – such an everyday item – briefly defying the laws of physics, that even she had to remind herself to breath.

"There's another!"

This time Amelia was able to read the title (*A History of the Great Western Railway*) as the book sailed unhurriedly past at shoulder height, turning slowly in mid-air as it went so it could slot easily into the recently vacated gap in Interior Design. Part of her brain was quietly peeved by this – there were few things she hated more than people who put books back in the wrong place.

"Look out!"

Customers scrambled to get out of the way as a pair of books, one from the bottom shelf, one from the middle, slid out and executed a complicated aerial manoeuvre between them, like literary Red Arrows. For a moment they remained poised in mid-air, hovering as if deciding where to go next, then they rushed towards the dais, across the small stage and soared over the empty audience. It might have been Amelia's imagination – she was too fixated by the books to be sure – but she thought the chairs moved as the books flew over them.

The two books now dashed the length of the central aisle, from the coffee shop to the main staircase and back again, leaving screaming customers in their wake, before finally coming to rest on the dais in front of the screen advertising *The Life of an Invisible Man*.

Everyone stayed where they were, feet frozen to the floor but heads twitching, eyes flicking anxiously this way and that, unsure if they were supposed to be scared or amused. What the hell was going on?

"There!"

A huge slab of a coffee table book, with hardcover and lavish illustrations, zipped along a few inches above the carpet, making people jump to either side as it approached, weaving around those too slow to move, making its way to join the pile on the dais.

As soon as it had landed, a stream of smaller books cascaded from the adjacent shelves, one after another, like divers diving into a pool. One, two, three, four, five, six of them landing on the pile as customers stared in wonder.

The attitude of the impromptu audience had changed. People had initially been shocked, even scared by the poltergeist behaviour of the books, but now those books were associating themselves with the launch this was assumed to be part of the entertainment, a clever publicity stunt that they were lucky to witness.

No one was quicker to spot this than Zita, who had an antenna for good publicity. Overcoming her shock and anxiety, she hurried to the table beside the dais, beneath which boxes of books had been stacked. The idea had been that people should buy them and then get them signed by the author, but it paid to be flexible.

"Copies of the Invisible Man's book, available now! Please pay downstairs."

People rushed forward to grab their copy, what had looked like

35

a sparse number of onlookers quickly concentrating into a throng.

Amelia saw Zita jump as the pile of books she had just unpacked levitated from the table beside her. Copies of the slim volume flew out across the crowd for people to catch, as if they were being thrown. These copies, people wanted even more. They wanted to see if they could find some clue on the book of how the trick was done, some mark left by the ingenious mechanism which had pulled this off and fired the books across the room.

For her own part, Amelia had not moved throughout the display, which had lasted barely a few minutes. What had she just seen?

Chapter 4 – #WhereIsTheInvisibleMan?

Safely back at the undisclosed location that he called home, the Invisible Man locked the door behind him, walked into the middle of the room and simply stood, letting each shivering breath in and out of his lungs. It felt as if the excitement that crackled through him might tear him apart if he did not pause to calm down. The thrill of the experience seemed to ripple across his skin. His mind fizzed with the present and the future and with sheer, pure, liquid joy, unlike anything he had ever felt; better than Christmas morning, better than drugs, better than sex.

"Yes!"

The Invisible Man leapt up, punching the air, then dropped to his knees to pound the floor with his fists before rolling onto his back and kicking his feet in the air.

That had gone… brilliantly!

In his wildest dreams he hadn't imagined it going that well! He had expected to cause a stir, he had anticipated scaring some people, but he had never thought that everyone would buy into it so quickly. It didn't matter whether they believed it or not – let them look for the wires for all he cared. Whether they adored him as an invisible man, a clever magician or a shill who had set something up with the bookshop in advance was unimportant; they adored him!

Books sales were great, and he was gratified that so many people had bought the book that he had tapped out here in this room over a fevered month of desperate creativity, but they were nothing compared to the public reaction, the public connection. That was what he wanted, what he craved, what he needed to do more of. Bigger and wider. He couldn't repeat himself. If he did the same thing at other bookshops – and he prided himself that they would all want him now – then he would become boring and *passé*. He had to find new ways to engage, to thrill, to entertain, to amuse and baffle the general public in ways that would make them believe and yet also try to figure out how it was done.

Oh, if only he could make this feeling last forever!

The sofa dinted as the Invisible Man flopped down onto it and stared at the ceiling, a beaming grin on his face – though no onlooker would have known it.

He glanced across the room towards his laptop and his breathing quickened again at the thought.

No. Not yet. Give it time to build. Parcel out these wild thrills to enjoy each one as a separate entity. When the excitement he was currently feeling from the book launch began to wane, then he could go online and see the reaction on social media. And probably on the regular media too by now! There had been at least two people in the bookshop today with the presence of mind to pull out camera phones. The shaky amateur footage would lend verisimilitude and add to the 'how was it done?' debate, because viewers would not be able to see clearly.

Would he make the national news? If he didn't today then he would tomorrow or the day after. Because the Invisible Man was not done yet.

Lying on the sofa he raised his hand before his eyes. Strange how that never ceased to give him an unnerving tremor down his back. It had been months now, and he knew that he wasn't going to see anything, but his instinctive reaction had still not acclimatised to his condition.

It had been an adjustment, of course. In some areas more than others. You never think about stairs; you never need to. You just go through life assuming that walking down stairs is something you could probably do with your eyes closed. Most people never had to find out how much, even if you are not conscious of it, you rely on being able to see your feet. He had never realised that he looked at his feet when going down stairs. He probably hadn't looked directly at them, but he, like everyone else in the world, saw them in his peripheral vision and his brain did the rest. Amazing thing the brain; it did so much without you being aware of it. Now his was struggling with suddenly losing that visual cue, and walking down stairs had become an extremely conscious process.

Typing had been worse. He had thought that as long as he could see where the keys were then he could hit them. Not so. In the end he had ordered skin-tight rubber gloves. If he hadn't done that then he would still be writing the book now.

He'd tried to come up with a similar life-hack for the stairs up to his flat, but tying plastic bags around his feet had been awkward when he'd met people coming the other way. Having a pair of specific 'going up and down stairs' shoes had seemed like a good idea at the time – he kept them at the top of the stairs then put them on in place of his invisible shoes when he needed to go down. When he met someone coming the other way, he just stood to one side, feet together, as if a pair of shoes had been left there. But then someone had tried to pick the shoes up and things had become weird again, as they wondered why some idiot had glued a pair of shoes to the stairs. It just raised too many questions.

That was what it was like being invisible; lots of little problems to solve. It had been an unexpected development to say the least. It had taken some getting used to. But after the initial shock and the furious confusion of it all, he had found a way to channel it. Being invisible was something that inevitably defined your life, but he was only just starting to realise that it might be the best thing that had ever happened to him.

He couldn't wait any longer. The sofa un-dinted as the Invisible Man sprang up. The chair at his desk pulled back, the laptop opened and the power button depressed. Seconds later he was on Twitter and the heady rush he had felt in the bookshop washed through him again.

It was big. It was BIG. Bigger than he could have anticipated.

The camera-wielding customers had posted their pictures and videos and those had been shared… how many thousand times? The store itself had security cameras, and some enterprising person in their promotions department – or perhaps that woman Zita from the publishers – had said; why are we sitting on this when we can use it? More shares, more likes, more comments.

Each one of the pictures and videos had invited thousands of comments; compliments, insults, endless theories about how it was done, which then invited their own sub-set of comments on how wrong they were and how dumb they were, which in turn became 'Well have you got a better suggestion?', and so on into vicious, hate-filled, 'big-talk in cyberspace' which is the ultimate destination of every social media argument.

The Invisible Man scrolled through the responses with wide-eyed wonder, reading little and taking in less. He didn't care what people were saying, only that they were saying it. They were talking about him. And it was spreading; it wasn't just Cambridge or even Britain – it was the world. A well-known pair of Vegas-based magicians had weighed in, saying that they knew a few ways this trick *might* be done but, cards on the table, they didn't think any of them were how it *had* been done. They congratulated the magician responsible and invited him or her to come on their show. The Invisible Man wished he could take them up on it, but it might be hard to explain.

Instagram, Facebook and other platforms likewise yielded endless interest; pictures being shared, comments flooding forth, everyone with a theory, everyone with an opinion. The social media revolution had democratised opinion so everyone had a right to their say regardless of qualifications. Not that this was a subject on which experts existed, so every opinion was equally valid anyway. It was all fine with the Invisible Man, all he cared about was the numbers, and those numbers were ever-increasing, snowballing into the stratosphere. He was fast becoming famous, and yet no one could pick him out of a crowd. Best of both worlds? Or an irritating anonymity when he deserved celebrity? Questions for another day; right now he was happy to wallow in it.

The most popular opinion online at the present, growing as it spread, was that this was a hoax designed to sell a book. You could do anything with computers these days and this would be easy to fake on film. It had only been witnessed by a handful of people, and everyone else had just gone a bit crazy.

As the Invisible Man watched his story unfold, he saw it describe a recognisable arc from wonder, through analysis and into cynicism. Within a matter of hours, even the idea of it being a clever magic trick was abandoned in favour of this being something cooked up by a special effects wizard in cahoots with the book's publishers. Too few people had been there to see the miracle first-hand for them to fight back against this turning tide. Just another internet hoax fooling the gullible into buying some stupid book. If it seemed too clever to be a magic trick then that was because it was fake – and not the magic trick kind of fake, which is clever and good, but the computer-generated kind of fake, which is dumb and pointless. Odd double-standard really.

With this growing development, the remaining faithful (those who thought it was a magic trick and a smattering who said he was a ghost), had begun a new campaign; #WhereIsTheInvisibleMan. They wanted him to speak. They didn't want him to say how it was done – that would spoil everything – but they wanted more. What would the Invisible Man do next? What trick could he pull to convince the doubters? How would he prove that this was more than computer wizardry, that it was a practical trick (or spiritual apparition) done in the real world for people to see?

#WhereIsTheInvisibleMan?

That evening, the Invisible Man turned on his TV to watch the news.

There he was (or wasn't), running through the bookshop holding a pair of books out in front of him – although of course that was not what it looked like. He was the final item in the local news report, occupying that space held back for amusing and quirky news. He had created an internet storm but not quite enough to interest the national news media, who presumably saw it as a publicity stunt (which, in a way, it had been) designed to sell books. And commercial endorsements had no place on national news.

The Invisible Man switched off, still smiling to himself. It was not all he had hoped for but perhaps his wild success elsewhere had led him to expect too much. Online and in person he had exceeded his expectations, so he had adjusted those expectations and the TV news had failed to meet them. Still, he had been on the news. He would have preferred to be on the national news rather than the local, and as a headline rather than an afterthought, but he had been on the news. And he was not done yet.

The Invisible Man went back to his computer.

Back in his old life, he had had a Twitter account which he had

41

imagined would be a necessity once he became famous, though in reality he had mostly used it to keep track of events and competitions that catered to his broad range of interests. He had about fifty followers, most of whom had just politely followed back. It was the same situation on other social media platforms and it was with these accounts that he had been keeping track of the sprawling spread of his new notoriety. It was still going on, new people discovering it and adding their thoughts.

Time he contributed to the conversation. The Invisible Man began to set up a new Twitter account.

By morning he would have half a million followers.

Elsewhere in Cambridge, another person had been watching the local news. They had missed the online storm – not really their area – but they checked it out now, watching the videos with blank-faced interest. Their reaction was very different to that of the Invisible Man. There were many emotions, but none of them could be called 'happy'.

Chapter 5 – The Date

The restaurant was nice. It was quiet, but not embarrassingly so, centrally located but off the beaten track, expensive enough to prove that this was an occasion but not so much to suggest that the person paying was showing off. It was nice.

Amelia looked nervously around, then picked up a breadstick just to give her something to do with her hands other than fidget with her clothing. She had not been on a date for… Actually this was the first date she had been on since Frank and they had been together a while, so her last actual date – like a *date* date – had been years ago. For the last few months her choice of clothing had been dictated by durability and wind-resistance, and wearing something that was supposed to be aesthetically pleasing (or at least make her more aesthetically pleasing) took some getting used to. Wearing heels was something she seldom did even when she was going out, but tonight she had tottered from her flat into the town centre like a baby giraffe learning to walk. The dress had been a favourite since she bought it but right now Amelia was struggling to remember why, and wondering if she had somehow changed shape since she had last worn it. It seemed tight in some places and loose in others which she didn't remember it being in the past. Plus the damn thing kept riding up, and while she did want to look as if she had made an effort, she didn't want to look as subtle as a shop window.

Lifting up from her seat she yanked the dress fiercely down again as discretely as she could. How had she let Zita talk her into this? Maybe she had caved just to stop her sister from talking? But then again, Jack had sounded like a nice man, and even if nothing romantic emerged from this evening, it would be good to have a meal with a nice man and get used to being in the company of one. It would good to be reminded that nice men actually existed in this world. If nothing else, dinner with Jack would be a way of easing back into the world of having dinner with men – call it 'dating' if you must.

Jack.

It was a good, solid sounding name. Nice people were called

Jack. Salt of the earth people who worked for a living, probably with their hands. Jack.

It sounded more like Frank than she was comfortable with. Jack. Frank.

They didn't rhyme but they had a similar cadence. Jack, Frank. Frank, Jack. Frank Jack sounded like the name of a loveable gangster in a Damon Runyon story.

Similar names didn't mean they were similar people. And Frank, as a name, didn't have the same solid credentials as Jack.

Then again, Frank was an open, honest, no-nonsense name, and look where that had got her.

It was almost as if you couldn't judge a man by his name. Jack. Frank.

The bigger worry where names were concerned was that she got them mixed up; that she might say Frank when she meant Jack. Saying the name of your ex while on a date with someone else was embarrassing. And could get more so in certain specific 'post-date' activities, when your mind was not necessarily focussed on details like names.

Amelia took a gulp from the glass of water by her place-setting.

Not that she was planning on any such 'post-date' activities. Although it had been a long time. She was suddenly very conscious of her underwear, something she hadn't had to think about while on an archaeological dig in the Carpathian mountains but which now dominated her thoughts. Not because she planned on anyone seeing it (although she had taken extreme care in choosing it, and then gone shopping for new underwear instead) but because it was bloody uncomfortable.

The lesson here was that you could not dress for comfort for months and then jump straight back into the deep-end of dressing for a date without some transition phase to ween you from one to the other. Did M&S have a transitionary underwear range? Buffer pants?

How obvious was it to everyone else in the restaurant that she was uncomfortable? How obvious was it that she was nervous and now starting to sweat more than she would have liked? How had she let Zita talk her into this?

"I've checked our coats." Jack sat back down opposite Amelia. He had been gone for no more than forty seconds and Amelia was quietly impressed with just how swiftly her mind had gone into full meltdown based on little more than the cadence of his name and an irritating bra strap.

"Great." Was there any more interesting response to '*I've checked our coats*'? What did people say on dates?

"Zita's told me a lot about you," Jack spoke again.

"Has she?" Oh God. "Good I hope."

"Well…"

Oh God.

"To be honest, no," Jack said, then hastened to correct himself. "Not that she said bad things about you. Just… I'm not sure *she* thought she was saying good things about you."

"Ah." Once again Amelia felt she was letting down her side of the conversation.

"She seemed to be making apologies for things that I wouldn't have said needed apologising for," Jack explained.

"I see."

Zita had been right; he was handsome. He looked like a 'Jack'. People didn't always look like their names but Jack looked as solid and reliable as his name suggested. He was tall (which Amelia did like), he had dark brown hair, slightly wavy, and hazel eyes. He had, Amelia noticed, strong hands. In fact, though it was hard to guess his physique while he was dressed in a smart-casual blue shirt and dark trousers, he seemed to have a strong frame in general. But it was his hands that Amelia noticed.

Jack gave an embarrassed laugh. "I'm not making myself very clear. Perhaps I should just be honest with you. When Zita said she wanted to set me up with her sister, I was desperately trying to think up a way out of it."

"Okay." No point criticising since Amelia had been doing the same thing.

"I like your sister a lot," Jack went on. "She's funny and full of energy; great to be around, but… She's really not my type and I was

45

scared you'd be like her."

"I'm not," Amelia finally knew exactly what to say.

"I'm not insulting Zita…"

"I know."

"I really do like her."

"Me too," nodded Amelia. "I love her to bits, but I still occasionally have the urge to beat her over the head with a chair."

"Well I wouldn't go that far," replied Jack, diplomatically. "The point is, like I said; I thought you'd be like her, and you're not. I mean you look like her…" He paused mid-sentence and then smiled. "And then again not. I've never seen two people look so alike and so different."

Amelia couldn't help smiling.

"Anyway – I seem to have got way off 'first date approved conversation' here – all I meant was, I'm glad you're not like your sister. Because she's not really my type. Not that I'm necessarily saying you are," he quickly added, now afraid of scaring Amelia off by being over-eager. "But I look forward to finding out. What type of person you are. Regardless of whether or not that's my type. Can you talk please? Just to stop me from saying anything else, because this is not going well."

Amelia laughed. "I think it's going fine."

After this awkward (but good-awkward) start, Amelia found that her clothes had stopped feeling uncomfortable. They ordered food and got down to the getting to know you portion of the evening.

"Romania?"

Amelia nodded. "Up in the Carpathian mountains."

"How does someone specialising in hieroglyphics wind up in Eastern Europe?"

"You'd be surprised how far the ancient Egyptians travelled."

"Really?"

Amelia laughed. "No."

"Oh. Sorry. Stupid."

"It's a long story," Amelia went on. "The short version is that I spent years trying to decode a form of hieroglyphics, only to discover that someone else had done it decades earlier. He just hadn't published his findings."

"Oh dear," said Jack, apparently at a loss for anything better to say.

"Yeah. I said something similar," nodded Amelia. "So I was kind of adrift, not knowing what to do, and this opportunity in Romania came up via a friend and I took it."

"Sounds pretty cool."

"Yeah. Yeah it is. We've discovered a whole new type of pictographic writing."

"Wow."

"Big wow," agreed Amelia. "If you're an archaeologist."

There was an awkward moment as Amelia reminded herself that ancient linguistics were not as exciting to everyone as they were to her.

"So what do you do?"

"Oh. I restore furniture," said Jack.

"Antique?"

"Mostly. You take the jobs you can get. I do build bespoke stuff as well."

"Interesting."

"Yes. That's how I met Zita. Her company hired me."

"So are you new to Cambridge?"

"Relatively. I mean I used to live here."

"Right."

"Yes."

"Are you liking being back?"

"Yes."

"Good." Pause. "Antiques, huh?"

"Yes."

The food arrived just in time to stop this blank spot from becoming a lull, and gave them something else to talk about.

"Is it good?"

"Yes. Very." Pause. "Yours?"

"Yes."

The conversational possibilities of good food are somewhat limited. It's actually better to have something to complain about.

Amelia began to notice that uncomfortable bra strap again. She scoured her mind for conversational topics. There were literally millions of things they could talk about; how was it possible she could not think of one? At least with the unfaithful Frank of dubious memory she had had common ground. They were both academics, they had stuff to talk about. She and Jack seemed to have a big, fat sod all.

"So what are you working on at the moment?" That ought to kill a few minutes.

Jack looked almost pained to have been brought back to the topic on which Amelia had already shown so little interest, but he manfully shouldered the burden.

"I've been restoring an antique desk for a college professor."

"Interesting," lied Amelia.

"Actually," Jack's tone changed slightly, "it's proved a little more interesting than I expected."

"Woodworm?"

"Murder."

Amelia stopped eating, forkful of food frozen on its way to her mouth. "Are you confessing to me? Did the professor piss you off and you hit him over the head with a mallet?"

"No."

"Nail gun to the head?"

"A proper restorer does not use a nail gun," Jack corrected. "Not even when murdering college professors. Have you heard about the Professor – what's his name? Digges, Professor Digges – who was found murdered in his office and the police don't know how the killer got in?"

"You're fixing his desk?" wondered Amelia. Who knew the world of antique furniture restoration was a gateway to murder? But then again; who could have known that studying ancient languages would lead her to battling the undead?

"I was," Jack looked crestfallen. "I've had to stop. And no, it's not because I'm a suspect. Usually people bring furniture to my workshop, but this desk won't go out through the door. It must have been at least assembled in there, if not scratch built. And it's too valuable to start pulling it apart. So I was working actually *in* his office. Then I turn up for work one morning and find police tape all over the place. The guy had been killed in that room the night before." Jack shook his head. "The desk is half-done. It's kind of bugging me. Half-done jobs make my palms itch."

"So you knew the man who was killed?" pressed Amelia.

Jack shrugged. "Not friends. But I'd met him. He seemed nice enough in a slightly condescending way. Strange to think of him dead. Strangled right in that room. The police interviewed me."

"Really?"

"They interviewed everyone who'd been in the building. I think they're grasping at straws a bit. Struggling."

"Why?" Amelia shuffled forward in her seat, the meal in front of her forgotten.

"The layout," replied Jack. "It shouldn't have been possible for someone to get in unseen. It's not as if this happened in the dead of night. People were about, there was a party going on. The University's got vicious security – cameras all over the place. And there's only one staircase leading to the Professor's office."

Amelia paused a moment, then reached for her bag, took out an eyebrow pencil and flattened out one of the white napkins on the table beside Jack.

"Show me."

Jack grinned. "You want to solve it?"

"You think we can't?"

As soon as the grizzly puzzle had been presented, a little thrill had ignited inside Amelia that she had not felt since Egypt. It was probably not the sort of thing to be encouraged, but what the hell.

Jack began drawing with the confident hand of a draftsman. "Something like that."

Amelia looked at the sketch on the napkin. "These are the stairs?"

"Leading up to the office. At the other end of the corridor are the double doors leading into the function room and they had a college porter standing on them at all times."

"At *all* times?"

"According to the police, someone tried to get through – just looking for the toilet or something – so the porter turned away from the corridor for at most thirty seconds, probably less. Later on he walked up to the staircase and looked up because he heard something. Those were the only times he moved. There's also a security camera on the wall here." Jack added a camera to his diagram. "They showed us some of the footage to try and jog our memories. It turns up and down the corridor."

"But it can't see the whole corridor?"

"No."

Amelia frowned. "Why not mount it at one end so it covers everything?"

"Listed building. There are some impressive armorials at either end of the corridor and nailing a camera to them was not allowed."

"Where do these doors go?" Four other doors led off the corridor, two on each side.

"These three go into offices." Jack labelled them 1, 2 and 3. "Door 4," he labelled the door to the right of the function room entrance and added some steps, "leads outside. Fire exit."

Amelia pondered the sketch.

"See what I mean?" grinned Jack. "No way in. You'd have been seen. And yet, somehow, the killer wasn't."

"Then he must have been in there to start with," declared Amelia, taking a sip of wine and smiling.

"But then; how does he get out?"

"Window?"

"Locked from the inside."

"Damn."

"Also, the Porter said that the Professor came down not long after going up, looked into the corridor and then went back up again. Why do that if there was a killer in there?"

"Why do that at all?" wondered Amelia.

"You'd have to ask him."

"Somewhat tricky now. I guess the room was under constant surveillance from the discovery of the body until the police got there?"

50

"Yep."

Amelia picked up the napkin again. It was a puzzle, but she could solve it. And the fact that the Cambridge City police had so far failed to do so did not deter her.

"Okay, let's say the killer comes in through the fire exit, up the stairs to door 4."

"That door is alarmed."

Amelia sighed. "Well it must be possible to unalarm it. Let's assume the killer has some skills."

"So he comes in through the disarmed door, up the stairs, but then door 4 is only feet away from the Porter."

"So he waits until the Porter turns away to speak to the guy looking for the toilet."

"How would he know that was going to happen?" Jack smacked the table. "An accomplice."

"Who agrees to distract the Porter at a specific time."

"Synchronised watches and all that."

"Then the killer dashes down the corridor. Thirty seconds is a long time."

Jack shook his head. "Camera."

Amelia deflated. "Oh yeah."

"In one of the bits they showed us," Jack went on, "the camera is starting to turn towards the stair end of the corridor just as the Porter is distracted. It would have caught anyone running that way. More wine?"

"Thanks."

Jack topped up her glass. "You're good at this."

"I read a lot."

"Sherlock Holmes?"

"John Le Carre, Stieg Larrson, Len Deighton."

"The Invisible Man?"

Amelia laughed. "Zi gave me a copy to read."

"It all seems to be working out for her."

Amelia nodded. "Zi's a born promoter and she's loving working for a born showman. Did you see the thing with the punt he did today?"

"I know. It's unreal."

Since the book launch (over a week ago now), the Invisible Man had not been idle and Zita was in raptures at the chance to work with an author who injected a bit of spectacle into their promotion.

"What about door 3?"

"What about it?"

"Was it unlocked?"

Jack shrugged. "They didn't tell us."

"Let's say it was unlocked." Door 3 was opposite door 4 and a few feet up the corridor. "The killer could easily get into there."

"To what end?"

"To hide," said Amelia triumphantly, taking a victory sip. "That's good wine."

"Thanks. My Uncle is a big wine drinker, taught me a lot. Mostly when to stop."

"Uncles are good like that. Mine taught me poker.

"Are you close with your family?"

"Physically, no; I'm the only one in this part of the country. But pretty close in other ways. Maybe less so with Zi."

"Different people."

"Yeah. So the killer can hide behind door 3 until the camera turns."

Jack pulled a face. "Camera turns on a fifteen second cycle. By the time it's turned, the Porter has turned back to the corridor."

"But then the Porter walks down to the stairs."

"How would the killer know he was going to do that?" Jack asked before answering his own question. "He said he heard something. Maybe the killer made the noise."

"Risky." Door 3 wasn't that close to the stairs. "But for whatever reason, the Porter does go towards the stairs."

"The killer creeps out of room 3 and…"

"Is immediately seen." Amelia sagged again and they stared at the napkin a while. "Do you have any brothers or sisters?"

"No. Only child. What if the killer waits until the Porter walks…"

"Back the other way!"

"Exactly. While the Porter's back is turned he runs for the stairs." Jack gave a little shrug. "Presumably on tip-toe but we'll let that pass."

"Where was the camera looking?"

It was Jack's turn to deflate. "Away from the Porter when he started but then it turned to meet him as he was coming back."

They both looked glumly at the sketch again.

"How come you left Cambridge?"

Jack sighed. "There was a woman. And then there wasn't. It was pretty amicable, we stayed friends. I think in many ways that was all we'd ever been."

"There are worse ways to break up."

"And worse reasons to get together."

"The killer could probably get to room 2," Amelia went back to the plan, "(assuming it's unlocked) when the Porter was walking up the corridor. But would he have time to run across to the stairs after the Porter turned but before the camera looked back?"

"Not based on what I saw."

Their food grew cold as Jack shifted around the table so they could both stare at the sketch more easily.

"Okay," Amelia tapped the napkin. "Let's say the killer was in the room to start with. Could he get *out* during any of these moments?"

"Not the first one," Jack shook his head. "Might be able to get as far as room 2 or 1, maybe 3 if he was light on his feet."

"So he gets as far as room 3," Amelia pressed on. "Then the porter walks towards the stairs, past the door he's hiding behind... But at that point the camera is pointing towards the function room so he can't get to door 4."

The waiter came to ask if he could get them anything else; dessert? Coffee? Another napkin to draw on?

"Give us another minute," asked Jack.

"Sarcastic waiter," said Amelia, after he had gone. "I quite like that."

"Better than the fawning ones."

"Exactly."

Back to the napkin.

"It's almost possible."

"But not quite," Amelia nodded. "He'd have to be invisible."

Jack sighed. "Plus, pretty much everything we've suggested would require the porter to be stone deaf."

"Was he?"

"They didn't say."

"Okay… How about…?"

They stayed for dessert and then had coffee, all while poring over the map, throwing out theories at each other, which became more outlandish as the probable proved impossible. And, because experimenting with the mechanics of a murder scene can only take you so far, between theories they spoke of family and personal history, of music and film, of how they had come to Cambridge and what plans each nurtured for the future.

The mysterious killing of Professor Herbert Digges was a pretty macabre icebreaker but it had done the trick, and perhaps the late Professor would have been pleased that his death had given two shy people something to talk about.

"It's going to snow soon," Jack commented as they stepped out into the cold night air.

"Maybe a white Christmas."

"That'd be nice. Did you want to get a late drink somewhere?"

"I think I'll leave it, this time."

"Cool." He might have been disappointed, but the words 'this time' had not escaped Jack's attention.

It had been a nice evening and Amelia did not want to gamble with that by pushing too hard too soon. Quit while you're ahead and guarantee a second date. Because she *did* want a second date.

"How are you getting home?" asked Jack.

"I'll walk. It's not far."

"Can I walk you?"

"It's not far."

Jack shrugged. "All the easier for me to be chivalrous."

Amelia laughed. "Your chivalry is noted, but seriously, you've got more of a journey. Call me."

"I will."

They stood there in that indecisive half-moment before parting when anything can happen, but only if someone allows it to do so.

Amelia moved first and Jack was there to meet her. It was not the longest kiss, or the most passionate. But it was a good kiss. A good first date kiss.

"Good night."

Heels precluded Amelia from executing a little skip as she rounded the corner and passed out of Jack's view, but the skip was implied. Damn Zita, she really did know her big sister.

It was obvious why one date had been enough between Jack and Zita. Zita demanded fireworks from the get-go and Jack was not a firework. Or if he was, then he was one of those slow-burn ones that starts small and then blossoms into something spectacular. At least that was what Amelia was hoping. It was early days yet, but she was prepared to allow herself to dream.

As she walked through the cold, wishing that her coat was long enough to cover more of her legs, her mind wandered back through their dinner conversation. They couldn't have missed anything but they had wound up at the same conclusion as the police; it was impossible.

'*He'd have to be invisible*'. That was what she had said.

After the spectacular events of the book launch, Amelia had asked her sister, hand on heart, if she had known any of that was going to happen.

"My hand on my heart, Amy." Zita placed one hand on her chest and raised the other. "Strike me down if I tell a lie, stick a needle in my eye and all that. I was there to meet the author, introduce him and get him to sign a few copies. I had no idea all that shit was going to kick off."

"What about the bookshop?"

Zita shook her head. "They said not. If they knew about it then the manager is playing it really close to his chest and missed his vocation as an actor, and I spoke to staff who were on the floor – just sounded them out, you know – and they all said the same. And looking at their faces I believe them, they were as shocked as anyone else."

Amelia nodded. "Do you have any idea how he did that?"

Another head shake. "Not a clue. My guess is the guy's a magician who decided to write the book – definitely reads like a first book – as much to promote his tricks as to sell copies. The whole thing feels like one big exercise in self-promotion."

And with that, Amelia had to agree.

There were still a lot of people online who subscribed to the magician theory over the computer-generated hoax theory. Obviously Amelia knew that the latter was wrong because she had been there, so the magician made the most sense, but…

A year ago (in fact, six months ago) she wouldn't have even considered another explanation. Just because you couldn't tell how a trick was done didn't mean that it wasn't a trick. She couldn't explain how her i-phone worked but that didn't make it magic. But since then, Amelia had gone through an experience that had opened her mind to a new world of gods and monsters. Monsters at any rate. She had seen the impossible made real before her eyes.

These days, because of advances in technology and education and general understanding of how the world works, we are less willing to believe the evidence of our eyes when we cannot explain something. In the past, people used gods and magic to explain everything they couldn't understand, and that didn't usually pan out well, but perhaps things had gone too far the other way. What Amelia had seen in Egypt made her more willing to ask the question; had she seen an Invisible Man?

Well… Obviously she hadn't *seen* one but that was just getting caught up in semantics. Had there been an invisible man there in the bookshop with them? She had seen a few stage magicians (not many, she wasn't a big fan) and some of them were absolutely amazing. People had walked through the Great Wall of China and made well-known landmarks vanish. What had happened in the bookshop was surely not beyond the wit of a clever magician.

But boy would it have taken some preparation.

And there were so many variables, so many people whose position the magician could not predict.

Most of all; she had been there. It had not felt like a trick. It might have felt like one a year ago, but not now.

None of which would have mattered except; '*He'd have to have been invisible*'.

Two impossible events in one week. Coincidence?

No one else was connecting a publicity stunt in a bookshop to a murder elsewhere in the city and there was a good reason for that; one was a trick and the other was a clever killer. Just because an invisible man *could* have murdered Professor Digges, did not mean that one had. There was no such thing as an invisible man. It was impossible.

But Amelia believed in the impossible.

Then again, maybe that was a problem. Because she had seen what she had seen out in Egypt, she now looked for miracles where none existed.

Amelia had arrived at her door without even realising and she shivered from the cold that she had not felt as she walked, so lost had she been in her thoughts. She opened the door, went in and began to climb the stairs slowly and quietly, cautious of disturbing other residents.

One night in Romania there had been strange noises in the camp where they were staying. Everyone else on the dig had put their pillows over their heads and gone to sleep, but Amelia and site manager Maggie (who had also been in Egypt) had leapt up, grabbed the nearest weapon and searched the camp for the supernatural creature coming to get them. They eventually found a stray cat sitting in a metal bucket, experimenting with the interesting acoustic effect the bucket produced.

Amelia remembered the look that she and Maggie had shared. Egypt had changed them and the way they saw the world. They saw monsters in every shadow.

That was all this was. She was imagining invisible men everywhere she looked. Which was easy because they could be literally anywhere.

But as she entered her flat, kicked off her heels and hung up her coat, Amelia spotted *The Life of an Invisible Man* lying on the arm of her favourite chair.

Really she should go to bed.

But after a night like this, after the excitement of meeting Jack and optimistic thoughts of the future, she would not sleep anyway.

Still wearing her best dress, Amelia sat, opened the book at page 1, and reached down to grab a notebook and pen – items she always kept within easy reach. She was now looking for something specific, and yet, curled up cosily in the chair with the book, she could not help being swept up in it once more. She was beginning to feel a strange affection for the protagonist to whom Zita had introduced her, his creepiness gradually morphing into the cry of a lost soul. He desperately wanted to be noticed, and in the nine days that had passed since the book launch, he had certainly achieved that.

Chapter 6 – The Rise of The Invisible Man

It was not that the Invisible Man was unfamiliar with Twitter or the other social media platforms. He had, in his previous life, attempted to forge an online presence by delivering pithy, capsule reviews of movies, TV shows and popular music, until he discovered that was pretty much what everyone else did and no one ever got famous that way, no matter how many pictures of himself standing beside movie posters pulling faces he posted on Instagram. But now that he had an almost instant following, he was not quite sure how to use it. He was inundated by questions, requests for appearances (people *always* made a joke about the word 'appearances'), what amounted to fan letters, what amounted to hate mail, and a surprising number of *extremely* explicit fantasies from people who described sex with an invisible man in a level of graphic detail that made him very uncomfortable.

What most wanted to know however boiled down to three things: was it a hoax? If not, how did he do it? Either way, what was he going to do next?

At first, the Invisible Man did not respond to any of these. This took a lot of restraint on his part – he had waited his whole life to have fans and was terrified of losing them by being stand-offish. But his silence only made them want him more, increasing the air of mystery in which he was already veiled. After a day's thought about the best way to play this, he posted his first message:

'*Parker's Piece*'

Parker's Piece was an iconic common in the centre of Cambridge, considered the birthplace of Association Rules Football. Roughly quartered by diagonal paths it was a busy thoroughfare that also attracted dog walkers, joggers, footballers and more, even in the colder months.

It was at 2pm that the first cry went up from the corner of the green where Regent Terrace met Gonville Place, and it was swiftly followed by others. The apparition was fast-moving, and many ran after it, phones held out in front of them to film the event (the standard 21st century response to any crisis).

All they saw was a bicycle. A riderless bicycle. A riderless bicycle that was apparently pedalling itself across Parker's Piece, corner to corner.

Astonishment spread in a wave across the common, following the passage of the bicycle and expanding outwards as the cries of amazement attracted the attention of others.

At the centre of the Piece stood a tall lamp-post, marking the intersection of the paths. The bicycle rode around it three times, before continuing on its journey, giving people a chance to catch up and take some really good pictures.

At the far end of the path, where it met Parkside, the bicycle suddenly fell to the ground, wheels spinning, as lifeless as a marionette whose strings had been cut. Those who were nearby at the time later claimed that they had heard footsteps running away, possibly down Melbourne Place, though it very much depended on who you asked.

Within minutes of the #ghostbike crossing Parker's Piece it was all over the internet. Videos crossed the world and debate about the Invisible Man sparked afresh. Arguments were rekindled but the naysayers had taken a hit because this trick had taken place in a far more public forum than the bookshop. It was still possible to fake this sort of thing with digital effects, but so many had seen it that that seemed less and less likely. The magician lobby grew and other magicians posted their own videos of self-propelled bicycles, showing how it might have been done, though none had the raw believability of Cambridge's Invisible Man. Key to which was the bike itself. That bike had been abandoned, fought over and eventually confiscated by the police before someone got hurt. Of course the police had better things to do than examine a bicycle that had played no part in any crime, but they released a statement saying that it was an ordinary bike, quite unmodified.

Once again, the Invisible Man made the local news.

'The Eagle'
As with any student town (and indeed most British towns full stop), Cambridge had a lot of pubs; from old-fashioned taverns where

everyone looked at you if you ordered anything but ale, to slick, chrome-polished bars where the drinks were brightly coloured and served in test tubes. But if you were looking for *the* Cambridge pub, then you were looking for The Eagle. It was central, a minute from Market Square and only seconds from the grand thoroughfare of King's Parade. It was old, first opened in the 17th Century. It was wood-lined, with creaking floors of warped planks, and a core clientele who looked to have been made from the same age-tempered timber. Above all, it had history, as everything in Cambridge did. The ceiling of the back bar preserved the graffiti of World War 2 airmen, and in 1953, it was to the lunchtime diners of The Eagle that Watson and Crick announced their discovery of the structure of DNA, commemorated by a blue plaque on the wall, to which someone had latterly added the name of Rosalind Franklin.

The Eagle was a Cambridge institution and a landmark. It was always busy, but even the staff who had been there decades were taken aback by how packed it became on the day of that tweet. From the moment doors opened at 11am, people were forcing their way in, anxious to claim a good viewing spot. But there was no such thing in The Eagle. The pub boasted a cramped, twisting layout, separated into rooms, split by wooden screens and divided by the courtyard outside which had been turned into the beer garden. There was no point from which you could see everything, so people just found a spot and stuck with it. They spilled out into the street, inconveniencing traffic, and it was standing room only in the courtyard.

This led to a number of accidents. Every time a glass shattered the whole room shifted as everyone strained to see if this was announcing the arrival of the Invisible Man, and for a few moments the conversation became high and expectant before dying back down again. The only subject of conversation was what today's stunt would be; what would the Invisible Man be able to accomplish in this confined space, and when would it happen?

It soon became apparent that it wasn't going to happen anytime soon. Hours passed. Some people gave up and left, others taking their places. The Invisible Man had not been specific about when he would be turning up and perhaps there was a reason for that. It must have been hard enough to pull off the illusions he was achieving – how much more difficult would it be in a crowded room?

As time passed the agitation grew, as people started to wonder if anything was going happen at all. They checked their phones to see if there had been any new posts on social media cancelling today's 'event'. But the Invisible Man remained as silent as ever.

It began with an argument. It was good-natured enough, as one man accused his friend of drinking his beer.

"I'm not saying you did it on purpose…"

"I didn't touch it. I'm on cider."

"I'm not mad, but I will get mad if you keep lying…"

"I'm not lying…"

"It just evaporated did it?"

"You've got half a pint there."

"But I *had* more than that."

"You just don't realise how much you're drinking."

The conversation was interrupted by a standing drinker. "Excuse me – sorry to eavesdrop – did you say someone drank your pint?"

"Yeah," the victim replied. "Him."

"I lost some of mine as well."

It was as if a veil of realisation had been lifted, and the actors in this little drama became suddenly aware of similarly aggrieved conversations elsewhere in the pub. They were not the only ones who had mysteriously lost a few mouthfuls of drink.

"Who took my crisps?" And it wasn't just drink that was going missing.

Word spread through the crowd like wildfire. The Invisible Man was here, and he was sampling people's drinks!

"I think he's had some of mine."

"You're imagining it."

Everyone wanted to believe that theirs had been one of those drunk, and so the effect of the stunt grew. The buzz swelled in the pub; never had so much excitement been engendered by pilfered drinks. People gazed at their glasses in wonder, trying to guess how it had been done, especially in this crush of people. And then...

"Bloody Hell!"

Joe Sutton had worked behind the bar in The Eagle for five years and as a barman elsewhere for fifteen. Like barmen everywhere he had seen some stuff, and thought he had seen it all. But now he staggered back from the bar in actual terror, eyes glued to the pint he had just placed there.

He did not see where the straw came from, and he could not tell where the beer was going. It seemed to go up the straw and out into the air where it remained briefly suspended before vanishing in front of Joe's astounded eyes, and those of the lucky few close enough to watch. The level of the pint dropped by about half an inch before coming to a stop. As those behind them jostled for a better view, everyone around the bar froze, waiting with baited breath to see what might happen next.

Nothing. The trick was over, and the room burst into spontaneous applause.

This time he didn't make even the local news. But that was okay because this had been a deliberately low-key event, getting up close to his public. The applause was more than enough for him, listening as he stumbled a weaving and drunken route out of the pub. He was their hero.

'*The Grafton Centre*'

The Invisible Man had not counted on how many people would show up at The Eagle, and had initially thought that it would be impossible for him to carry out his plan in that press. In the event, there were so many people that one more made little difference – everyone was pushing each other so no one stopped to wonder who had pushed them. Still, he thought it better for his next 'appearance' to try a larger space. The announcement was general enough that people had no idea where in the large shopping centre they were supposed to go. Was the trick going to happen in one of the shops? In one of the courts? Perhaps even outside the grand entrance lobby? Some settled down to wait, others hurried from shop to shop in quick succession, checking each one before going back to the start and round again.

This was set against the already crowded Christmas season, as people tried to get their shopping done and parents queued up with little ones at Santa's Grotto, situated in the main hall. The Grotto was shaped like an igloo, festively decorated with lights, the queuing area festooned with tinsel, and featuring a small replica of Santa's sleigh pulled by the requisite reindeer, led by Rudolph.

For the brief period that they were in the Grotto children loved it, but the long wait bored both them and their parents (who spent it wondering how the price of one minute with a fat man went up so much every year). The queue had a background murmur of whining, moaning and general dissatisfaction.

And then the sound hushed. Children who had been slumped bonelessly on the floor or hanging over the guide ropes were suddenly upright and alert, eyes wide, mouths open, all staring in the same direction; towards Santa's sleigh.

Rudolph was moving.

He shook, shivering as if life was animating his fibreglass body. Then he tugged at the tinsel reins that attached him to the sleigh. One of Santa's elves (for whom the festive season was already wearing thin) strode up to see what the problem was, but before she reached the sleigh Rudolph shot forward, trailing snapped tinsel in his wake, leaving the other reindeer behind as he took to the air.

In fairness, Rudolph did not achieve much of a height, particularly not when you considered the size of the hall, but that did not matter to the children who screamed in excitement and cried out with glee, while their parents just screamed and cried out. One enterprising child took the initiative and ran after Rudolph, setting a precedent that the others were not slow to follow. A stream of children charged after the flying reindeer, forgetting their parents' warnings and cautionary tales about Pied Pipers, laughing and squealing as they went. They, in turn, were followed by a much less happy stream of jostling parents, all trying to get past each other to lay a hand on a fast-departing collar and reclaim their errant offspring.

To either side of this unlikely parade, staff stood gaping, wondering if this was a publicity stunt they had not been told about or if they were supposed to be doing something to stop it. Other shoppers stopped in their Christmas rush to gaze in disbelief. They knew they were seeing something special, they knew this was going to be on the news tonight, they knew they were in the presence of the Invisible Man.

This time he was at the top of the local news.

'*Cambridge United*'

Cambridge United hadn't sold out a match in years, but it was fair to say that not everyone was there to watch the game. That might have been a little unfair on the players, but they were as eager as anyone else to see what might happen.

The two teams ran out onto the pitch. The Captains met and shook hands. The referee flicked a coin up into the air.

And there it hung.

Most of the crowd could not see what was happening, but they saw the reactions and heard the United Captain swear in shock.

After about five seconds the coin dropped to the grass and the referee inched nervously forward to pick it up, as if afraid it was going to explode.

Suddenly, the ball he was holding popped out from under his arm and took off down the pitch, weaving between astonished players all the way to the goal and flying into the back of the net.

The stands erupted.

"Invisible Man! Invisible Man!" Difficult words to chant but they made it work.

Though none of them saw him, the Invisible Man stood in front of the goal, arms in the air, turning slowly around and letting their adoration wash over him in a crashing wave.

This was what being alive was all about. This extraordinary feeling.

He made the national news that night. He was the final item – the joke item – but he was there. The presenter spoke to a stage magician who called him the most gifted illusionist of this generation. Books sales were through the roof. The publishers couldn't print them fast enough.

'Silver Street Bridge'

The onlookers only took a moment to spot the punt out on the water that seemed to be unmanned, the pole that drove it moving of its own accord.

Camera phones were whipped out and people struggled for position to take their video. The excited voices became louder as the punt headed towards them, the bridge becoming an aggressive tussle, no one willing to give up their spot to the crush of people behind, blocking the road and holding up traffic. He was going to go under the bridge!

Cameras were thrust down over the parapet to get a good shot (more than one finding a permanent home on the bottom of the river) as the punt passed into the darkness beneath the arch. The crowd did an abrupt about-face, the frenzied jockeying changing direction as they stormed the other side of the bridge to watch for the punt's reappearance.

But now the pole was laid flat along the narrow boat, and there was no sign of anyone in control. The punt drifted on, describing a path determined by the current.

The Invisible Man had vanished. Sort of.

Instantly people took to the river, claiming the punt and dragging it back to shore where they upturned it, looking for the mechanism that had driven it and held the pole in place. People dived into the water to search beneath the bridge. They roamed the banks hunting for a man with a remote control.

From his seat on the bank, where he had leapt out at the last moment, the Invisible Man watched them and took a strange pleasure in their fanaticism. It made him tingle to think that they were so desperate to find him.

The day after the events on Silver Street Bridge, Cambridge City Council put out an online video to speak directly to the Invisible

Man, describing him with self-conscious irony as '*Cambridge's most famous face*', and inviting him to turn on the lights on the Christmas tree at the corner of Market Square that Saturday night at 9pm. They knew, they said, that he would likely not respond, but the offer was there and they would not invite anyone else to do it.

The night arrived, and the Mayor, with various other local bigwigs, stood beside the big, red button on the dais erected beside the tree. It was a local tradition that usually attracted a reasonable crowd of parents with children still young enough to enjoy coloured lights, but tonight the square was packed with people.

Time ticked by, and the hired band did their best to keep the crowd amused while the organisers exchanged glances and wondered if this had been as good an idea as it had seemed two days ago. After all, this set-up had been constructed by council builders to council-approved specifications. There had been no chance for anyone to monkey around with the mechanism, which would surely be necessary to pull off this trick. If nothing happened then the Mayor would have to press the button himself and even he was prepared to admit that would be a serious anti-climax.

As the time drew near, the Mayor led the crowd in a countdown.

"10… 9… 8… 7… 6… 5… 4… 3… 2…" The Mayor swallowed. "1…"

It was the longest second of the Mayor's life. A second was all it was but it felt as if time hung frozen in the air as all eyes turned to the big red button and, as that frozen second finally defrosted into the next, the button pressed down.

The lights sparked into life up and down the Christmas tree, flickering on and off in attractive patterns that made the children ooh and aah.

But those oohs and aahs were inaudible over the raucous roar of approval from the crowd.

The Invisible Man had done it again.

Chapter 7 – The Lecturer

As she did every morning on arrival at the Chemistry Department, Professor Evelyn Herrick picked up her mail before going to her office. She flicked from envelope to envelope in her gloved hands as she walked, sorting the correspondence into personal, professional and people who wanted money. One envelope stood out; her name handwritten and the letter hand-delivered. She put this to one side when she entered her office and removed her hat, coat, scarf and gloves. She gave the radiator a kick – the central heating was a hit and miss affair that froze up at the first sign of wintry weather.

Having smoked a quick cigarette out the window, she turned to the mail. With a letter-opener shaped like a swordfish she filleted the first envelope, working through the pile with curt precision till all that remained was the hand-delivered anomaly. A swift incision of the swordfish and a sharp upward jerk opened the envelope to reveal single sheet of paper inside. Professor Herrick frowned at it. The letter was written in the style of a kidnap note, in letters cut from newspapers and magazines, and consisted of a single sentence.

'You won't even see me coming.'

Evelyn Herrick snorted and dropped the offending article into her departmentally mandated recycling bin. She was a lecturer who did not mince her words and this would not be the first piece of hate mail she had received from a student. At least this one had refrained from sending a dead animal of some sort (it was usually a mouse or a fish).

It was possible that, for a moment, her thoughts turned to the recent death of Professor Digges, but if they did then it was only momentary. Though they were both 'scientists', that term was a broad umbrella and nowhere more so than at Cambridge, where specialisation was encouraged down to the microbial, molecular and atomic levels. In the same way that the great evolutionary biologist Stephen J. Gould had declared that there was no such thing as fish, at Cambridge there was no such thing as a scientist. There were macro-biologists, analytical biochemists, condensed matter physicists and chemoinformaticists, but no one was just a 'scientist'. If there was someone else with the same area of study as you, then you were sitting at the academic kiddie table.

This letter was just another childish prank as might be found at any university. Students away from home for the first time had a habit of regressing to an infantile level of humour just because you tore up their work in front of them, berated them for their spelling, or called them a half-witted dunce with less understanding of biocatalysis than that possessed by an artichoke in front of their friends and contemporaries. Professor Herrick did not suffer fools lightly, and her definition of fools was a very broad one indeed, including anyone who disagreed with her but also those who slavishly nodded away at everything she said as if they had never had an original thought of their own. If the price one paid for high standards was hate mail, death threats and the occasional deceased rodent in her in-box, then it was one Professor Herrick was happy to pay.

The letter was excised from her mind as easily as it was dropped in the trash, and she turned to her laptop to answer online correspondence before her first seminar.

Despite the Professor's reputation, the seminar would be well-attended because she had an equally well-deserved reputation for brilliance. It is a feature of people like Professor Herrick that others hate them and desire their approval in almost equal measure.

The seminar room was on the same corridor as the Professor's office. Unlike Professor Digges, Professor Herrick preferred a working place that was right at the centre of her department. Professors like Digges did everything they could to avoid students, and treated the University like a retirement home with more intelligent conversation and better booze. Those like Herrick, who was still an active researcher, enjoyed imparting wisdom to the next generation, and berating them for the lack of it. Teaching ran in her blood in the same way that pillage ran in that of Genghis Khan.

"Take your seats."

The students hastened to find a place to sit and fumbled laptops and personal devices from their bags. Nobody wanted to be the one holding up proceedings. At some point during the seminar, someone was almost guaranteed to be singled out for the kind of humiliation that made Professor Herrick's seminars a spectator sport, and nobody wanted to give her an excuse.

"Today I shall be talking about enantioselective catalysis. Specifically; asymmetric hydrogenation. I will doing so very quickly and I expect you to keep up. I also expect you to pay attention. There will be questions. They are not rhetorical. If I ask you a question it is because I expect you to be able to answer it, because it will be a question on the subject about which I have been talking and on the subject which you are supposed to be studying and in which I presume you take at least a mild interest. If you are unable to answer the question there will be no direct consequences but I would beg you to seriously consider redirecting your studies to one more suited to you. Shapes and colours perhaps. Or if even that seems too taxing then I'm sure they are looking for students at ARU."

There was a nervous murmur of amusement. Anglia Ruskin University was the 'other' University in Cambridge, an ex-poly with an excellent reputation for music and optometry, and an institution that Evelyn Herrick never missed an opportunity to mock, as she still resented the idea that the word 'university' could just be tacked onto such a place.

"We shall begin."

For the next twenty minutes the Professor talked and her students listened. Most had the good sense to record these seminars rather than trying to type, because even if you were quick enough to keep up with the Professor, it was hard to take in the sense of what she was saying while acting as a stenographer, and when a question was fired at you then you were left there like a deer in headlights desperately scanning the last few sentences you had written in the hope that the answer might lie somewhere in them.

As the clock hit twenty past ten, Professor Herrick held up her hand sharply. "We will pause there for a five minute break. You may step out to stretch your legs. Do not be late back. I shall start speaking again at twenty five past exactly and if you are not in your seat then I guarantee the first question will be directed at you."

The Professor turned on her heel and went back out the door

that led to her office. The room breathed a collective sigh of relief. So far the rapidly fired questions had produced answers that had been adequate enough not to lead to an outburst. One of the few good things about Professor Herrick's seminars and lectures (besides their brilliance) was that they came with regular breaks because the Professor could not go for longer than half an hour without a cigarette. You could set your watch by her cravings.

The students stood, stretched and talked amongst themselves, though quietly because the door to the corridor, and the door beyond to the Professor's office, remained open. Some stepped out of exit on the far side of the seminar room to get a drink or...

SLAM!

Every head in the room whipped about at the sound of the Professor's office door slamming violently shut.

That couldn't be a good sign. The Professor had seemed in a comparatively sunny mood so far today but none of them had ever known her angry enough to start slamming doors. Perhaps the open window in the Professor's office, through which she smoked (in direct contravention of University policy), had somehow caused the door to...

Another noise.

Less sudden and not as loud, but just as unexpected. Professor Herrick was not a noisy person; she moved like a shark, silent but deadly. This noise was like a scuffling or a scrabbling, as if the Professor was taking secret dance lessons, which seemed unlikely.

Now a tumbling, rattling clatter, as of items falling to the floor, followed by sharper noises; a thumping against wood, the stamping of a heeled shoe. And then; more human sounds, but muffled, straining to be heard.

"Professor?" It was Leon who first amongst the students summoned up the courage to speak.

No response. The noises continued.

Swallowing his fear, and preparing himself for the verbal tirade that was sure to follow, Leon stepped into the corridor and knocked on the door.

"Professor?"

The noises peaked. And stopped.

"Is everything alright?"

The silence that now came from the room beyond seemed louder than the noises had been.

Leon knocked again. "Professor Herrick, are you alright in there? Should I get someone?"

"Try the door," urged Anne, who had come to join Leon in the corridor.

"You try the door."

"You're closest."

"I knocked."

Anne reached out and turned the knob.

"It's locked." She sounded relieved. "Professor Herrick? Professor Herrick?!"

Leon turned back to the rest of the room. "I think we should get someone."

When Inspector Harrigan arrived, he found the room exactly as it had been when the caretaker, fetched by the students, had unlocked the door. It was a mess. Papers and books were strewn across the floor, making a mockery of the stringent organisation Professor Herrick had imposed upon them. The chair was overturned, the laptop lay nearby, its screen broken, the contents of the desk and shelves had been likewise reduced to chaos. Sprawled across all this was the lifeless body of Professor Evelyn Herrick, eyes starting from their sockets, tongue protruding, a swordfish letter-opener sticking from between her ribs and a crimson blood stain spread across her white blouse.

"I suppose we can rule out suicide," said Sergeant Stubbs, dourly. Stubbs seemed to have been hired specifically to fill the role of the lugubrious sergeant.

"Accidental then, you think?" suggested Harrigan.

"Or natural causes."

Harrigan sighed. "Tell me Sergeant, before the doc gets here; you ever see a face like that on a stabbing victim?"

Stubbs shook his jowly face. "No, sir, I haven't. That's a

strangle face if ever I saw one."

Harrigan nodded. "That's what I thought. Do we know if the knife – looks to me like a letter-opener – belonged to the victim?"

"First question I asked, sir. It does."

"So what we're looking at is maybe an attempted strangling in which the victim fought back and the killer was forced to use whatever was to hand to finish the job."

"That's the way I see it, sir. Victim may have grabbed the letter-opener to defend herself and the killer took the opportunity."

Harrigan stared at the scene, his glum features reflecting his Hangdog nickname.

"You were at the Hopkins Building two weeks ago, weren't you Sergeant?"

"I was, sir."

"Am I alone in seeing a similarity?"

"You are not, sir."

"Bugger."

"The very word I used myself, sir."

Harrigan took a step further into the room and heard a crunch beneath his feet. He looked down gingerly; when something went 'crunch' at a crime scene it was usually something nasty. He frowned.

"Are there seeds on the floor?"

Stubbs nodded. "Victim was a bit of a health nut. There was a bowl of nuts and seeds on her desk. Knocked over in the struggle."

"Do you think it might be an important clue?"

"I do not, sir."

"Neither do I." Harrigan puffed out his cheeks. "Well, at least there's an open window here. So no questions about how they got in and out this time."

The window was on the far side of the office and there was no way to reach it without disturbing the chaos of the scene, which Harrigan didn't want to do until forensics had been in to pick it apart piece by piece. But how the killer had got in was not what was currently concerning him.

A second murder. It had been almost two weeks since the

death of Professor Digges but there was no question in Harrigan's mind. Sometimes you just got a sense of these things. How long could they keep it from the press that the two might be related? Not long. Cambridge professors did not get strangled in their rooms every day. The media would be on it like tweed on a University don.

More stress. More pressure. More stuff he didn't need on the last case of his career.

'*I'm taking you with me.*' Good last words, but first he'd have to find someone to say them to.

He took a deep breath. Put it from your mind. Not your problem. Be a detective and leave the press to the higher ups. A second murder was unexpected and not good news (certainly not for Professor Herrick), on the other hand it did provide more information, more potential for clues. Above all, there surely had to be a connection between these two professors (beyond the fact of their both being professors) and that connection would be the biggest clue of the bunch. That, more than anything, would lead him to the killer.

"Right," Harrigan took charge, "I've got to phone in." No avoiding it unfortunately. "You get this sealed off and tell the students they can't go anywhere for now. I want to speak to all of them. I want to speak to everyone in this department and anyone who knew this woman. I want every bit of information there is on her."

For two weeks he had floundered with the case going nowhere, but now he had something. Somewhere, there would be a connection between Digges and Herrick, and Harrigan found himself almost light-hearted as he stepped outside to phone Chief Inspector 'Growley' Lane.

Lane reacted about as Harrigan had expected and instructed his detective to speak to no one about this. Which was fine with Harrigan, who hated talking to the press; his media interviews were blooper reels of 'umm's, 'err's and mumbled excuses for why he hadn't got any answers.

"I'm going to take a look outside to see how he got out, then I'll speak to the students."

"Don't waste too much time on that."

Lane hung up and Harrigan went for a stroll around the building.

The Chemistry Department was housed in an ugly, twentieth century block that squatted on Lensfield road, unintimidated by the much nicer buildings around it. Harrigan soon located the open window of Professor Herrick's second floor room which overlooked the carpark. The killer had been pretty brazen to scale the wall at this time of day in sight of anyone parking, but a convenient drainpipe made it a relatively easy climb, so presumably it had been worth the risk.

Harrigan examined the ground at the base of the wall, more because that was what detectives were supposed to do than because he expected to find something helpful like a footprint on the wet stone. It had been raining on and off today, and even if someone had left a print then it would be gone by now. He found a single unsmoked cigarette, which he bagged without much optimism.

He turned back to the carpark and smiled. This second murder continued to move more easily than the first. Directly opposite him was a security camera, positioned to take in the whole space. Gotcha.

A pigeon chose that moment to crap on his shoulder, but Harrigan decided to take it as a good omen.

While Stubbs went to secure the camera footage, Harrigan spoke to the students. The conversations were brisk and to the point; there had been nothing untoward about today's seminar; Professor Herrick had been in no more vindictive a mood than usual; no one knew anything about her personal life and they would have been surprised to learn that she had one; yes she had enemies, how long have you got? The one thing that seemed worth gleaning was that Herrick always took a cigarette break at the same time, which suggested that the killer was familiar with her routine and had known when to strike.

"She couldn't go long without a fag," Leon confirmed what others had already said. "She tried switching to an e-cig last year." He shook his head like a trauma victim recalling a horrific memory. "That was a bad fortnight for everyone."

Harrigan nodded. It did strike him as a little odd that someone who was enough of a health freak to have nuts and seeds as their snack food of choice should also be a smoker, but perhaps she tried to offset the one with the other. Smokers were good at justifying themselves. He himself had quit in the mid-nineties and, outside of a brief relapse after his divorce, had stuck to it, despite missing it every single day.

"Got the security footage." Stubbs stuck his head in as Harrigan was winding up with the students, whose main concern seemed to be what effect this might have on their grade. "Is that bird-do on your shoulder?"

"Pigeon."

"Supposed to be lucky."

"Let's hope. Give me the security tape."

It wasn't a tape of course, it was a USB stick, and officially he was supposed to send it in for analysis, but Harrigan was too impatient to wait.

Advances in digital technology have surely had an effect on the security industry and yet, at least as far as Harrigan could see, the quality of security camera footage had remained unchanged from the early eighties. There was some evidence that juries did not believe in crisp, pixel-perfect security footage, thinking it had to be faked, and so a conscious decision had been made to keep it grainy and horrible.

Harrigan watched the morning arrivals in the carpark, checked the time-code and fast-forwarded. At this point Professor Herrick's window was closed but, yet more luck, the angle of the camera gave a partial view into her office. Harrigan watched. Just after nine he saw movement at the window and rewound to watch again. Professor Herrick had arrived for work. Harrigan saw an arm at the window as she removed her coat, a brief full figure and then; there was the murder victim herself. She opened the window and leant out to light and then smoke a single cigarette, which she stubbed out on the sill. This done, she closed the window and – Harrigan peered closely at the grey image, rewound and peered again – fastened it shut. At ten o'clock Harrigan caught another passing glimpse as

Professor Herrick left the room to attend the seminar.

For the next twenty minutes, nothing happened. People passed through the carpark, heading for the main doors, bundled up against the wind. None seemed suspicious or even looked up at the locked window.

At twenty past ten, Herrick returned and opened the window to smoke a second cigarette. Harrigan shifted in his seat; it had to be now. Sure enough, just as Professor Herrick leant forward, she was suddenly and violently jerked back into the room, the unlit cigarette flying from her hand. Harrigan stared intently at the image. There was Herrick again, flung back against the open window, clutching at her throat. Then she was on the move again, perhaps fighting back against her attacker. Harrigan's frustration grew as he peered at the obscured image. Here was a flailing arm, there a passing body or a flung back head, but all seemed to belong to the Professor. Had the killer known about the camera? Finally, he saw the Professor's left arm, straining upwards, clawing at the air desperately. Then a spasm. Then it dropped. She had been stabbed.

Harrigan's eyes were glued to the window. The caretaker had found the office door locked from the inside, there was one way out.

Nothing.

For long minutes he stared, knowing that the murderer had to still be in there, waiting.

Then; movement!

But it was the caretaker. Harrigan recognised him as his horrified face flicked past the window. Then the man looked out, removing all doubt. The killer *had* to still be in the room; there was nowhere else for him to be. But he hadn't been there.

Harrigan felt a sense of crushing defeat overwhelming him. This was as impossible as the first.

Reaching home that night, after an afternoon spent in fruitless interviews with staff, colleagues and friends of Professor Herrick, and finding no connection between her and Professor Digges, Harrigan collapsed into his chair. There had to be a connection. There *had* to be. If he couldn't figure out *how* either murder had

77

been committed, then that connection was all he had.

On the shelf beside him was a picture of his two sons, William and Don. He hadn't spoken to them in… Well, it had been a while. He ought to call really. But it always felt like an imposition; either that he had called at the wrong time or that he shouldn't have called at all. If he didn't call then he could cling to the fantasy that they wanted to speak to him but knew how busy he was.

'*Tell my boys I love them.*'

Harrigan's gaze slid to the phone. It wasn't that late…

The phone rang, and he answered it half-expecting it to be one of his sons, but it proved to be O'Connor from forensics asking if they had a comprehensive list of the contents of Professor Herrick's office.

"The secretary's putting something together. There's going to be a lot of paperwork. We're not looking at robbery as a motive anyway."

If either Harrigan or O'Connor had known *exactly* what was in the room before the death of Evelyn Herrick, then they might have spotted that one thing was now missing. But not even the secretary knew, because the letter that was absent from the Professor's recycling bin had only been delivered that morning.

Chapter 8 – The White Rat

The text from Jack arrived in late afternoon, the day after the date.

'Have you seen the news? Had a great time last night. Hope we can do it again somewhen.'

The news in question was the murder of Professor Evelyn Herrick. Police were refusing to confirm a connection between this new killing and that of Herbert Digges, but they didn't need to because the media was doing it for them.

Amelia read the text three times, making sure that it had no levels of meaning that she was missing. It seemed to be a straightforward checking-in text. Calling someone the day after a first date can sound a bit needy, while not getting in touch at all seems like a rejection. A text strikes the right balance of casual but interested. Amelia had sent such messages herself, and spent long hours crafting the few sentences they called for. Most interesting, to her practiced eye, was that Jack had chosen to open with the murder, as if that was why he was texting and the rest of the message was an afterthought. If Amelia was any judge then that had been a calculated decision, and one that Jack had gone back and forth over. He had probably been wondering what to text and been delighted by the breaking news that had given him an ideal icebreaker.

On the other hand, perhaps Jack was normal and didn't put this Napoleonic level of planning into saying *'Had a great time last night'*.

Amelia broke off from what she had been doing to craft a considered and yet apparently off-the-cuff reply.

'Yeah, saw it. Weird, huh? I had a great time too.'

Here she paused. She didn't want to be the one to say *'How about next Tuesday?'* or similar. On the other hand if she failed to address the last sentence of Jack's text then it was as if she had consciously decided to ignore it.

In the end she went with *'Call me.'*. Which she wasn't completely happy with but there was only so long you could spend on something like this and she had already spent an hour and a half.

Finally putting the phone down, she turned back to the project that had consumed the better part of her day. In a sprawl of maps, sheets of paper and post-it notes, it had spread across the floor as she worked, making her living room look like a conspiracy theorist's attic.

Had today's events given this project new urgency? Maybe not. The police had not yet released any details that suggested the second murder had the impossible aspect which had distinguished the first (no matter how much the media goaded them into doing so).

Besides, Amelia was not trying to find a killer, she was trying to find an Invisible Man. Not to expose him or to put him on trial, but because…

Amelia paused in her train of thought. Why was she doing this? Probably didn't matter. She was doing it because. Would this approach work? Maybe.

Last night, when she had got in after her date, Amelia had turned back to the start of the Invisible Man's book and begun to go through it again with a highlighter and a notebook at her side, marking any references to location and/or surroundings. The book contained no place names other than Cambridge, which suggested that the Invisible Man was deliberately keeping his location secret, but it did contain descriptions. Actually, it contained a lot because the Invisible Man stressed how the world seemed different now he was invisible; '*It was as if there was no barrier to every sound in the world. The regular roaring of trains, the clanking of heavy machinery, the cacophony of children's laughter, all assaulted my ears.*'. Taken individually, they were not that helpful, but when you put them together then maybe she could start could start to narrow things down.

Once she had marked up the book and noted down all the descriptions, Amelia went to bed. She rose early, unable to sleep, too many thoughts in her mind. As she ate a bowl of cereal she got out her notes and began putting them in order of usefulness.

Finding the Invisible Man's home seemed impossible as there were only the most general descriptions, but the lab in which his transformation had taken place was a different story. It was as he left the lab that the book began, taking his first wobbly steps into a world that seemed new to him even before he understood why. The descriptions of what he saw through newly invisible eyes '*still burning with the after-effects of the process*' were vague in their location, but specific in detail. It had to be near railway lines and probably near the station itself ('*The train whipped by in a blur; colour and speed bleeding together.*'). The '*heavy machinery*' could be the railway but there was also '*the acrid stink of exhaust and the stinging tang of oil*'. The '*cacophony of children's laughter*'? Perhaps a school? He went on to note '*I clutched the iron railings for support, trying not to be sick*', and the book's first line referenced breaking '*though the undergrowth*'. Most cryptically, the very first thing he saw was '*...a white circle, a silver man pointing back the way I had come, to the House of Pain.*'.

Gradually, point by point, Amelia began to narrow down the list of places it could be. Tearing sheets from her notebook, she assigned each sheet to a place and kept track of which salient points each place had and what they lacked.

It was an inexact science because children's laughter could be a birthday party; clanking machinery could be a train, a truck or a garage door; and what constituted 'nearby' varies from one person to the next. But by evening, Amelia had managed to put together a list of areas in which the Invisible Man's lab might be located.

When she went to bed that night, she felt different. Lying in the dark, she felt a frisson of excitement, of something just on the horizon. There was still a chance that it was all in her mind, but then again…

Amelia started early the next morning. She showered, had a proper breakfast, then made sandwiches to take with her on what might prove a long day's hike. Cambridge was not a big city – one of the things that recommended it to Amelia was that you could walk across it in an hour – but she did not know how long this trek might take. She felt like an explorer going into unknown territory.

The first cluster of spots she tried was on the north side of the city. This was where the Science Park was located and where Cambridge's second railway station, Cambridge North, had recently opened. The tracks ploughed a path through the east side of the city so trains could be heard and seen elsewhere, but the number of times the Invisible Man referred to the sight and sound of trains in those opening pages suggested proximity to a station. Certainly it was a good place to start, and Cambridge North's proximity to the Science Park made it the leading candidate – a lab near a Science Park seemed almost too logical. It was also a far less densely populated area than that surrounding the older main station, not far from where Amelia lived. That area was thick with houses, student accommodation and new builds, and while an invisible man was easy to hide, a laboratory was less so.

Probably. Actually ascertaining if there was a lab in the vicinity was something Amelia hadn't put a lot of thought into. She'd narrowed the possible locations, now she was going to them, and she had sort of expected it to just pan out, like unlocking achievements in a computer game. But the book contained no actual descriptions of the lab itself – '*The House of Pain*'. It could be in the basement of someone's house for all she knew.

For the next hour, Amelia checked those streets which she had identified as clear possibilities (those near schools and/or garages). White circles of one sort or another abounded but she found nothing resembling a silver man. She spent the next two hours traipsing around and around the station, trying to walk every street. But with every step she became less convinced. The silver man could be a post-invisibility hallucination, but that absence aside, this just didn't feel right to her. Even without a specific description, the Invisible Man's words had left her with an impression of what sort of place she was looking for. She'd read the words so often that she felt she had been there, and this all felt wrong. It was the perfect location; but it wasn't right.

Eating her sandwiches as she walked, Amelia trekked back across town towards the main station. This felt like a quest now, and she was not going to waste a second.

She crossed the footbridge that spanned the railway tracks, and immediately felt better. This was a much less suitable area for a secret lab, densely populated and with people around at all times of the day and night thanks to the proximity of Anglia Ruskin University, but it *felt* like the place the Invisible Man was describing.

Amelia stopped in her tracks.

In many ways, and as her sister had inferred, the Invisible Man was not a very good writer, but he did have a flair for description. On the road was the large white circle of a mini-roundabout at a three-way intersection. Growing from the verge beside it was a silver birch tree that had an accidentally, but unmistakably, humanoid shape to it. One of its branches pointed across the road at a paved path to Amelia's right, hemmed in with bushes, cramped between new build flats and the industrial estate beyond, from which Amelia could hear the sound of clanking machinery. Shivers whispered their way down Amelia's spine as she heard the laughter of children coming from a park just past the birch tree, surrounded by an iron fence.

This was it. And that path to her right; that was the way from which he must have come that day.

'*My body still shaking, my heart trying to tear itself apart, I broke through the undergrowth and stumbled blindly onto the path, and into the light of a new world.*'

Amelia felt almost lightheaded as she walked, conscious that she was treading in the footsteps of the Invisible Man. She kept her eyes on the fence to her left, thickly grown through with plants that wound twigs and tendrils through the wire diamonds.

There!

The torn gap in the fence was hard to spot because of the undergrowth on the other side. You had to be looking for it to see it, and Amelia had known that it would be here.

For the first time, she paused. Was it possible that the Invisible Man lived here? Up to now she had been too consumed with the pursuit to think about what would happen if she actually found the man she was looking for. There was nothing in the book to suggest that he was dangerous, but there was plenty to suggest that he did not want to be found. And what if she was right to make some tenuous connection between the Invisible Man and the insoluble murders? She could be walking into the lair of a killer.

It wouldn't be the first time, but in Egypt she had had back-up from people who knew what they were doing, or at least knew how to handle a gun.

Then again, what use would a gun be against an invisible man?

Amelia checked up and down the quiet path, finding it empty. She stooped to the tear in the fence and forced her way through, the tangle of bushes scratching her skin and tugging her clothes as she crawled forward.

"Ah, ah, ah…" Her head was dragged back as her hair caught in the scrub and she had to stop to free herself before going on, her body contorted at an awkward angle.

"Ow!" There were thorns as well.

Scrabbling out the far side of the thicket, face scratched, hair a mess, hands dirtied and clothes snagged here and there, Amelia looked around her. Surrounded by a verge of thick, wet grass was a blank, faceless building, its only distinguishing characteristic its lack of windows. Possibly an abandoned military building of some sort.

Could this be The House of Pain? Amelia had thought a lot about the name that the Invisible Man had given to the lab that created him. It made her shiver.

She wiped the mud from her hands onto her jeans and took a walk around the building. The grass verge continued all the way around and the building was enclosed on every side by thick, impenetrable bushes, all evergreen needles and bramble spikes. At the far end there was a door which Amelia skirted nervously away from on her first time around. Having established this was the only entrance in the otherwise featureless walls, she went back and knocked.

She wasn't quite sure what she would do if someone answered – she could hardly ask if anyone had seen an invisible man – but it seemed the polite thing to do. No one came to answer, but the door swung open. Or at least it appeared to. Was it possible that the Invisible Man had seen her arrive, waited for her by the door and opened it himself, making it seem as if it was swinging naturally?

Amelia checked her imagination and tried to control her breathing. It was all possible. That was the problem with an invisible man.

"Hello?" She wasn't sure if she would prefer to get an answer or not, but none came. Cautiously, Amelia stepped inside.

Even allowing for the weather, the building was cold with that damp chill of emptiness. Using the torch on her phone, Amelia located a light switch and flicked it on. Buzzing halogens snapped into life revealing a space as blank and anonymous as the exterior.

From the outside, all the signs had seemed right, but now Amelia began to wonder. This didn't look like a laboratory. The place was divided into three rooms, all with bare concrete floors and white, paint-flecked walls, smeared with mould. Dust-heavy spiders' webs hung thickly in the corners. It might have been empty but it certainly wasn't clean, and her understanding of labs was that cleanliness was important. It didn't look as if anyone had worked in here for years, if ever.

That said, there was something about it. Something uneasy. Amelia felt a prickling sensation on the back of her neck, as if she was being watched.

A scratching sound made her turn and Amelia started at the sight of a rat, trotting along the base of the wall. It was large and white, and took scant interest in the tightly clenched woman intruding in its home. Amelia held her breath until she was sure it had left the room.

You had to expect rats in place like this, but white ones? Did that mean something?

Did any of it?

Before setting out that morning, Amelia had gone into her purse and found a business card given to her earlier that year. On the back of the card was a single word, printed in a black, unostentatious script: 'UNIVERSAL'. On the front was the name 'Boris' and a phone number. For so little detail it was barely worth having the card.

Boris was the man who had got her involved with a Mummy. He was also the man who had saved her life. At the end of her Egyptian adventure, Amelia had still been unclear on exactly who Universal were and what they did, but when it came to the inexplicable and impossible she could not think of anyone else to call. She had thought about it this morning, but all she really had was her own vague suspicions. Did she have more now?

Not really. Perhaps this was still a belated hangover from Egypt. She wanted it to be more than it was. She wanted the Invisible Man to be real. She wanted the murders to be connected.

Amelia forced a smile. "Idiot."

And in the corner of the room, an unseen figure, watching her, nodded in silent agreement; Idiot.

Once she was back outside, Amelia felt a sense of relief. Though she had found nothing suspicious, the atmosphere within had been tense to the point of being oppressive. She had felt it weighing down on her. Perhaps it was just her imagination. Her expectations.

There was nothing here to suggest anything untoward. If this looked like the place that the Invisible Man described then what of it? Why should the writer not base the fictional lab in his book on a real location? Lots of writers did that and it did not mean that the events were real. She needed to get her head back in the game. The game in question being life. She wanted a second date with Jack, she wanted a nice Christmas with her family, she wanted to return to the Carpathian mountains in the New Year with a renewed sense of purpose. All of these were achievable goals and had nothing to do with murder and invisible men – real or imagined.

Closing the door of the 'lab' behind her, Amelia headed back around the building to crawl back out the way she had come in.

Inside, the white rat watched the door close. It sniffed the air and tensed as it heard footsteps far heavier than its own on the concrete floor, coming its way. The rat's body chemistry changed subtly as fight and flight instincts kicked in. For a moment it flickered briefly, waves of invisibility passing across its white fur. Then it winked out of existence, and scurried for a hole that led down to the basement.

Chapter 9 – Nuts In May

It was a normal mid-December afternoon in Cambridge's Market Square. Which was to say that it was horrible. This close to Christmas, the market became a seething sea of irritable people, all convinced that, despite evidence to the contrary, that pair of gloves that was just the right size and colour for Auntie Millie was the last such pair in creation and there would never be another. The rudeness of the British shopping public, which comes in at a pretty high level to start with, goes up a notch with every day closer to Christmas. Like the Mongol hordes, they roamed from stall to stall; nothing would distract them from their focussed pillaging.

The first scream came from Rose Crescent, followed by more cries of terror. Then the tone changed as an object of fear transmuted into one of wonder, and people realised what was happening, or at least *who* was happening. But the loud reactions of the Christmas shoppers to the apparition that now entered Market Square were not enough to drown out what people afterwards remembered most about the extraordinary event. The Invisible Man was singing.

"Here we go gathering nuts in May, nuts in May, nuts in May. Here we go gathering nuts in May on a cold and frosty morning..."

The voice rang out high and clear in the cold air as, to the jaw-dropped bewilderment of passers-by, a pair of trousers skipped into Market Square, turning right and beginning a circuit of the central stalls.

They were, witnesses later agreed, beige, held up with a belt, and appeared to be loose-fitting, although it was hard to tell when you could not see the person wearing them. They were open at the top, and taller people would later claim that they had been able to see right down into the legs. At the bottom they terminated approximately three inches from the ground – although that measurement was speculative as the trousers were constantly in motion, skipping energetically through the crowds who hastily got out of the way, not sure what they were seeing but certain that they would prefer to see it from a distance.

By the time the trousers started on their second lap, people had recovered themselves enough to grab their phones. No one would believe this, there *had* to be evidence. Round the trousers went again, still singing loudly, before breaking into a run as they completed the second lap and dashing off the way they had come down Rose Crescent, leaving stunned silence behind them, broken only by a wailing child, who had foolishly run into the path of the trousers and hurt himself.

This time there had been no announcement in advance, because the Invisible Man had wanted a bit of space, and because it no longer seemed necessary. His celebrity needed no introduction.

Within the hour, social media was on fire with the news of what everyone agreed was his most remarkable feat yet. People were stumped. Elaborate robotic machines were proposed to animate the trousers whilst a drone disguised in each leg maintained that floating position off the ground. But no one who had seen the trousers in action could seriously believe that. They had been too lifelike. It had been impossible.

It was everything that the Invisible Man could have hoped for. Wall to wall acclamation. Whether people thought it was a magic, science, an internet stunt, some combination of the above or the second coming of Christ, there was nothing but admiration and excitement.

Was he on the national news? Damn right he was. And more. He had finally broken internationally. The pictures of his previous stunts had gone around the world, but with distance comes disbelief, and people in other countries had been happy enough to write this off as a cleverly stage-managed hoax, using digital effects to fake the video. But not this time. There was no refuting it. Now he was a star in Europe, America, Africa, Asia, everywhere! He was no longer Cambridge's Invisible Man, he was the world's.

And yet, when he arrived back at his home having chucked the trousers over someone's fence, the Invisible Man sat on his couch a while and stared at the carpet where his feet ought to have been, a horrid cold sensation spreading through his stomach and crawling across his skin.

The child.

It had not affected the outcome of the stunt; few enough people had even noticed that the boy had been hurt. And it was not as if he had been badly hurt. Besides, when an invisible man goes for a run then there is a chance of people running into him. It was an accident waiting to happen and no big deal.

Except that was not what had happened.

He had not run into the child. He had hit him.

Deliberately.

He had seen the boy and something about his face or the noise that he was making had sent a pulse of hatred searing through the Invisible Man and, without even thinking about it, he had lashed out to backhand the child across the face. Even looking back at it now he could not quite believe or understand it. He had never done anything like that before in his life. When he remembered it, it was as if he was watching the event from a distance. That could not have been his hand striking the child.

Of course no one had seen the blow. No one had seen his hand. No harm had been done.

And yet he had done it and he had no idea why.

He had been under a lot of stress lately; trying to come up with all these stunts and execute them, staying hidden, feeding himself when he could not go shopping. There were a lot of pressures on an Invisible Man. Simple things became difficult. Sleep had been a problem since day one because closing his eyes made no difference; he saw straight through his own eyelids. And there was no sense in pretending that this sudden fame had not affected him. Didn't people who became overnight successes sometimes do uncharacteristic things? A lot of them seemed to turn into total jerks.

Yes. That was it. A combination of all of that had boiled over when the child had annoyed him. Obviously it was regrettable but it was a one-off event that would not be repeated. He could cut back on his public appearances – he had already established himself and it was better to leave people wanting more than to become boring through over-exposure. He could focus more on himself; his health and well-being. And now that he was aware of the problem he would be better able to control it. It was all fine. It would not happen again.

He watched every news bulletin he could on TV that night, then went online and tracked down news reports from around the world. He could not understand them but he could watch the pictures and the reactions of the presenters. He was big news. He was huge news. He was fast becoming the most famous man in the world without anyone knowing his face. It felt wonderful.

And it got better. In amongst the weight of fan tweets and other online messages that he received as a matter of course, was one that was a little bit special. He read it three times just to make sure he was not mistaken. It was an invitation to appear on TV morning show, *Wake Up!* in two days' time (or whenever he felt like it). He could just turn up and make his presence known by whatever means he wanted.

Television. The Invisible Man had been dreaming of appearing on television for most of his life. His dreams were coming true.

But when he went to sleep that night, his dreams were of a different kind. He saw the boy's face, he felt the boy's cheek as the backs of his fingers smacked against it, he heard the cry of pain. And he felt a rush of delight at the thought that he had caused it.

Chapter 10 – The Guest

Rather than driving back to his house (a rather nice four-bedroom in one of the small villages that peppered the landscape surrounding Cambridge), Dr Sampson Cranley chose to spend the night in his college rooms, because they were comfortable and convenient. They were also isolated, something that he had come to value more this month.

On the table by the sofa was a pile of newspaper cuttings about the murders of Herbert Digges and Evelyn Herrick, which he now took to the fireplace to burn. He had read them all multiple times and had no more idea than the police of how they had been committed.

But he could guess at why. And he could guess at who.

The death of Professor Digges had come as a shock, but had not given Cranley any sense of the untoward. That of Evelyn Herrick coming so hot on its heels and apparently committed by the same hand had been different. That had given him pause. He had put the question to the others and they had agreed that caution was indicated but that there was no sense in involving the police. It could still be a coincidence, or a run of the mill serial killer targeting Cambridge scientists (not massively comforting but preferable to the alternative). None of the messages that passed between them mentioned the name that hovered on the tip of every tongue.

Broadly speaking, Dr Cranley agreed with the this course of action, but when night fell that agreement got a lot less certain. Still, he was at the top of the college, behind many locked doors and with any number of inconvenient witnesses (students) littering the building.

Before going to bed, Dr Cranley walked through his rooms like Ebenezer Scrooge before Marley showed up, turning off lamps one by one as he went, carrying a torch with him because the dark suddenly held a quiet horror that it never had before. He checked that the door was locked; checked the latch and shot the bolts. He stepped back, running the beam of his torch over these precautions. Then he went to the dining room to fetch a heavy, straight-backed chair which he carried back to the hall to wedge under the door handle.

He checked the windows one by one, twisted the bolts until his wrist ached to be sure that they were as tightly closed as they could be.

In the dining room was an old dumb waiter which had been boarded up years ago. Dr Cranley made sure that it was still closed up, peering intently at the nails by torchlight to see that the patina of rust remained, indicating that no one had tampered with them.

He was sealed in.

And as soon as that thought crossed his mind, Sampson Cranley began to wonder if that was really such a good thing. No way in. But no way out.

Torch in hand, Cranley moved from room to room again, now looking for a hidden intruder. He peered under the table, the bed, and even the sofa, which had a ground clearance of about two inches. He checked every cupboard, every corner and behind every curtain. When he was a child, his father had unintentionally terrified him with the story of a ninja in feudal Japan, who had hidden in a toilet and waited there five days for his victim before inflicting a fundamental injury. Although the toilet in question had been nothing that Thomas Crapper would have recognised, and had probably been nothing more sophisticated than a hole, the young Sampson had spent the next year carefully peering beneath the lid for concealed ninjas every time nature called. Much to his own surprise, he did the same thing now, because these childhood fears die hard. Despite the fire, he checked the chimney too, because Santa was obviously a home-invader and no one ever bothered to call him on it.

He found nothing. He was alone and sealed in.

Returning to the living room where the fire still crackled, he turned on the table lamp by the sofa, picked up the phone and called the porter's lodge.

"Good evening Doctor." The comforting, familiar voice of Bert Hobbes.

"Good evening, Bert. All well this evening?"

"Yes Doctor."

"Nothing out of the ordinary?"

"No."

"Even the slightest thing. Might be anything."

Bert thought about it. "Three of the chaps," to Bert all the students were 'the chaps', even the female ones, "went out carrying a *papier mache* crocodile, singing *Delilah* while one played the ukulele."

Dr Cranley nodded to himself; nothing out of the ordinary there. "Do me a favour would you Bert? Give security a buzz and ask them the same question. Anything at all."

"If you want, Dr Cranley."

"Thanks, Bert. Call me back."

Dr Cranley hung up the phone and sat brooding. He switched on the TV to distract him from the horrible thoughts that processed through his head, but found it too loud. With that on he would not be able to hear anyone creeping up on him.

Sampson Cranley knew that he was flawed. He had made mistakes in life. He had missed opportunities, he had screwed others for his own betterment and some of the experiments he had performed were not one hundred percent 'kosher'. You couldn't make an omelette without breaking eggs, and in neuroscience some of those 'eggs' made a hell of a mess when you broke them. He thought that he was a better person than either Professor Digges or Professor Herrick had been, but he hadn't known them all that well and they would probably have felt the same way about him.

You didn't really get to know the others. It wasn't as if they were all friends together. Their deaths had therefore been less of a shock in the 'terrible personal loss' vein, and more one in the 'what does this mean for me?' vein.

The phone rang, causing Dr Cranley to spring three feet into the air, crashing back onto the uneven springs of his sofa. He grappled with the receiver before raising it to his mouth.

"Hello, yes?"

"Bert, Dr Cranley. I've called security, they said the same as me. Nothing unusual."

"Thanks Bert."

Hanging up the phone, Dr Cranley relaxed back and allowed

himself the luxury of a smile. The only danger to him was himself. He was making a ridiculous fuss over what was probably an unfortunate coincidence. And even were it not a coincidence, he was safely ensconced here.

Although it was an unworthy thought, he took a moment to wonder if the others were taking similar precautions, and quietly hoped that they weren't. Surely the ones who were easy to reach would fall first.

Getting up from the sofa he crossed to his drinks' cabinet to pour himself a glass of something that might aid sleep.

"Nothing for me, thank you."

The bottle and glass crashed to the floor and Sampson Cranley spun around, his wild eyes scanning the shadowy corners of the room for the unseen speaker.

"Who are you?"

"Do you really want your last question to be such a profoundly stupid one?"

Cranley stumbled back towards the lamplight at the centre of the room, broken glass crunching under his slippers as he went – there was safety in light.

"Show yourself!"

Only laughter met him.

"What do you want?"

"Another stupid question."

A faint chink of daylight seemed to show itself to Sampson Cranley. "It's not too late, you know. Our decision wasn't final."

"It seemed pretty final at the time."

"Well," Cranley's tongue tripped over itself in its haste to find excuses, "a lot of that was down to Digges. He was senior. And Herrick. And they're… well they're no longer obstacles. So I'm sure we'd all be more than happy to reconsider your proposal."

More laughter. "Yes. I'm very sure that you would."

The voice seemed to be moving about the room but Cranley still couldn't see anyone by the light of the table lamp and the flickering remnants of the fire.

"Where are you?"

"I've been here all along."

Cranley swallowed. He wasn't dead yet, there had to be some room for manoeuvre. "What do you gain by… by any of this?"

There was a pause, and for the first time Cranley got the impression that the unseen intruder was stopping to think.

"Do you know? I'm really not sure."

Which ought to have been an answer that gave Cranley some hope, but the tone in which it was spoken allowed for none.

"What can I do?"

"Do?"

"What can I give you?" Cranley sounded desperate now. "I'll give you anything."

He had feared laughter, but the silence that met him was somehow worse.

"Can you give me back my dignity?" The reply was almost growled. "Can you take away the echoes of supercilious laughter in my head? Can you take back the mockery?"

It was in that moment, listening to the cold, hard clarity of the questions that sounded more like accusations, that Sampson Cranley realised this was not a negotiation. It never had been. It was not even a trial. He had been found guilty in his absence and all that remained was to carry out the sentence.

He was locked in. If he ran for the door, he would never get it open in time. Was there a gun trained on him? There might be.

Safety in light.

Cranley didn't run for the door, instead he ran for the light switch, determined to look his accuser in the face.

The light flickered on and Cranley stood by the wall staring in terror at an empty room.

"Where are you?"

The voice came from right beside him. "I told you, Cranley; I've been here all along."

The first two murders, Harrigan thought to himself as he looked down at the strangled corpse of Dr Sampson Cranley, had been impossible. This one was just taking the piss.

No one had seen the killer come and go in the first murder, but Harrigan remained convinced of a logical, if devious, outcome. The impossibility of the second relied almost entirely on the evidence of a security camera and, while he didn't understand it himself, Harrigan was happy to believe that such things could be hacked and faked to disguise what had actually occurred. They had been impossible, but in ways that suggested their impossibility might be eroded with time.

But this…

The door had not just been locked. It had been locked and bolted with a chair shoved under the handle. The windows were all fastened from within, the old dumb waiter was nailed shut. Harrigan had even checked the chimney, and found it closed off with an iron grill to stop pigeons falling down and getting unexpectedly roasted. If he listened he could hear them on the roof, cooing down the chimney at him mockingly. There was no way in.

That was not necessarily an issue because you assumed that the killer had secreted themselves in advance. But how had they got out? They couldn't have.

After an odd conversation the night before, the college Porter had decided to check on Dr Cranley first thing in the morning and, getting no answer at his door or from his phone, had called ambulance and police rather than breaking down the door himself. In light of recent events, it had seemed like the thing to do.

This meant that there had been a police guard on that door ever since it had been broken down. Harrigan and his team had searched every room, looked under every item of furniture, opened every cupboard. There was no one there.

It was impossible.

On the other hand, people didn't strangle themselves.

"Bit of a puzzler," said Sergeant Stubbs.

Harrigan looked at his Sergeant. He liked Stubbs as a no-nonsense, down-to-earth sort of individual but right at that moment he could have gleefully throttled the man.

"How do you think he got out?" asked Stubbs, adding insult to injury.

"I have been wondering about that," replied Harrigan.

"Clever sod," nodded Stubbs. "Why are psychopaths always clever?"

"They aren't," Harrigan corrected. "Regardless of what comic books would have you believe, the majority do not have PhDs. If they did then Cambridge would be overrun with super-villains."

Stubbs shrugged. "I sometimes wonder."

"So do I," admitted Harrigan.

At some point he would have to face Chief Inspector Lane. If you were fired before you reached retirement then perhaps you didn't have to die. Or maybe that just increased the irony of your death.

'*See you in hell.*' He probably couldn't pull that one off. He wasn't the type.

After Lane there would be the press, and he had nothing to tell them either. He was making the force look bad. Two weeks had separated the first two murders, but there had been just four days between Herrick and Cranley. Who was to say there would not be more?

After exhaustive interviews with everyone who had known Evelyn Herrick, Harrigan had gone back to re-interview everyone who had known Herbert Digges, and had been forced to conclude that, beyond both working at Cambridge University in scientific fields, the two were unconnected. In fact, they were so unconnected that that in itself almost became a connection. It ought to have been impossible for two people who had lived in the same city and worked in the same institution (five minutes' walk from each other!) for this length of time to have remained this distant. As far as Harrigan could ascertain, not only had they never been in a room together, they had probably never even been in the same street. They had no friends in common, no students in common, shared no interests, had different books on their shelves, watched different TV shows and voted for different political parties. In a long career, Digges had worked in many different areas but never with the big pharmaceutical companies to whom Herrick was connected (not always to her credit, so gossip said). They could be the poster children for how diverse Cambridge University had become, dispelling the myth that only one type of person went there.

It had been a lot of work to achieve precisely nothing and that fact had not been lost on 'Growley' Lane.

Despite all this, Harrigan intended to pursue this worthless line of enquiry. Partly because the death of Sampson Cranley gave him more to work with, another circle in his Venn diagram of acquaintance. But he was also continuing with it because he had damn-all else.

"Sweep the place," he said to O'Connor, as the forensics man entered. "The bastard must have been hiding in here somewhere. Find me a fingerprint, a hair, anything."

O'Connor shrugged. "We'll do what we can, but someone lived here. There's going to be fingerprints and hair everywhere."

Harrigan deflated. He had known that. In his heart he knew that anyone clever enough to get out of here by magic was clever enough to know about forensics and take precautions.

"Just do your best."

His gaze lingered briefly on the mantelpiece where a handful of Christmas cards stood.

He needed to post the boys' cards. Come to think of it, he needed to buy their cards. He had, in the past, missed birthdays, anniversaries and other significant dates, but never Christmas. Even when he stopped getting cards back, he always sent them. Because it was Christmas. Harrigan loved Christmas. He had happy memories of his own childhood and wondrous ones of when the boys were young and he and his wife were still happy. Christmas mattered to him.

Which made the ones he spent alone all the greyer. He always decorated, but did that just make it worse? Sitting alone in a flat decked-out with tinsel and baubles, eating a turkey drumstick and overcooked roast potatoes.

He could ask.

He knew that the boys' and their families had started spending Christmas together. Their kids – the grandchildren he had never met – got along well. It was what Christmas was supposed to be. But perhaps that was a good reason for him not to intrude. They did not need the ghost of Christmas past sitting in the corner making everyone uneasy. It shouldn't be about him. They would enjoy it more without him there.

But cards were a necessity. Would 'William and family' and 'Don and family' cut it? He was pretty sure that he had the names of their respective wives written down somewhere, assuming they were still together – stuff did happen and he wouldn't have known either way. But the kids? He had no idea what their names were. Someone must have told him, but if he had had the foresight to write it down then he had no clue where. If he wrote to 'William, Jennifer (or whatever) and family' then that made it obvious that he had forgotten the names of his grandchildren. While 'William and family' sounded like a card for his son that just included the rest of the family. Neither was good, but the second was better.

Perhaps if he joined something like Facebook then he could stalk the boys and find out their children's names. But, as he understood it, you could only look at someone's personal details if they accepted you as a friend. They might. But he could not take the risk. He could not have borne actually seeing the rejection.

"Tall," said the student, firmly.

Harrigan tried to hide his frustration. "I rather meant; what was he like as a person?"

"Oh." The woman considered this a moment. "I don't know really."

And so onto the next interview.

"Leader in his field."

"Not the best lecturer."

"Not a social butterfly but he had his crowd."

"Enemies? Probably. This is a university."

"Friends? I doubt it. This is a university."

"Herrick?"

"Digges?"

"No."

"Nope."

"Not that I can recall."

"Was she the short one with the teeth?"

"Classics Major?"

"From Anthropology?"

"Oh. Then no, I don't think so."

The people came and went and Harrigan mentally beat himself up with each failure. He was clearly asking the wrong questions but he didn't know what the right questions were, and had a sneaking suspicion that if someone told him the right questions he still wouldn't recognise them. He had hoped that Cranley would be the missing link in the chain that had to exist between Digges and Herrick. More than that, he *insisted* upon it, and for one reason: Cranley had locked himself in. Not just locked himself in, but stuck a chair under the door. He had *known* he was at risk. He had seen the deaths of the other two and had taken precautions. There *was* a connection.

But knowing it and finding it were two different things. Cranley proved to be yet another who seemed to live in a parallel dimension, occupying the same physical space as the those in which Digges and Herrick lived but distinct from it. If they met, then they passed through each other. They could not have had less to do with each other if they had actually set out to avoid one another. Harrigan thought about that for a while, and then tried to picture Chief Inspector Lane's face if he started talking about conspiracy theories.

By the time he got around to Cranley's secretary, Harrigan had more or less given up hope.

"When did you last see him?"

"That would be the day before he died." Gale Bevan was a bright, thirty-something who was taking the death of her boss in a way that suggested they had not been close. She had been shocked, but far from distraught.

"You weren't in on the Friday?" Harrigan dared to hope that Cranley had been doing something interesting on the Friday.

"Called in sick," Gale replied. "Flu. Actually," she leant in, "it was a hangover. I tend to go out on the Thursday night because he never needs me and I went a teensy bit overboard this week."

"Why does he never need you on the Thursday?"

"That's his club night," Gale explained.

Harrigan looked up. "I assume we're not talking about loud music and dancing?"

Gale laughed. "I should think not. Although I suppose I don't actually know. It was just his club."

"What sort of club?" Was that a dim light Harrigan saw at the end of the tunnel?

"I don't know," Gale shrugged. "When I started the job last year – haven't even been with him a year – one of his students wanted a sit-down and Thursday night was empty in his diary so I put it in. Then, later that day, he told me to re-schedule it and never to schedule anything for Thursday evening because that was his club night."

"And you never asked what club he belonged to?"

Gale nodded. "I asked. But he said, 'Just a University club'. And something about the way he said it…" She pursed her lips. "You know when you can tell that it's a brush off and you're not to ask any more?" She smiled. "Secretaries get to know that look. Usually it means an affair, but he wasn't married. Although I suppose it could have been with a married woman. But that's very regimented don't you think? Every Thursday? I'd get bored. More fun to mix it up. So I think it was probably a club."

After Gale had left, Harrigan took a break from interviews and made himself a cup of coffee. But the coffee sat undrank, slowly cooling on the desk in front of him. There was nothing suspicious about a man being a member of a club, in fact in Cambridge University it would stranger for him not to be. His secrecy about its nature was a little odd but, again, Cambridge liked its traditions and some clubs and societies were not to be spoken of.

So why had this information set off a flashing light in Harrigan's head?

There was something he was missing. Something he had forgotten.

Wasn't there…?

Harrigan grabbed his notebook, opened it and began to flick

back through the multitudinous interview notes. He was old-fashioned enough to prefer writing everything down by hand – one more source of infuriation for his superiors. Sometimes it was so illegible, written at such speed, that even he could not read it but it was more of an *aide memoir*, and the act of writing seemed to lodge the facts in his brain better than typing or recording.

There.

'*Thursday*'.

The word seemed to leap out at him from in amongst the blue scrawl. It was on a page of notes taken during his interviews with the guests at the Faculty of Biochemistry Christmas party, on the night of Professor Digges' death. Harrigan squinted at the spidering loops and sweeps of his handwriting.

'*Party originally scheduled Thursday – changed by Prof. D.*'

Yes. Now he remembered. The Departmental head had told him that the party had originally been scheduled for the Thursday night but Digges had said that he was unavailable and so it was changed.

Harrigan scrabbled back through his notes then grabbed the phone. "I need the number for that woman who ran the Biochemistry party… That's her."

He scratched down the number in red on his notepad, hung up and redialled. A secretary.

"Could I speak to Professor Sutherland please?... Inspector Harrigan, Cambridge City Police… Thank you."

"Inspector?" Professor Sutherland picked up after what seemed like an eternity to Harrigan.

"Professor, thank you for taking my call…"

"I do have a class."

"It's only a very quick question," Harrigan's voice was trembling. "You told me that the Faculty party was originally on a Thursday night but was re-scheduled at Professor Digges' request, is that correct?" Please let him have remembered this right.

"That's correct. Really, Inspector, I…"

"Just one more question; did he tell you why he wanted it moved?"

102

"He said it clashed with his club."

Chapter 11 – Wake Up!

"Hi, it's Jack."

Amelia ran a hand through her hair and worried that she looked a mess before remembering that she was on the phone and couldn't see her.

"Hi. Good to hear from you."

"I'm sorry I didn't call sooner."

Amelia bit her lip. "You did, didn't you? You left a couple of messages."

"Yeah." Tone of voice could be so hard to judge on a phone. "I wasn't sure you'd got them."

"Yeah."

"Okay."

"So I should probably be the one apologising for not replying," admitted Amelia.

"Not necessarily," said Jack, still uneasy. "Hard to tell at this point of the conversation. It might be me who should apologise for not being able to take a hint."

"No," Amelia almost shouted. "No, I'm glad you can't take a hint. Not that it was a hint. It wasn't a hint. I wasn't trying to… you know."

"Get rid of me?"

"Yes. That's what I wasn't trying to do. I just didn't want to…"

"Be the one who makes the call."

Amelia couldn't help smiling. "Wow, you just get me."

Jack laughed. "So, you did want me to call?"

"And you did!" Amelia enthused. "So you see; it worked."

"Just. This was going to be my last try, I was pretty sure I was turning into a stalker."

"Haven't you seen those movies where guys never give up? They always get the girl."

"Yep," Jack replied. "Been badly misled by them in the past. You try pulling that shit in real life and you get a restraining order."

"You haven't…"

"No! No. Definitely not. I was just… I'm relieved. You know? I thought I'd made a good impression and it was worrying that you seemed to be dodging me."

"I can see how that would be worrying."

"It was."

"Well now I feel like a bitch." She had been waiting for his call (sort of) but calling back just felt… Sadly, Zita's doom-laden pronouncements about Amelia letting Frank ruin men for her did have some grounding. She was over him, but taking this next step was proving harder than she had thought it would. Perhaps she should tell Jack about it, but talking about the ex who broke your heart was bad first date etiquette. Probably second date too.

"I'm really glad you kept trying and I'm really sorry I didn't reply."

"Okay," Jack sounded relieved. "Okay. Would you be interested in going out again? And please don't think you *have* to say yes because I've revealed myself to be painfully needy."

"I didn't think you were painfully needy," corrected Amelia. "I just assumed I was worth the effort."

"That sounds much better. Let's go with that."

"I'd love to go out again."

"That's brilliant." She could hear Jack's smile down the phone. "How about Tuesday?"

"I'm free." There was still a voice inside Amelia advising caution, telling her not to be too keen, too trusting – but frankly she was sick of that voice.

"Okay. I'll book us a table."

"Where?"

"How about I surprise you?"

Amelia grinned. "I would like that."

Surprising her had never been one of Frank's moves and anything that differentiated the two men was good.

"So that's sorted. It's a date."

"It's a date."

"So how's things with you?" asked Jack, dangerously pre-empting conversation they might need on Tuesday. "Did you see the news this morning?"

"Three now," nodded Amelia.

"Should I bring pen and paper in case you want to solve these two?"

"How about we try to keep our second date as murder-free as possible?"

"I guess we could try that. And if the conversation slows then murder is always there."

"Exactly. Look, I've got to be up early, but we can catch up properly on Tuesday."

"Okay. I'll text you."

"Okay. Bye."

"Bye."

Amelia hung up. '*Got* to be up early' was an exaggeration, but she did *plan* to be up early. After the hunt for the Invisible Man's lab, and its flat conclusion, Amelia had put aside all thoughts of that other man in her life; of tracing him and of his being connected to the mysterious killings. Even if he was real (and she had found no evidence of that), the more she read the book, the less likely it seemed that this desperate and lonely individual could be a killer. The Invisible Man might be a little creepy, but really he just wanted to be loved. Or at least that was the impression she got; of a shy man who found it difficult to put himself out there in the world. Amelia could identify. Whether he was real or not, the Invisible Man had struggled to be seen long before he became invisible. And becoming invisible had enabled him, for the first time, to be seen. Apparently the book's author was big on irony.

The point was; she was done, it had all been in her imagination.

But then, just this morning, TV morning show *Wake Up!* had announced that they would be interviewing the Invisible Man live on air, while the news was filled the murder of Sampson Cranley. And Amelia was hooked once more.

She still didn't know if it could be real. She still struggled to see the Invisible Man as a killer. But whatever was going to happen tomorrow morning, she wanted to be there to see it.

Her alarm wrenched her rudely from sleep at a quarter to six and Amelia – not one of nature's morning people – lurched sleepily for the shower. With a robe around her and her hair in a towel she made it to the TV in time to see the start of the show and then busied herself in the kitchen making dangerously black coffee, always keeping one eye on the screen.

"We've had no word from the Invisible Man to say he's coming but we did tell him just to turn up, visible or invisible, and he hasn't said no either, so…" the host shrugged. "Don't go anywhere, you might miss a piece of television history."

After the first cup of coffee had kicked her brain awake, Amelia made a second and started on breakfast. She found that getting up this early she wanted an actual cooked breakfast and made fried egg on toast to eat in front of the TV. Her mind strayed as the hosts talked, passed things over to news teams, weather persons, sports presenters and inane 'local interest' items that for some reason were screened on national television. Tomorrow she had a meeting with the head of the Faculty of Archaeology, for whom she still, in theory, worked. She would present what she had found in Romania and try to get backing for a grant application. She wasn't that worried; her boss liked her and what she had found definitely warranted further study. The only real question was whether someone specialising in Egyptology was the right person to conduct such research. But since the pictographic writings were unique to the region there was probably no one else better qualified, and Amelia was relatively sure she could keep getting paid, at least for the foreseeable future.

Her eyelids drooped, the sound of the TV becoming an atonal wash of sound passing over her. Amelia shook her head, drained the second cup, and went to toast the last fruit muffin in her bread bin to see if that might wake her.

"…can announce that the Invisible Man is in the building!"

Amelia had got as far as the kitchen when her brain successfully filtered the only words that might interest her out of the miasma of sound which *Wake Up!* had become. She started back into the living room, standing behind the sofa, kneading it with her fingers.

"He should be here soon," host, Bruce MacBride, continued. "It's not like he has to go through make-up. And this is very exciting, isn't it?"

"It really is," nodded Kitty Russell. "Obviously we'd made the offer, but we hadn't heard anything from him, he just showed up at the studio."

"And said, 'I'm the Invisible Man'."

"Which we should be able to prove without too much trouble."

"It is very exciting."

"Very exciting and... Here he is! Ladies and gentlemen, in his first TV appearance – if appearance is the right word – The Invisible Man!"

Without letting her eyes leave the screen, Amelia manoeuvred herself around the sofa to sit, as a man joined Bruce and Kitty. He was tall – very tall – and walked in a slightly awkward fashion, which might have been due to his attire. He wore gloves, a hat, and a long, loose coat that tented his body. Wrapped around his head were bandages, tightly wound to show some rough contours of the face beneath, and a pair of large, wrap-around dark glasses covered his eyes. No wonder he seemed ungainly, he was probably struggling to see where he was going.

"Welcome, welcome." Both hosts pumped his hand.

"Thank you." The Invisible Man spoke, his deep voice muffled by the bandages that covered his mouth.

"Take a seat."

"Thank you."

"It's wonderful to see you here," Bruce enthused. "We didn't expect to 'see you' at all."

The Invisible Man laughed. "Well, I thought your viewers would want to see *something*, otherwise you'd just have an empty seat and no one would believe you."

"There have been a lot of doubters online," Kitty nodded. "Have you come here to set them straight? Or did you just feel that it was time for the Invisible Man to talk?"

"Bit of both, I suppose. I mean, who doesn't want to be on

Wake Up with Kitty and Bruce?"

"So," Bruce said, "I have to ask. The running trousers. How on earth did you do that?"

The Invisible Man shrugged. There was something about the gesture that was off, though Amelia couldn't put her finger on exactly what.

"I put on a pair of trousers and I went for a run."

"Ah," Kitty raised a finger. "So, this is what people really want to know, because there has been much debate about it. Some people are saying that all of these videos are faked using digital effects."

"They are absolutely not," the Invisible Man said, defiantly.

"Others are saying they are amazingly well-planned magic tricks, the sort of thing that David Copperfield used to do. But no one is clear how something like the running trousers can be a trick."

"That's because they are not tricks."

Kitty and Bruce exchanged glances and Amelia shuffled closer – had she been right all along?

"Let's be quite clear about this," Bruce said, "you're saying these are not tricks of any kind. You are actually invisible."

"I expect you'd like me to prove it."

Now the looks that passed between Kitty and Bruce were of '*I can't believe we're going to get this lucky*'. They were about to snag the exclusive of a lifetime.

"You can do that?" asked Kitty.

"Why else would I come on your show?"

Amelia felt she could not even blink. And yet there was something bothering her. She had read *The Life of an Invisible Man* multiple times and the way in which this man spoke… It just didn't sound like the man she knew. On the other hand, onscreen was some pretty compelling evidence.

Kitty's intake of breath was audible as the Invisible Man stood and removed his hat. The bandages stopped around his forehead and beyond them was nothing but air where his head ought to have been.

"Viewers of a nervous disposition should probably look away," advised the Invisible Man.

Reaching up to his head – still so very awkward – he untucked the end of the bandage and began to unwind it. Bruce and Kitty edged away down the sofa, as turn after turn of bandage unwound from the invisible head beneath.

"Voila." The Invisible Man tugged the last of the bandage aside to reveal; nothing. An empty collar with no head above it.

Bruce and Kitty were both lost for words. Amelia could only stare.

And then, all hell broke loose.

From off-camera came a scream of animal rage. Moments later the Invisible Man was back on the sofa, hitting it hard and then jerking back and forth as if he was having a fit. The lapels of his coat started forward into the air in front of him and seemed to be dragging him back and forth, left and right, as if they were attached to something. He dropped back onto the sofa, his gasping cries captured by the radio mic on his lapel which now reported a solid thump, and the Invisible Man went sideways as if he had been hit. Back and forth he went, again and again, accompanied by corresponding thumps and by the cries of the Invisible Man.

Kitty and Bruce were frozen in shock, staring at their guest, not knowing what they were seeing. The rest of the crew were presumably in the same state. Was he having an attack of some sort? Was this part of his 'act'? Or was there some third option that no one could understand?

The Invisible Man was now lying limp, moaning in pain. But it was not over yet. Another animal cry came from nowhere and the Invisible Man's coat was yanked open, followed by his shirt, already stained with blood, buttons flying. And…

Kitty screamed as the open shirt revealed a face. Amelia shifted closer, on the edge of her seat as she realised why the Invisible Man had seemed so awkward moving his arms; because he was a small man wearing a carefully designed coat that made it seem as if his shoulders and arms were higher than they were, to allow a fake head on top of his own. It had all been trick.

But this, surely, was not.

The terror on the revealed face was all too real, and that terror was replaced with pain as the face was flung violently to the right, the skin of the cheek seeming to mash and the man spitting blood onto the sofa beside him. He yelped in agony as his face went back the other way and the microphone picked up the sickening crack of his teeth breaking in his mouth. More blood flew, spattering the sofa, the floor, the table, the newspapers laid out ready for the 'paper review' later in the program. As Amelia watched, and the camera stared relentlessly, its operator as unable to look away as she was, the 'Invisible Man's nose was suddenly flattened and he screamed in pain. Amelia saw it break. She actually saw it move without anything touching it, as if the nose had a life of its own and had decided to commit suicide.

Blood poured from the man's nose as his head continued to go left and right, his eye sockets imploding, his face a welter of blood and swollen bruises as he received the beating of a lifetime. But from nobody.

Then, as suddenly as it had started, it stopped. The fake invisible man lay on the sofa looking like the victim in a horror film. His breath came in slow, bubbling gurgles, his chest rising and falling erratically.

It was then that someone had the intelligence to cut to the weather.

Amelia continued to sit staring dumbly, wondering what on earth she had just witnessed.

His name was Oskar Cole, though professionally he was Oskar the Omnipotent. Once he had been stabilised in hospital and was able to speak, he confessed that he had seen the invite on *Wake Up!* and had decided to take advantage of it. He could not have fooled the presenters indefinitely, nor had he wanted to, his plan had been to give Britain a good show then reveal himself; an exercise in self-promotion. He had nothing to do with the book or the stunts in Cambridge, he had never even visited the town. He claimed that he had never intended to take credit for those stunts, which no one believed.

What people did believe was now up for grabs. The majority verdict was that this was the Invisible Man's biggest stunt yet, to a national audience, and that he and Cole together had staged this whole 'fake Invisible Man attacked by real Invisible Man' thing. Which seemed reasonable; someone who could make a pair of trousers run around a market square was surely able to make it look as if a man was getting beaten by a pair of unseen hands, especially if the producers of *Wake Up!* were in on it. But Cole's doctor's spoke out strongly against these theories; the man *had* been beaten, and to within an inch of his life.

However it had been done – and consensus remained that this had been another clever trick by a master of stagecraft – the overwhelming conclusion was that the Invisible Man had gone too far. People watched this show at breakfast, children had seen it, and even if they had not, what sort of sicko would want to watch a man beaten like that?

In one instant the world turned its back on the Invisible Man. His followers deserted him. Admiring messages turned to hatred. Charity shops were suddenly so overstocked with his book that they started putting them straight into the recycling.

As with many a celebrity, the precipitous rise of the Invisible Man was followed by an equally precipitous fall. His fifteen minutes of fame were over.

"He never tells me anything," Zita pleaded ignorance on the phone to her sister. "I didn't know about the bike, or the trousers, or the football, just like the bookshop; he never runs any of this past me, I just make sure it gets out afterwards, although God knows I wish I could stop news of this one getting out – I'd have told him what a mistake it was."

"You think it was another stunt?" asked Amelia.

"Don't you?"

What did Amelia believe? A few days ago she had been ready to give up all her suspicions about the Invisible Man; that he might be real; that he might be involved in three impossible murders. She had been ready to write it all off as the inevitable side-effect of her own unbelievable experiences. But now… What she had seen on TV had not looked fake. And she had clearly misjudged the Invisible

112

Man in thinking that he was not capable of killing someone, he had damn near done it on national television.

What did she believe? She didn't know. But she was unwilling to discount anything. Which was why, when she was done talking to Zita, who could shed no more light on the matter, she located a card in her purse and picked up the phone again.

The phone was answered after one ring. "Universal."

It was a name that told you nothing, and Amelia remained unsure about what they did, but where else could she turn? If she went to the police then they would say she was crazy.

"Can I speak to Boris please?"

"Please hold."

A tinny version of Swan Lake played for a minute before the woman returned.

"Boris is unavailable at present, would you like to leave a message?"

"Sure." Amelia tried to collect her thoughts. She didn't mind sounding a fool in front of Boris, but having to explain to someone else was hard. "Tell him it's Amelia. Evans. Amelia Evans. Tell him… Tell him this Invisible Man thing in Cambridge is looking like more than a publicity stunt."

"Anything else?" If the woman thought Amelia was crazy she gave no sign of it.

"No. That's it's. Thanks."

"Thank you for your call."

And that was that. Amelia wondered if it would make any difference. Boris wouldn't discount it out of hand. At the very least he would look at the footage from *Wake Up!*. Amelia shivered. No one – or at least no one who knew that there are things in this world that go beyond what we understand – could look at that and think it was fake.

It was supposed to have been his big day. The best day of his life. For as long as he could remember the Invisible Man had wanted to be on TV, to be famous. And now…

He had taken the train up first thing – which was cheap and

113

easy for an Invisible Man. Getting into the studio building had been likewise easy. He'd wandered about a bit, looking for the right studio and generally enjoying himself. It was exciting. He'd been happy.

And then, from one of the many TV screens that dotted the walls (because if you didn't watch your own shows then who would?) he heard the words that had changed everything.

"Ladies and gentlemen, in his first TV appearance – if appearance is the right word – The Invisible Man!"

By the time the Invisible Man located the studio, the interview was already underway, and there, seated on the sofa in the spot that he himself was supposed to occupy, was some *asshole* with bandages wrapped around his face. This person who was stealing his moment. This thief.

And the Invisible Man saw red.

He had never felt anything like it before, a rage so white hot streaking through his veins that it actually seemed to take possession of his body. He had no control of his own actions and seemed to watch as a spectator as he descended on the interloper.

But if he was only a spectator to the violence that followed, then he was a gleeful one. He revelled in each meaty smack of his fist against the face of the bewildered fraud, he delighted in the man's cries of pain, in the crack of his shattered teeth and the crunch of his broken nose. With each gout of blood he enjoyed himself more, spurred on to inflict even more damage with his next blow. He had loved every second of it.

Now, sitting back in his room, the Invisible Man looked at where his hands ought to be. Perhaps it was just as well that he could not see them. He had washed off the blood of his victim before leaving the building, that would have been a giveaway, but he knew that his hands must be bloodied, scratched and swollen. He could feel the pain, but see none of the damage.

From out of nowhere a drop of blood fell to the floor. That was how it seemed to work; as long as it touched him, as long as it was part of him then it remained invisible. It was the same for food and drink or when he went to the bathroom.

He watched another drop of blood fall. Now he was the one who needed bandages.

He would have killed the man.

Right now he was doing his level best not to think about it, but he knew it was true. He would have killed him, and it was only a small voice at the back of his mind that had held him back.

It had been righteous anger. No one could say that this man, this Oskar Cole, was in the right. But however hard he tried, the Invisible Man was struggling to justify what he had done. However much in the right he had been, he had done the wrong thing and quite unnecessarily when he could have just demonstrated who was the real Invisible Man.

That was what really hurt. It would have been so easy to walk out there and prove himself. Everyone would have loved it and everything would have been different. But the anger had taken him, and much as he had enjoyed it he was also paying for it.

He couldn't bring himself to look at Twitter again. The names they were calling him. The hatred. He would have liked to talk to someone about it but... Suddenly he was very aware of the fact that he had not talked to anyone for months.

It would pass. It had to. The Invisible Man would rise again. He just had to think of a stunt that would win back the public's love. Tomorrow he would issue an apology, maybe come up with a clever way of giving it, and then everything would be alright again. It had to be.

But while he was worried about his fast-diminishing celebrity status, the more needling worry was the one at the back of his mind about what had happened today. Something was wrong. Being invisible was making something go wrong in his head.

Chapter 12 – One Snowy Night

The interview had gone well and Amelia's faculty head had agreed to support her funding application. In real terms nothing would change except the wording on a form somewhere, but it still felt like a victory and Amelia celebrated by going out to buy a new dress. She was not, in general, someone who shopped as a celebratory activity, or as the holy rite that some treated it, she shopped when she needed to. She had never put any great stock in pretty dresses and nor had Frank, so why worry? As yet, she did not know Jack well enough to have gleaned where he stood on the pretty dress question, but she wanted to look her best for Tuesday night and had already worn what she considered her 'best dress', so buying another seemed less like a frivolous extravagance and more like a necessity. She spent a long time strolling up and down clothing rails looking for something that leapt out at her, until she realised that she was looking for something Jack would like to see her in rather than something she would like to wear. Eager as she was to look good for Jack, she drew the line at pandering. It was going to be bloody cold on Tuesday night and wearing anything that showed more flesh than dignity would result in frostbite in some unusual places.

In the end, she found something she liked in dark blue that was seasonal as well as attractive, and flattering while still modest and moderately wind-resistant. It was also nice that it cost less than some of the dresses she'd been considering earlier, and Amelia wondered why there seemed to be an inverse relationship between the cost of a garment and the amount of fabric it used.

She did a bit of Christmas shopping while she was out, finding a book for her Mum and a DVD boxset for her dad. When she returned, the message light was blinking on her phone.

"Amelia? Maggie. Keep missing you. Just to let you know, I'm stopping here over Christmas. Word's got out. About the tomb. Need to keep an eye on things." Maggie Moran was always on guard against tomb robbers and any she met would need to run fast if they wanted their future to include walking, chewing their food or fathering children. "Speak soon."

116

Amelia listened to the message over. Maggie cared enough about the dig to sacrifice her Christmas and spend the festive season waist deep in snow watching over an archaeological site. Amelia now had funding to keep working there, but her commitment still felt lukewarm by comparison.

Jack had texted to suggest they meet at a bar, not far from the restaurant he had selected.

'It's new so I'm taking a chance.'

New restaurants came and went with unseemly speed in central Cambridge, the penalty of starting a new business in a town in which people clung to the old like grim death (*'We've always gone to this restaurant and we're not going to stop now just because the health inspector has stamped a skull and crossed bones in the window and the rats are leaving to find somewhere more hygienic'*).

Amelia found herself less nervous and more excited as she walked into town that Tuesday night, concentrating on walking in heels, her breath showing before her as white clouds in the thin, frosty air. She had ended up really enjoying her first evening with Jack, and now that she knew she liked him, she could enjoy the second from the start. She was genuinely looking forward to it, and when she saw him waiting for her at the bar, her heart executed a little somersault of glee. It was too early to be using big, deep, emotional words, but after all that had happened and then hadn't happened in her love-life over the last year or so, being pleased to see a man was nice. And nice was a pretty good starting point. You could build on nice a lot better than you could on instant, gotta have you now passion; something you only learn as you get older.

"Hi," Jack leant in and kissed her cheek. "Great to see you, you look great. You're cold – can I get you a drink?"

Amelia said that he could and he did and they perched at the bar chatting over what they had been doing since they last saw each other. This time the conversation flowed freely from the get-go, and there was no need to introduce murder to break the ice.

"It's a great job," enthused Jack. "And I kind of need it right now, what with my last client dying and no one sure if they want me

117

to finish."

"Not exactly your usual work though," Amelia smiled. "Building Santa's Grotto?"

"Well I'm not building all of it," replied Jack. "The Grotto itself is being built by someone who apparently specialises in this sort of thing."

"Must be a busy time of year for him."

"Yeah. Pretty slow January through November, but then it all kicks off."

Amelia giggled. She didn't often giggle; must be the cold, the alcohol or the company. "So what's your role?"

"Santa's chair."

"Really?"

"They have something pretty grand in mind," nodded Jack.

"And the Grotto guy doesn't do chairs? Is it a union thing?"

Jack laughed. "No. He did design a chair that I was supposed to build – he mostly works in fibre glass and polystyrene, not wood – but the committee wasn't happy with the design. I took a look. It's possible he'd watched too much *Game of Thrones*."

"Not kiddie-friendly?"

"No. Kind of made Santa look like some sort dreadful warlord who was about to pass judgement on them. So I got upgraded from builder to *designer* and builder. I've gone for something jollier."

"I don't know if I've ever seen a jolly chair."

"Well you should come and have a look," Jack urged. "If you're not doing anything the day of the Festival."

The Winter Festival, for which this was being designed, was on the 23rd of December and would close down King's Parade for the day. It was a last chance to buy presents before the day itself and something to do with the kids in that stressful lull between the end of school and them having new toys to play with.

"At the moment I'm free."

"Cool," Jack nodded and smiled. "At the moment, it's a date."

"We've planned a third date before we finished the second."

"Might even end up being the fourth. There is time."

Amelia sipped her drink, trying not to look more cagey than

she was. "Well I don't want to drag you away from making jolly chairs."

"So what have you been up to?"

Amelia told him about the interview with her faculty head, but decided not to mention her trip around Cambridge searching for the laboratory of a quite possibly fictional character. Someone who hadn't been through stuff along the lines of her Egyptian adventure might struggle to understand why she believed in an invisible man.

They finished their drinks and Jack led the way out onto the street, holding the door for Amelia like the gentleman he was.

"Now I can't vouch for this place. I haven't eaten there, it's very new, but it seemed like the sort of place you would like."

It was amazing that no one had previously thought of a restaurant like it in Cambridge. Or perhaps someone had but it had not lasted long enough to make an impression. The Stacks was a library themed restaurant, and Amelia's eyes grew wide on entering. Books lined the walls – real books, not those fake things just designed to look good – the tables were supported on a central column that looked like a stack of books, and the whole place had the mahogany and brass decor of a college reading room.

"I booked a table for two; Jack Travers."

The man at the door scanned a list. "Ah yes, Mr Travers. We put you on Wells."

The tables were named after authors, whose names was embossed in gold on the leather table-tops, designed to look like old books.

"The War of the Worlds," read Amelia, before the waiter spread a white cloth across it.

"Read it?"

"I have. Also liked *The Island of Dr Moreau*."

"There's a good film of that with Charles Laughton, called *Island of Lost Souls*."

The menus were of course designed to look like books and a literary theme ran throughout. They advertised 'Chapter 1' rather than 'Starters', and coffee and cheese was to be found under 'Epilogue'.

" 'Bleak House Wine'," read Jack. "Do you think they may have taken this too far?"

"Would you prefer a 'Mary Wollstonecraft ale'?" asked Amelia. "Or a cocktail? T. H. White Lady? Longfellow Island Ice Tea? I think it's pretty awesome."

"Yeah?"

"It's like the perfect combination of classy and incredibly cheesy."

Jack nodded. "I think that was a compliment, but I'm honestly not sure."

Amelia grinned. "You got it absolutely right. You earned big points for this."

They ordered and returned to chatting. It was not that Amelia was keen to talk about the Invisible Man, but he had been such a talking point everywhere, and especially in Cambridge, since the *Wake Up!* interview that it was almost inevitable.

"What do you think that was?" asked Jack.

Amelia shook her head. "I honestly don't know. I watched it live."

"Really?" For obvious reasons it had not been re-shown and attempts to post the footage online had been quickly shut down.

"Yeah." Amelia sighed. "None of the explanations people have come out with really work for me. I don't know what I saw but that guy was terrified in a way I don't think you can fake."

Jack nodded. "Grim stuff."

"Yeah. Why do we always end up on violent subjects?"

"Don't know." Jack gave a rueful smile. "I guess your sister went from having the easiest job in the world to the hardest, pretty much overnight."

"Yeah. Zi's not too happy about it."

"He was doing so well."

"He was," Amelia agreed. "Although I don't know how all that other stuff was done either."

"The trousers were amazing."

"It was all… impossible."

Talking to someone else about it just crystallised the certainty in Amelia's mind that it *was* impossible and only an impossible solution would suffice. She still hadn't heard back from Boris or anyone at Universal. Were they ignoring her as an hysterical idiot? Had they looked into it and decided there was a perfectly reasonable explanation? Perhaps they made no connection between the murders and Invisible Man? Amelia wished she had explained herself better on the phone. If she could have talked to Boris it would have been alright.

She looked around the room. It was a dream library, the way that everyone imagines old libraries to look and they never do. Except one. Boris had shown her the Universal Library, the collection of books on the supernatural, occult, ancient and impossible, around which the organisation was founded. This place reminded her of that; though food would be strictly forbidden in the Universal Library.

"Look," Jack drew her back, pointing out of the window. "It's starting to snow."

And with that, Amelia once again cast the Invisible Man from her mind. There were so many better things to think about; she was at her perfect restaurant, on a perfectly Christmassy night, with... Maybe she wouldn't call Jack 'perfect', but Frank had seemed her perfect man and look how that had gone. She could see the plus points in imperfection; someone who was different enough that you could learn things from each other and have your own lives while still being together; someone who was a little uneasy in his own skin so you didn't feel awkward about being uneasy in your own; someone who was ordinary in the best possible way, who didn't inspire love at first sight, who wasn't all fireworks and flash, but who was worth discovering. Maybe she just needed to redefine 'perfect' in more useful ways.

By the time they left the restaurant, the snow had landed a light expeditionary force on the ground.

"You don't want to walk home in this," said Jack. "I'll call you a cab."

Amelia rolled her eyes. "Are you kidding? I definitely want to walk home in this. How often does it snow in Cambridge? I'm

121

boozed up enough to stay warm. Besides, I'll be standing around twenty minutes waiting for a taxi, by which time I *will* be cold and I could have walked home."

"Well that told me. At the risk of being all over-protective, can I walk you home?"

"No," Amelia shook her head. "But thank you for asking."

She leaned up to kiss him and Jack met her halfway. It was a longer kiss than the one they had shared at the end of their first date. That had been tentative, this was inevitable, and spoke of a desire that went further than kissing. They didn't have to act on that desire right this minute, but the kiss communicated that both parties were walking the same path, in the same direction and at more or less the same pace.

"You're good at that," said Amelia, as the kiss broke.

"You're a little tipsy, aren't you?"

"Only a very little."

They kissed again, and for a long time. After which they said their good nights. There was no need to ask whether there would be a third date. There was going to be a third date. And then, maybe other things would happen. Maybe. The whole 'third date sex' thing was a social construct that Amelia believed to be the invention of American sitcom; a cliché with no solid footing in reality. On the other hand, right now, walking through the snow with the taste of Jack still on her lips and a certain amount of alcohol buzzing in her brain, Amelia thought it sounded like a damn good idea.

A snowball fight on Trumpington Street made Amelia turn off to take Tennis Court Road instead. It didn't extend her journey by much and she was happy enough to wander a little longer in the snow. Alcohol and thoughts of Jack cushioned her from the cold. Maybe she was getting ahead of herself, maybe the wine was having an effect, and she knew that tomorrow morning she would feel differently, but right now she felt good and right and was determined to enjoy that sensation as long as she could. It had been too long.

While the main roads had become filled with people out enjoying the first fall of snow, Tennis Court Road, buried in the middle of the university district, was deserted and dark; wide spaces between the dull, orange street lamps. Amelia listened to the sharp clack of her heels on the pavement. She was getting used to walking in them now; despite the snow and her slight inebriation she had only slipped once and had managed to retain her balance.

She turned her face skywards. Bare trees standing behind the wall to her left thrust spindly branches out over the road, but the snow still found a way through to light on her face, making her skin tingle.

It happened without warning. She didn't hear approaching footsteps or see someone rushing from the shadows. One moment the world was happiness and snow and wine and Jack, the next there were hands around Amelia's neck, grabbing her from behind, fingers digging into her flesh.

Amelia tried to cry out but her throat had other things to do. She scrabbled at her neck, trying to pry loose the grip, straining for breath. Her legs skidded away from under her and she fell to the snowy street, which felt suddenly hard and wet and cold. With nothing else to do and with breath fast deserting her, she flailed with all her limbs, flinging her arms backwards to claw at her attacker, kicking out with her legs along the snowy ground.

As a red mist descended, Amelia felt her assailant's grip shift – it is hard to effectively strangle someone from behind. She tried to take advantage of the moment but the man was too quick, now digging both thumbs into her windpipe. Amelia stared up to look her attacker in the face.

But there was no one there.

Her eyes started wider, swivelling left and right as the panic and terror, that had already been running riot inside her, reached new levels. There was no one there. She was being attacked by no one. Was she having an allergic reaction? Her throat closing up of its own accord? No. She could feel the individual digits as they dug into her, she could touch the arms in front of her and even tug at them, and as she stared, she could now see snowflakes hanging suspended in the air before her, seeming to describe a shape that might be that of a person on whom they had settled.

She was being killed by the Invisible Man.

"AAAAGGGGHHHH!" The war cry seemed to explode from the night, and a split-second later the owner of it cannoned into Amelia and her attacker.

The grip was released from around Amelia's throat and she gasped painful breaths. Her saviour hit the ground hard and rolled smoothly into a crouching position.

That saviour was a woman; short and slightly built, wrapped in a great coat that might once have belonged to the Russian military. Beneath a mountain of curly, red hair, tied back with an elastic band, she had a pixie-ish face that seemed at odds with the toughness of her demeanour. Standing quickly, the woman scanned the ground with sharp, green eyes.

"There!" She pointed, and Amelia saw footprints appearing in the pristine snow on the road up ahead of them. The Invisible Man was running way.

The unidentified woman shot a look back at Amelia. "Well don't just sit there. Come on! Don't you want to catch him?"

She took off like a hare after the footprints, and Amelia found herself following. The world swam as she forced herself to her feet, but neither that nor the pain in her throat mattered as she ran after the strange woman. Damn right she wanted to catch him.

Inevitably the heels were more of an encumbrance now than before. Walking in heels on snow when you've been drinking is an art, running in them is a crap-shoot. Amazingly, driven by adrenalin, Amelia managed a decent turn of speed without slipping up, falling on her arse or turning an ankle. She couldn't catch up to the strange woman, but didn't give too much ground either and skidded to a halt beside her as they reached the busier thoroughfare of Lensfield Road.

"Damn," the woman snapped. The footprints led into the road, already a mess of greying, car-mangled slush. The trail was dead.

Amelia put her hands on her hips, getting her breath back as she took in her unlikely saviour. Amelia was not tall but the woman was inches shorter, though the attitude she projected made her seem bigger than she was. She was like the sparky sidekick in a Disney film; a fairy who would kick an ogre's ass in the final reel. She was probably in her mid-forties but had an animation that made her seem younger. Also very good skin.

"You alright?" the woman asked, almost as an afterthought.

"Yeah." Amelia touched her neck. The skin was tender and it hurt to swallow, but she was alright. "Thanks."

"Not a problem. Amelia, yes?"

"Yes." How did she know that? "Who are you?"

"Call me Elsa."

The choice of words rang some familiar bells in Amelia's head.

"You're from Universal."

Elsa pulled a face. "Not quite as clandestine as we might have hoped. Oh well, not my problem. Let's have a drink."

Chapter 13 – Elsa

There were not many pubs in Cambridge that stayed open past the old limit of eleven thirty, because in a student town it was asking for something to clean up the following morning, but one that had made that bold decision, and lived with the consequences, was The Lion's Head, which was only a ten minute walk away.

Elsa talked as they walked. "You been out somewhere?"

"Sorry?"

"You're all dolled up. Theatre? Symphony? I don't know what people do around here."

"I had a date." The conversation seemed quite incongruous to Amelia.

"And he didn't walk you home? You should ditch his ass."

"He offered, I said no."

"Well I bet you feel like a fool now, don't you? Or were trying to avoid putting out?"

"Are these questions important?"

"Nope," said Elsa. "Just making conversation. I find that people who've had a near death experience don't necessarily like to talk about it. Especially if, as in your case, it seems likely they're going to have another one."

"I am?"

Elsa shrugged, the collar of her big coat moving up around her ears. "Well he clearly wanted you dead and you're not. Might have been a random attack, but I think we both know that's pretty hopeful. *Ergo*; he'll have another try. Maybe not tonight. But somewhen. Soon, I'll bet."

Amelia felt a cold knot of terror in her stomach. "You were right."

"Probably. About what?"

"I didn't want to talk about this."

"Too late now."

Though she had met a couple of Universal agents during the Egyptian affair, Boris was the only one with whom Amelia had spent any time and, without realising it, she had mentally put all Universal operatives into a Boris-shaped mould, assuming him to be typical. Boris had been well-dressed, well-spoken, quietly polite and closed-lipped about much of his work. Elsa was none of these things.

The Lion's Head was not over-crowded but was still busy for a weeknight and they were lucky to get the table by the wall.

Elsa shrugged off her coat, hanging it over the back of the chair, revealing a woolly jumper and jeans. She flicked a look at Amelia.

"You look over-dressed. It's possible people think we're on a date."

"Two in one evening." Amelia managed a wan smile. "Nice to be wanted."

Elsa smiled. "I'm starting to see why Boris liked you for Universal. You bounce back from someone trying to kill you."

"I've been thinking about that." Amelia leaned forwards. "Last week I went to this abandoned building…"

Elsa held up a hand. "Drink?"

"What?"

"I'll get you something."

As Elsa headed for the bar, Amelia slumped back in her chair. She didn't want to judge someone she had only just met, but she couldn't picture Boris prioritising a drink over talking about a potential killer on the loose. It had occurred to Amelia that the only thing she had done that might provoke the Invisible Man was tracking down his laboratory. In which case she had almost certainly found the right place (and had been observed to do so, which was a chilling thought). It also probably meant that there was more there to find and it was worth a second look. But Elsa had seemed completely disinterested.

Amelia's phone pinged a text alert and she fished it out of her pocket.

'Don't freak when you read this, but he's watching us right now. E.'

Amelia did not 'freak'. At least not on the outside. On the outside she remained composed if somewhat stiff and blanched, as if someone had dropped an ice cube down her back. On the inside, her conscious mind had leapt out of its chair and run screaming from the pub, and it took a dint of effort for the rest of Amelia not to join it. Eventually her mind returned, somewhat shame-faced and making excuses. Amelia put the phone back in her pocket, and tried to remember what people did with their hands when they were being casual and nonchalant.

"Hell of queue," commented Elsa as she sat back down and plonked a drink in front of Amelia.

"What is this?"

"Coke," Elsa replied. "And I had them put something else in it. You've had a shock and it's cold out."

Amelia sipped the drink and tasted the sharpness of the alcohol through the coke. There were a hundred questions she wanted to ask but they were being eavesdropped upon and she had already given away more than she should have.

"The footprints were a surprise." Elsa seemed happy to lead the conversation, keeping it natural but steering clear of anything that might alert the Invisible Man.

"The footprints?"

"I'd been thinking we maybe had a ghost on our hands."

"And ghosts don't leave footprints?"

Elsa shrugged. "No idea. There aren't any confirmed sightings of ghosts. But we don't like to discount things where I come from and a ghost seemed to fit the facts. But if ghosts left footprints I reckon there would have been a confirmed sighting by now. So I guess 'invisible man' is the best explanation we have."

"I'm assuming that's not common either?"

"Nor is it really within our purview," admitted Elsa.

"You're not an invisible man specialist?" Boris had been an expert in Egyptian mummies, which was why he had been assigned that case.

"No such thing," replied Elsa, ever unconcerned. "I'm the one they call when there's science and technology involved. Our people don't always 'do' science. If you work with things that science cannot explain then you tend to have scant regard for it. I'm as close as Universal gets to an expert. Which in practice means I'm also the one they call when the wi-fi goes down. Plus I get the occasional DWBC."

"DWBC?"

"Doctors Without Brain Cells. Your basic mad scientist. Reanimation of the dead, tampering in God's domain, meddling in things men should leave alone, that sort of thing."

"That sort of thing." Amelia recalled that her first meeting with Boris had left her with a similar feeling of being rubber duck adrift in a large and bewildering sea.

"This is a new one on any of us, so who knows? But I'll look into it. See where we end up. You finishing that?"

Amelia looked at her half empty glass. "I don't think I am."

Elsa swallowed the remainder of Amelia's drink. "Waste not want not. Come on. I'll walk home with you."

It was pushing towards one in the morning when they left the pub. The snow had stopped and was already vanishing beneath the cold drizzle that had replaced it. Amelia wondered what the purpose of this little excursion had been. Though Elsa seemed a bit erratic, Amelia was fast getting the impression that the woman was shrewder than she let on.

"This way." The route Elsa took was not the most direct but Amelia soon realised why as they passed a series of noisy bars and clubs, still open at this late hour.

"He shouldn't be able to hear us now," Elsa whispered, careful to keep her demeanour open and casual as she spoke. "Not over that racket."

"Why did we go for a drink?" asked Amelia.

"To put him at his ease. To let him think that *we* think he's gone. Now he's following us."

"Are you sure?"

"Nope. I can't be even be certain he was in the pub. I'm making all this up as I go. Like I said; invisible man is a new one on us."

Amelia felt wretched and sick to her stomach.

"Can't we lose him?"

"Why would we do that?" Elsa turned a big grin on Amelia. "Here's thing; what we do in Universal is we track down monsters. But you can't track an invisible man. That is their most fundamental trait; they are hard to find. Famous for it. You can't go to him, so you have to make him come to you. Which is creepy as hell, I know, but it's the way we always do it."

"You said you'd never done this before."

129

"True. But if we had, then it's the way we always would have done it."

It was hard to argue with that sort of logic, particularly because they now passed the last conveniently noisy bar and Elsa whispered, "Shh."

They walked on a few paces in silence.

"So what was the guy's name?" Silence was suspicious.

"The... Oh. Jack."

"Good name," Elsa nodded. "Solid name. I went out with a Jack once."

"Nice guy?"

"Nope."

A car drove by and Elsa took the opportunity to whisper, "Walk lightly and listen."

Amelia tried to moderate the click of her heels on the slippery pavement, holding her breath and straining to tune out the background sounds of Cambridge by night. At first she heard nothing, but then, alongside her footsteps and those of Elsa, who wore stout, heavy boots, she caught the faint sound of a third set, a few feet behind them.

Invisible men are incautious. They have a tremendous advantage in that they cannot be seen and tend to forget that they *can* be heard, and that rain or smoke will reveal their outline. They forget that being invisible does not make them intangible or invulnerable. Being invisible can mess with your head in a lot of ways.

Again, Amelia strove to be as cool as possible and not give any physical sign that she knew they were being followed, while her heart performed calisthenics at the back of her throat.

"Which way?" asked Elsa.

"Left up here."

As soon as they turned the corner, Elsa grabbed Amelia's arm, rushed her forward and dragged her into the deep doorway of someone's house.

"What the...?"

Elsa silenced her with a look, then pointed to her ear. Amelia listened.

There they were. Footsteps. Barely audible at first, but then... They stopped. When they re-started the footsteps were louder, throwing caution to the wind, the panicked footfalls of someone who had lost their quarry. They came closer.

While Amelia had been listening to the approach of the Invisible Man, Elsa had silently stripped off her great coat and now stood tensed, holding it ready. As the footsteps drew level with their hiding place, she threw out the coat like a fisherman casting his net. The coat landed over what had seemed to be mid-air, revealing the shape of a figure beneath, who immediately tried to fling it off again. But Elsa followed like a rugby player, hurling herself at the blinded invisible man, wrapping her arms about him as he struggled under the coat, which seemed to float a few feet above the ground. He thrashed desperately but Elsa clung on with a wiry strength. Locked together, they staggered out into the road, lit by hazy moonlight from above.

Amelia rushed out of the doorway, wondering if she should help or leave this to the professionals.

But before she could decide, a pair of bright lights rounded the corner, harshly illuminating the scene. Brakes screeched. Tyres fought for purchase on the slippery tarmac, finding none. The car skidded forwards, out of control, and Elsa flung herself aside, rolling on the ground.

As soon as it had come to a halt, the car's door opened and a man leapt out.

"What the hell are you playing at?"

Ignoring the irate driver, Elsa sprang to her feet and ran back into the road. Her coat lay in a damp heap under the car's bumper and she retrieved it, feeling around for anything else.

"Are you listening to me?" the driver asked, relieved he had not hurt anyone but understandably furious.

"Not really." Elsa was on hands and knees now, feeling her way from one side of the road to the other. "Back up a few feet, would you? I seem to have lost something."

There was, Amelia had noticed, a kind of authority to Elsa's voice. Earlier that night it had brought Amelia to her feet to chase the Invisible Man when she would have preferred to sit on the ground and recover, now it made the driver get back into his car and do as he was told.

Elsa hurried back up the road, bent double, sweeping her hands from side to side. Amelia joined her and together they covered every inch of the road and pavement.

Finally, Elsa straightened with a rueful expression. "Gone. I doubt we'll get the drop on him like that again."

"Are you two quite alright?" asked the driver, leaning from his window.

"Fine. You can go now."

The man looked non-plussed, but once again did as he was told.

Elsa swore. "Right idea. Unlucky timing."

"What now?" asked Amelia.

"Sleep," replied Elsa. "I can crash on your sofa, can't I?"

Back at her flat, Amelia finished the sentence she had begun in The Lion's Head, explaining to Elsa how she had found the abandoned building, and possible laboratory, by going through descriptions in the book.

"Clever," nodded Elsa. "And perhaps productive."

"I didn't think there was anything to it at the time," continued Amelia. "Just a place the author had found and used in his story. But I can't think of any other reason for me to get attacked. So now I'm wondering if I found something important."

"And if there's something there worth hiding." Elsa slapped her thigh in decision. "That's where we'll start tomorrow. But first..." she patted the sofa. "Thanks for this. I'm in the Travelodge but its way across town and I can't really be bothered."

She said it chattily, setting to work unlacing her enormous boots, but Amelia wasn't buying the easy-going attitude. Elsa wasn't stopping on the sofa because it was long walk to the hotel, she was staying there because Amelia was a target.

Amelia thought back to a night in this same room six months ago when Boris had first brought her into this new world. In the months since then her life had been in danger more often than in all the years leading up to it. It could be a hard world, and sometimes a sad one, and it had changed *everything*. She had come very close to saying no to Boris. In fact, thinking back, she *had* said no and he had tempted her with promises of the Universal Library. What might her life be like now if she had not taken that leap? She would have no need of the diminutive bodyguard currently bedding down on her sofa; her life would not be in danger; and she would not have some bad and bloody memories that popped into her dreams all too frequently.

132

But she did not regret the decision. It had opened her eyes to a bigger world, of course, and let her see things she could never have dreamed of, bringing her closer to Ancient Egypt than any researcher before her. But more than that; it had made her a stronger, more confident woman. Zita would have introduced her to Jack either way, but Amelia did not think she would have taken the chance with him if she had not been through all that she had that year. She would have taken more time to get over Frank.

There were things that had happened that she wished she could change. But not the decisions she had made. Even if those decisions had had some unforeseeable consequences.

Before going to bed that night, Amelia got the broom from her kitchen and swung it round the room, poking it sharply into corners, waving it under the bed and ramming it into the recesses of her wardrobe. To a casual observer she looked like someone practicing either an obscure martial art or some form of extreme housework, but she was checking for invisible men.

When she finally got into bed, she lay awake a while. She was unnerved by the night's events, but mainly because this was not behaviour she had expected from a man she felt she had come to know, and even to like. She felt betrayed.

Chapter 14 – The Lair of the Invisible Man

Amelia was shaken awake at eight in the morning.

"Mmrf?" she said, as her eyes focussed on Elsa, looking wide awake and impatient.

"You've been asleep for hours."

"I usually do sleep for hours," Amelia replied. "It's a habit I got into as a child and haven't been able to break."

"Come on. Big day ahead."

The Universal agent had already showered, dressed, breakfasted and been out to buy supplies, which she had packed into a rucksack that was waiting by the door. She was eager to get going, further evidenced by her shouts of encouragement as Amelia got ready.

"We need to check out the maybe-lab before our invisible friend goes back there to cover his tracks."

"Sorry," said Amelia, as she dragged a hurried brush through her hair. "I shouldn't have opened my mouth in the pub."

"You didn't know." Elsa wasn't one to dwell. "Come on. I've made breakfast, you can eat on the way."

Breakfast was coffee in a travel mug and a protein bar, but Amelia was happy with that and they set out, weaving their way through the rush hour traffic that was redoubled this close to Christmas.

"Haven't these people got any homes to go to?" wondered Elsa.

"They're going Christmas shopping. Probably in London."

Elsa just grunted in reply. They were on an urgent mission, but Amelia got the impression that Elsa was one of those people who did everything at top speed regardless, because why wouldn't you? If you were walking somewhere then presumably where you were going was the place you needed to be and the place in which you were was not; so why would you not go from one to the other as speedily as possible? It was logical, but Amelia sometimes struggled to keep up as her companion snaked a path through the people trailing down Station Road.

As everyone else headed straight on for the station, they turned left to take the footbridge across the tracks.

"We haven't talked about the murders," said Elsa,

conversationally.

"I guess I don't know if the two things are related."

"The connection between them was initially pretty circumstantial," agreed Elsa. "Just some tricky murders occurring at the same time as someone who does damn good magic tricks. But the TV show suggested what he's capable of and last night proved it. Now we know he's real, I think we're pretty safe making the connection. Have you thought about the victims' professions?"

"University professors."

"Scientists," Elsa stressed. "I've seen some weird things in my job, but I don't get the impression that this bloke just woke up one day and thought '*Hello, where's my hand gone? And where are my legs while we're about it*'. This was done deliberately."

A noticeable absence in the book was that it never addressed *how* this had happened; that was not important to the Invisible Man's story.

"You think he might be a scientist? A DWBC?"

"And scientists know each other. They read each other's papers, work on each other's projects, compete for the same funding and argue over who came up with what theory or solved what hypothesis."

"Maybe the Invisible Man knew these scientists?"

Elsa shrugged. "I'm just spit-balling here, but revenge is an awfully strong motive."

"Three murders over who came up with a theory?" Amelia wasn't sold.

"I'm not saying I've got all the details," Elsa admitted. "But remember the TV show. This isn't just revenge; this is the revenge of someone who clearly had some violent tendencies to begin with."

"Or perhaps being invisible has a bad effect on you?"

"I've been wondering about that too," Elsa nodded. "But I'll tell you what's bugging me. I've checked recent missing persons reports. Cambridge isn't missing any scientists."

"So maybe he can go back and forth? Make himself invisible then visible again at will."

Elsa pulled a joyless smile. "I can't tell if that would make things easier or more difficult. At least with an invisible man, you know him when you don't see him."

They reached the footpath near the potential laboratory.

"Here," said Amelia.

Elsa slowed. She didn't come to a complete stop, but the energy she poured into walking seemed to be redirected into an intense stare, taking in the round-about and the silver birch.

"The silver man. Well spotted." She shook her head. "Our invisible man has the soul of a poet. A bad one, but still."

"This way." Amelia led the way down the path and through the hole in the wire. The frozen ground crunched beneath her knees as she crawled into the undergrowth, and the cold bit at her hands, even through her gloves.

On the other side, Elsa did exactly as Amelia had done, circling the building before going back to the door.

"In we go."

They entered.

"Lights?"

Amelia flicked the switch and the lights snapped into life, revealing the bare room as she remembered it.

"I should warn you; there are rats. At least one."

Elsa nodded absently, scanning the room, her eyes seeming greener with concentration. "Close the door."

As Amelia shut the door, Elsa took off her rucksack and opened it to take out some of the supplies she had bought that morning.

Amelia frowned. "Silly string?"

"Good thing about the Christmas season," said Elsa, "shops open early and stay open late. You can pick this stuff up any time of the day."

"Well you certainly wouldn't want to be without it."

Elsa handed Amelia a can before closing the doors that led to the other rooms. The hinges screamed as if they had not been moved for years.

"Follow my lead." Elsa ran down one wall, spraying the brightly coloured string out into the centre of the room, watching carefully as she did so. Amelia mirrored her, running along the opposite wall. They both turned and went back again, then took a more random path, spraying wherever they went and revealing nothing.

This done, Elsa returned to her bag and took out a jar.

"Glitter."

"Glitter?"

"You ever got glitter on you?"

Amelia shrugged. "There were some parties when I was at university…"

"And how long did it take you to get it off?"

Amelia recalled the days after those parties, finding glitter in the most unexpected places, even after she had showered.

Elsa hurled handfuls of glitter around her, watching it settle, alert to the slightest disturbance, till she had systematically covered the whole room, by which point it looked as if a children's birthday party had been thrown in a disused bomb shelter.

"This room's clear," nodded Elsa, confidently. "No invisible man gets past silly string *and* glitter."

They went into the next room and repeated the process, finding just as little. Amelia was grateful that there was not an invisible man in there, and was not sure what she would have done if they had discovered one, on the other hand, she had rather hoped to see the glittering, silly string-festooned shape emerging out of nothing. In the third room, she almost got her wish.

"Wait!" yelled Elsa, as they were spraying string. She pointed.

The two women watched as the strings by the wall moved, something passing over them. Elsa grabbed a handful of glitter and tossed it at the movement.

As the glitter settled, the tension of the moment eased to be replaced by something else.

"It's that damn rat," breathed Amelia.

"Was it invisible last time?"

"You don't think I'd have mentioned that?"

"Interesting."

The glittery outline stopped and Amelia could see its head turning from one side to the other. She could even see its little nose twitching in the movement of the glitter.

Everything had happened so fast last night that Amelia had still been in two minds; there had to be a logical explanation, didn't there? But presented with the reality of an invisible rat covered in glitter sitting right in front of her, she was finally reconciled to the truth. This was not a trick.

And yet it still felt like one. Perhaps it was the incongruity of a glittery rat, but staring at it, Amelia still found herself wondering how it was done. Her brain was so overloaded with astonishment that it seemed to have tempered it with disbelief.

The rat set off again. It had had enough of this and made for its more private retreat.

"Interesting," Elsa repeated as the sparkly rat vanished into a hole. She put an ear to the wall. "Not in there." Stooping to one knee, she examined the floor.

Beneath the glitter and silly string, the floor was filthy, caked in concrete dust overlaid with dirt and mould. Thick enough to hide secrets.

"Ah." Elsa grinned and ran a finger along a thin gap in the floor.

"What is it?" asked Amelia

"Well, unless I miss my guess, it's a trapdoor."

It was hidden in a corner of the room where there was little light, fitted so snugly that it barely left a line and disguised by dust and dirt.

Reaching into her coat, Elsa produced a pocket knife which she used first to clean the gap and then to pry the metal trapdoor open. Leaving Amelia to peer uneasily down into the shivering darkness, Elsa went back to her rucksack and returned with a torch. The bright, white beam cut through the blackness to reveal a steep, bare, concrete staircase leading down into a basement room, as featureless as the one in which they stood.

"Are we going down?" asked Amelia.

"I think you know the answer to that. Fetch my rucksack."

Elsa held the torch in one hand and in the other a can of spray paint which she fired out ahead of her as she walked slowly down.

"I should really be writing all these good ideas down, you know? For when Universal encounters invisible men in the future. Nice to know you can face them with a few bits from the nearest craft shop."

She sounded relaxed, but Amelia thought that was just for her benefit.

"That door didn't look to have been opened for a while," Elsa continued. "But if you didn't want anyone to find it then maybe you'd brush all that dirt and crap over it. Press it into the gap. Make it hard to find *and* make it look like no one's been down here. Ah, light switch."

The lights were the same as the ones upstairs, starting with a bang then buzzing continually. They revealed a bare-walled basement similar to the rooms above in all but one respect.

"It's clean," said Amelia. She remembered thinking that the upstairs rooms were too filthy to be used as a lab. Down here it looked as if someone had scrubbed the walls. For the most part. "Are those scorch marks?" One wall bore evidence of a recent fire.

"You thought about what this place was originally?" wondered Elsa.

"Not my primary concern," admitted Amelia, who was now feeling very uncomfortable, and not just because her imagination was populating the room with invisible rats.

"I'm guessing something military," Elsa was fishing in her bag again. "There's a nuclear bunker not far from here – did you know that? This has got a Cold War feel to it. Abandoned or never used. Forgotten. Right; you stay here to guard the stairs – just blast the silly string out around you. I don't think there's anyone down here, but if there is then I don't want him leaving."

She did not add '*Because if he leaves then he can close the trapdoor on us and we're stuffed*'. Nor did she mention that, because Amelia had let slip about finding this place in the pub last night, the Invisible Man might have guessed they were coming and set a trap.

As Elsa repeated her movements from the rooms above over this larger space, covering it with silly string then glitter, Amelia stood at the base of the stairs, firing the string out in front of her. Each strand she fired, she imagined hung in the air before her, draping over the invisible body of a psychopath who had already tried to kill her once. But, thankfully this was just in her head.

"Clean," announced Elsa. "Grab yourself a can of spray paint and let's give this place the once over."

There was not much to find. If anyone had ever used this place as a secret laboratory then they had done a good job of removing all signs. But there were a few points of interest.

"What have you got there?" asked Amelia.

"I think they're rabbit droppings. Want to see?"

"I'm good."

Elsa smiled. "Rabbits and rats. Interesting, no?"

"I guess this is a pretty nice place if you're a burrowing rodent."

"Rabbits aren't rodents," Elsa replied, casually dropping wisdom. "But my point was more that they are animals commonly used in lab experiments."

"The rat I saw was white." It had struck Amelia as odd at the time, now it made sudden sense.

"If they were just living down here," Elsa went on, "I'd expect to see piles of crap. There's barely any. Not enough crap means someone cleaned it up."

The next thing Amelia found.

"Ugh!"

"Are you alright?"

"Stepped in something. Please tell me I haven't trodden on a rabbit."

"I don't think so," murmured Elsa. She was examining the offending article and poking at it.

"What is it?" There was nothing to see but a line of silly string laid across an invisible lump on the floor. The dust beneath it moved when Elsa prodded it.

"I think it's a brick."

Elsa directed her spray paint at the object and revealed something that was indeed very brick-shaped. There was one problem.

"You put your foot through it."

Elsa placed the toe of her boot onto the remains of the brick and pressed. It crumbled like a stale biscuit, revealing the invisible interior beneath the paint-sprayed surface.

"Maybe it's not a brick," suggested Amelia. "Just something brick-shaped."

"Either that," said Elsa, darkly, "or invisibility doesn't work as well on bricks as it does on people. Or at least as it appears to on people. Not all experiments go as planned." She glanced at the scorch marks on the wall. "Called it 'the House of Pain', didn't he."

A slight shiver ran down Amelia's back. They had talked earlier about the possibility that being invisible might have a bad effect on a person; what if the fate of the brick was what awaited the Invisible Man?

"Interesting to know that it works, at least partially, on something other than people," commented Elsa. "I thought he was wearing clothes the other night, but it was hard to tell under my coat while we were struggling."

"I guess he'd almost have to be dressed in this weather," considered Amelia. "He'd have died of pneumonia by now if he was wandering around naked."

Elsa sighed. "More questions, more problems. It works on clothing and people better than it works on bricks. Does it work on metal? Could we have an invisible man with an invisible gun wandering about?"

"If we do then he's going about killing people the hard way."

"True," Elsa nodded sharply. "Let's assume metal is a no-no and... What's that?"

That proved to be a black rubbish bag, which they had missed when they came in because it was in the shadow of the staircase.

There was a tense silence between the pair as Elsa fiddled with the knot at the top. Thus far, what they had found had been of interest but little use, this felt like their last chance to find something that might take their investigation forwards. There was also something creepy about abandoned bin bags found in the basements of empty buildings. It seemed guaranteed to contain the dismembered remains of a murder victim, weapons grade plutonium, or the answer to the question; what happened to all those rats and rabbits?

In fact what it contained was disappointingly anti-climactic.

"Crisp packets, used tissues, empty bottles (tch; hasn't he heard of recycling?)..."

It was generic trash, and the only thing to do was sift through for items of interest amongst the grossness.

There were some balls of screwed-up paper and these were carefully unfolded to reveal a domestic shopping list, a receipt that corresponded to the shopping list plus a bottle of wine, some train times, the phone number of a local pizza place, and what they eventually identified as someone trying to work out an anagram, perhaps for a crossword puzzle.

"I'm starting to think someone just dumped their shit down here," mused Elsa. "I mean it's a lot of trouble to go to just for fly-tipping, but no one's going to catch you and look how much space there is."

"What about this one?"

Amelia plucked another ball of paper and unfolded it. It was an

141

envelope, and although the name had been torn off in opening, enough remained for the Cambridge address to be legible.

Amelia and Elsa looked at each other.

"Is this…?"

Elsa shrugged. "I don't know. But it's where we're going next."

For as long as anyone can remember there have been two Cambridges; Town and Gown.

Gown is the Cambridge that people think of, the one tourists come to see and the one the city likes to project. It is the image of the University town, untouched by history even as it crams high-end boutiques into listed buildings; the ancient traditions and well-kept greens; the attractive market where you expect to be gouged because this is Cambridge and stuff is supposed to be expensive. This is a Cambridge of intellectual estimation, quality and money. Plus quite lot of students, but even they are of a better sort than you get elsewhere.

Town was what Cambridge would be without a university; just a town in the east of England without even a cathedral to give it city status. It was a place where people lived and worked and never even noticed that their home was a world-renowned seat of learning – they knew it, but it didn't have any impact on their lives. It was the part of Cambridge that the tourists did not come to see and were herded away from by clever signage. If it had been a viable option then the council would have erected a screen. It was a Cambridge that was not affluent, where the roads went unrepaired and where unemployment was a fact of life. It was a Cambridge that went against the image that the word 'Cambridge' projected, but which also underpinned it. On the great Monopoly board of life it doesn't matter whether you are Mayfair or Old Kent Road, somebody has to do the shit jobs.

Amelia was Gown – she had attended the University, she now worked for it and she didn't get out of the city centre much because everything was there. But she was also not blind; she knew that the Town side of Cambridge existed.

It was not, therefore, the area itself that surprised Elsa and Amelia when they made their way out towards the Arbury end of town in search of the address on the envelope, it was that this was not where they had expected to end up.

"I'm going to stick my neck out and say not many Cambridge University scientists live round here," commented Elsa.

"I don't really know any," admitted Amelia. "But I think not."

The University was not just the buildings and the vast tracts of land it owned, it was also the people, and those people clustered about it, creating their own little world in a bubble. Central Cambridge was an expensive place to live (almost comparable to London) but the University paid well and owned a lot of property, so could act as a generous landlord. It was easy to be a generous landlord when you could fire your tenant if they refused to clean the oven every six months.

"This is it."

'It' was a five-storey block of flats looking very much like a block of flats anywhere in the country; bikes locked to the railings, graffiti on the walls, an optimistic washing line catching what December sunlight it could, strung along a balcony. A handful of kids kicked a ball against the wall, ignoring the snow that had started to spit from the slate grey sky. It did not look like the home of a revolutionary scientist or an academic-slaying psychopath. It looked like a place where people lived.

"You ever stop to wonder," Elsa asked, as they climbed the stairs to the third floor, "how different classic cult literature would be if the protagonists lived elsewhere?"

"The Council House of Doctor Moreau, you mean?"

"Exactly. The Creature From the River Avon."

"If that bald guy from James Bond…"

"Blofeld."

"Sure – if he couldn't afford a hollowed-out volcano then there really is no low-budget substitute that would have the same impact."

They reached flat number 37 and Amelia rang the bell.

"Are you expecting someone to answer?" asked Elsa.

"We said he might be able to change back and forth."

But no answer came.

"There's a turn up," said Elsa. "The Invisible Man can't see us right now."

She checked up and down the corridor to make sure no one was about.

"Keep an eye out." She dropped to her knees, fishing some

143

long, thin tools out of the side-pocket of her rucksack.

"Are you picking the lock?"

"Ask louder why don't you? I don't think they heard you on the fifth floor."

"Are we sure this is quite alright?"

"We are hunting a murderer. I think it's fine."

The lock clicked and Elsa pushed the door open. "Hello? The door was unlocked, we're coming in."

Still no answer. The pile of junk mail on the mat suggested that no one had been here for a week at least, and that they never got any interesting post.

Elsa picked up a letter as Amelia closed the door behind them, feeling terribly guilty and sure that a policeman was about to spring out from behind the sofa to grab her.

"Stuart Price," Elsa read. She sifted through a few more letters. "Not one of these is addressed to a Dr or Professor Stuart Price. I suppose he could live with someone." She scanned the room. "But I rather doubt it."

The room screamed 'single male'.

While Elsa began to conduct a swift search, Amelia turned her attention to the bookshelves. It was something she always did when she was in other people's homes, she liked to see what books she had in common with the occupant and thought it was a pretty good way to get to know someone. People might lie about themselves to project an image, but their bookcase never lied.

At first glance she did not have similar reading habits to Stuart Price. There were a lot of How-To books for budding artists, writers, actors, singers, stand-up comedians. There was an obvious breadth to the aspiring talents of Stuart Price, and Amelia wondered how much of that was backed up by actual talent.

On the wall by the little kitchen area, was a calendar that had come free with something and Amelia flicked through it. The boxes were mostly filled with annotations she couldn't make head or tail of outside of the obvious 'b-day', but a couple attracted her attention because they were in red and vigorously circled. Some were once again acronyms that meant nothing, but she spotted 'BGT'. Wasn't that *Britain's Got Talent*? It didn't have to be – other things had those initials or he could be planning burgers for tea – but here too was '*Voice*', another talent show. If all these annotations were talent

144

competitions – some big and well-known, others less so – what picture did that paint of Stuart Price? One of a man desperate to be seen.

Had Stuart found a way?

Her phone blipped a text alert and Amelia felt suddenly guilty as she read the message from Jack, checking in and tactfully mooting a third date. She shoved the phone back into her pocket; she couldn't answer him while she was in another man's home.

She looked about the room again. It was all so very… ordinary.

"I don't think this can be him." Elsa strode back in, all business. "So we should get out of here, because if this is not the flat of a serial killer then the whole breaking and entering thing becomes swiftly much less cool."

"I think it's him."

Never one to waste seconds, Elsa had already been halfway to the door when Amelia spoke. She turned back. "Why?"

"It feels like him."

It would have been very easy for Elsa to completely dismiss her at that point, but Universal agents do not survive long if they dismiss the ridiculous.

"Explain to me. How?"

Amelia showed her the books, the calendar, the sketch pad, the water colours, the overflowing '*Ideas Book*' filled with scribbled plotlines, the demo cds dating back to when you might put a demo on a cd. Everything in the room painted Stuart Price as a frustrated artist, and more specifically, Celebrity.

"Think of all those stunts he's done," Amelia went on, her words speeding up as she warmed to her subject, "but in the context of this room. Being invisible is one of those major fantasies (especially for men), it's right up there with flying. And when you ask people what they would do if they were invisible for a day then it's always 'go into the women's changing rooms', followed by 'find out what people say about me when I'm not around'. Those are the standards. There's none of that in the book – not even a hint. What does Stuart do? He writes a book that no one else can write and finds a way to promote it that no one can resist. Suddenly he's a celebrity – what he's always wanted. One slight problem; he can't make public appearances. So he does the next best thing. Think of all these stunts. What do they all have in common? The public. He works with an audience. That's what he wants. Based on this place I'd say that's what he needs."

It all spilled out of Amelia in a torrent, her mouth barely keeping pace with her thoughts. In the reading and re-reading of his book, she had come to know the Invisible Man better than anyone, and in this room she recognised the man who needed to do *something*, faced with the horror that he never had and the fear that he never would. He might not be the man she had thought he was – her throat was still tender after last night's attack – but that aspect of his nature still spoke to her. To Amelia, the need to be seen was more a personal than a public one, but she understood how it felt to be invisible to those around you.

"All very neat and empowering," Elsa sounded a note of scepticism, "but I don't follow how the murders fit in, or how an aspiring celebrity did this to himself."

Nor did Amelia. Not yet.

"If being made invisible is affecting his mind, like you thought…"

Elsa pulled a face. "When you start riding the 'if train' then who knows where you're going to end up. Show me proof."

It was actually easier to find than either could have predicted. Hiding in plain sight on one side of the desk was a notebook. On the cover Amelia saw '~~The Invisible Man~~' '~~The Memoirs of an Invisible Man~~', '~~The Confession of an Invisible Man~~', '*The Life of an Invisible Man*'. And on opening it she found that familiar first line '*My body still shaking, my heart trying to tear itself apart, I broke through the undergrowth and stumbled blindly onto the path, and into the light of a new world.*'.

Elsa put her hands on her hips and sighed. "Well, I'm a big enough person to admit I'm wrong. At the very least this Stuart Price is involved. But, call me a science snob, I still don't see him doing this to himself. There's nothing here to suggest he could tell a test tube from a tube train."

A thought lasered its way through Amelia's cerebellum and looking at Elsa she realised that her new friend had had the same thought.

"Someone else did this to him."

146

"Someone he might have reason to be angry at."
"And now he's looking for revenge?"

Chapter 15 – Uncomfortably Numb

Relatively early in his new life, the Invisible Man realised that living at home was more a habit than a necessity. He could not walk through walls, nor had he suddenly acquired the skills of cat burglar, but it was strange how swiftly moral guidelines dropped away from you when you knew that you could not be caught. Helping himself to food was something he had done almost immediately – largely because it was hard to get the cashier's attention and money floating out of mid-air caused more problems than it solved. Helping himself to somewhere to live did not seem a big step.

The first time had just been a case of right place, right time. He had seen a middle-aged couple outside one of those nice houses at the Common end of Maid's Causeway, taking bags out to a taxi, and had thought; why not? He strolled in while they were still ferrying luggage and sat down to wait as they bustled to and fro making sure they had not forgotten anything. From scraps of their conversation he picked up that they were going to be away for the weekend. Before they left, the man set the security system by punching a code into a box at the door. The Invisible Man watched over his shoulder and deactivated it the moment the man had gone. He was not sure if he would set off motion detectors, but it was better to be safe than sorry. There were a lot of specifics of his 'condition' that he wasn't sure about. He had signed some papers to say that he understood what was being done to him but that was standard boilerplate – no one ever read that.

For the next two days he enjoyed being the owner of a large and expensive property with a big screen TV (one of those that covers most of the wall in eyeball-melting hi-def), a well-stocked larder, and a bed that was like sleeping inside a marshmallow. He even found a spare set of keys, so was able to come and go at will.

On the Sunday night he watched through the window for the lights of the taxi, then went to the front door, turned the alarm back on, and waited for the owners to enter, at which point he went on his way, back to his flat. He had left the house spotless, without a sign that he had been there (unless they kept careful inventory of their food). It had been easy, and rather like an all-expenses paid holiday.

It had been so easy in fact that, the following day, he went to an eye-wateringly expensive hotel in the centre, helped himself to a key card, and took a room for the remainder of the week. This was fun, but not quite as good as house-sitting (as he liked to call it); he couldn't order room service because there wasn't meant to be anyone in the room, and helping himself in the restaurant was liable to attract comment.

It was too much to hope that he would wander by when people were off on holiday again, so instead he decided to simply adopt a new home – an empty one. Squatters, he was given to understand, did this all the time and were only caught because they could be seen and demonstrated a lack of hygiene. He would treat the place well, keeping it clean enough that when people came to look around there was no sign that he was living there. In fact, he was arguably doing the sellers a favour by giving empty, but furnished, properties that homely, lived-in feel that is hard to put your finger on but also hard to fake.

He spent less and less time at his flat, popping in irregularly to check the mail or spend a night in his own bed.

It was hard to say if *Wake Up!* changed things or if it made him aware of a change that had been happening anyway. Previously he had justified his new living situation easily: he wasn't hurting anyone. But after *Wake Up!* he did not even try. Did he now feel that the world owed him something? Or had his moral compass been skewed for a while and he just hadn't noticed?

Sometimes he actively tried to feel guilty, but got no reaction from himself, as if he was trying to awake sensation in a paralysed limb. There were no longer any nerves feeding his sense of morality; it was dead.

A day or two after the *Wake Up!* debacle, an assistant in a Cambridge bookshop – the same bookshop in which it had all started – was engaged in the dreary task of marking down. From day one *The Life of an Invisible Man* had lived on the bestseller shelves near the front door, reserved for those books you *had* to buy your loved ones this festive season. But the TV show had precipitated a backlash and now the bargain bin beckoned. The price was being slashed to more than half what it had been and even then there were few takers.

The assistant carried a stack of books from the bestseller shelves to their new home in the 'embarrassed to exist' corner, and began to affix the markdown stickers.

Afterwards, he struggled to accurately describe what happened next, but he had the clearest memory of a sudden hiss of rage before the book was wrenched violently from his hands. Before his astonished eyes, the sticker was torn off and flicked aside. More books – the ones he had already stickered – flew from the shelf, tumbling to the floor where the stickers began to peel away, as if the books were rejecting them, refusing to allow themselves to be marked down.

The pile of unstickered books now rose from the floor and floated back towards where they had come from, and where they apparently felt they belonged; the bestseller shelves. The assistant had been stunned to immobility throughout, but drew the line at this; he had been given a job to do and he would damn well do it.

"Hey, come back here!"

He gave chase, grabbing the top book from the pile. But as he did so the next book down sprang at him like a striking snake, catching him in the face with its spine, knocking him back then leaping into the air only to descend violently on his skull, bringing him to his knees. The book leapt up again then flew at him, hitting him full in the face, its pages flapping, paper cuts scoring his cheeks.

And it was not alone. One by one the books in the floating pile sprang to life, diving on him in quick succession like kamikaze planes, then tumbling lifeless to the floor. All the assistant could do was hold up his hands, crying out for help until, as suddenly as it had begun, the assault ceased.

The books lay around him as still as death, the anger that had animated them now expended.

Only a few people saw what had happened and the events were dismissed by the online community as a cheap publicity stunt by a bookshop desperate to unload the now unsaleable copies of a book they had massively overstocked. This just went to prove, people said, that the events of the book's launch, and probably all subsequent stunts, were fake.

Sitting on the comfortable sofa in the well-appointed town house he was currently calling home, the Invisible Man tried to recall the events of the day. It had been something he could not have done and yet he knew that he had done it. The memories were indistinct and tinged in red hues, but he recalled the sensations with pin-sharp clarity. Above all he remembered the pleasure he had taken in beating that assistant senseless. And why not? The man had treated his book with complete disregard.

But did that justify what he had done?

The Invisible Man was very aware that he would once have recoiled from such behaviour, and now did not. His mind was in flux between two points of view, fighting for supremacy, but there was so much crossover between them that he could not say who was who; where one ended and the other began. It was not black and white simple. It was a battle painted in shades of grey, and he wasn't sure how he felt about either. He wasn't sure how he felt about anything anymore.

Except when he had been attacking that man. Then he had known very well how he felt. He had spent his life trying to achieve notoriety and now it was being taken from him for the sake of one careless transgression? Not if he had anything to say about it!

Absently he shook his hand. It had been tingling all afternoon, a strange numbing sensation. He had probably damaged it during the... 'incident' in the bookshop.

A few days later, the staff of every bank in Cambridge sat up long after closing time, attempting to locate the thousand pounds that had somehow gone missing during the day. Banks will often have trouble cashing up – accidents do happen – but a thousand pounds was a lot to lose. It was only when calls started to be made to respective head offices that the extent of the problem became gradually clearer.

Which was a relief to managers. A branch being a thousand pounds down was a branch problem, but every branch of every bank in the city being a thousand pounds down? That sounded like someone else's problem. It was hard to say whose, but the managers took the view that 'not mine' was the salient point.

That night, every homeless person in Cambridge suddenly had a fistful of notes thrust into their hands by a shadowy figure, swathed in coats and scarves.

Some of them recalled hearing a whispered voice, "A present from the Invisible Man."

The Invisible Man was not remotely guilty about taking money from the banks, and he was pretty sure that no one was going to judge him for giving it to those who were more in need. Sure, some of them would use it to get bombed out of their skulls but he had enough faith in mankind to think that most would put it to good use. He had a right to feel good about it.

But he didn't.

He felt as little pride in giving money to the poor as he felt guilt in taking it from the rich. He had taken considerable pleasure in robbing the banks, after that he had just needed a way to get rid of the money. The homeless had seemed as good a place as any. Perhaps he had just done it for the brief human interaction it gave him. It had been so long since he had really *talked* to anyone. He had not even spoken to the woman, Zita, from the publishers since *Wake Up!*. Some days the loneliness was crushing. Others he felt nothing.

But if his emotions in certain areas seemed to be letting him down, in others they were running hot, as if lava was in his veins. The loss of his celebrity burnt him from the inside, leaving his nerves raw and ragged. He had to come up with another stunt to win back the hearts and minds of Cambridge, of Britain, of the world.

Fifteen minutes of fame. That was what they said, wasn't it? And that was all he had got. A few whirlwind weeks.

He had kept a masochistic eye on developments online. Perversely, the *Wake Up!* affair, the most impossible of his 'appearances' because it had been the least planned, had rekindled the old idea that it was all fake, just a bunch of pixels in someone's computer. He had been downgraded from the century's most brilliant public entertainer, to the level of a novelty video on YouTube. He did not dare let himself think about it for too long, because when he did, he started to hear his heart pounding in his ears, to feel his muscles tensing rigidly in his invisible limbs, and the red mist began to rise.

His right foot was tingling now, and he stamped it on the floor, trying to get the feeling back into it.

It was 4 days before Christmas. In the home he had appropriated, the Invisible Man had hung some tinsel and put up a tree. But right now he was seated at his kitchen island, staring at his hands.

He could not see his hands of course. But he could see the

blood on them; the blood all over them. If he held them up then he could see the dried blood from within, like looking at the inside of a glove. It creased and cracked as his hands moved. It was mesmerising. But he had no idea whose it was.

His memory had been unreliable of late; he forgot to switch things off or where things were or what food was in his fridge. But this…

He had woken up like this, his bed smeared with blood. He had no memory of it getting there. He had no memory of the map laid out on the worksurface in front of him, no idea why he would have circled one particular building, no recognition of the name written beside it in block capitals.

What had he done?

Who was Una Jaffers?

Chapter 16 – Harrigan's Shoe Leather

In his office, Harrigan drummed his fingers on his desk, daring himself to continue with this line of enquiry. Finally he got up and stuck his head out of the door.

"Stubbs?"

The sergeant looked up. "Sir?"

"Do you know if we collected a diary from the second victim?"

"Professor Herrick?"

"That's her."

Stubbs shook his head. "Don't know, sir. Would you like me to find out?"

"Please. In fact, bring me the diaries of all three victims."

The sergeant hurried off and Harrigan returned to his office to pace. This was so tenuous you couldn't even call it a lead, it was a coincidence at best.

A knock on the door heralded the sergeant's return, holding three desk diaries sealed in evidence bags.

Harrigan sat down to look through the diaries. Dr Cranley's had nothing specific marked down for Thursdays, though there was always a cross in the bottom right corner, indicating that the evening was spoken for. The diaries of Herbert Digges and Evelyn Herrick were, on the face of it, even less instructive; Thursday evenings were simply blank. But that in itself, Harrigan consoled himself, could be important. Herbert Digges' college existence was defined by the jollies he attended; a port-tasting here, a class reunion there. His diary looked as if he had dedicated his life to never having to pay for a meal. Evelyn Herrick's by contrast was fuelled by work. In the evenings she conducted tutorials, discussion groups and study sessions into the night. She might not have been well-liked, but she had been much in demand. Both professors had busy diaries, albeit for different reasons, and yet neither of them ever had anything scheduled for a Thursday evening.

Harrigan went all the way back through the year to January and could not find a single Thursday with anything happening after six in any of the three diaries. He could not confirm that they had all been at the same club, or that they were at a club at all, but after weeks of failure this still felt like a lightning flash of inspiration, the sort of thing that could blow a case wide open.

But what next?

Heading down to the evidence room, Harrigan scoured the inventory of materials collected from the three crime scenes. Inevitably there was a lot of paper, a lot of notes, a lot of books, a lot of records. Harrigan started reading. Pretty soon he switched to skimming, scanning the pages for stand-out words like 'club', 'society', 'Thursday' or 'death cult'. He thought about enlisting others to help but held off, partly because he didn't really know what he was looking for, but also because he was nervous. This was an almighty longshot, bordering on fantasy. Ending your career on failure was one thing, ending it on embarrassment was much worse.

At the end of the day he signed out an armful of paperwork to take home with him and pored through it long into the night until his eyes started to cross and the words ran together.

Come the morning, he was ready to try something new. If a club was so secretive that it was not even marked in a diary, then hoping to find some record of it amongst the victims' papers was wildly optimistic. He had to take what he knew and work his way back.

Trying to identify a Cambridge club that met on a Thursday and might have some connection to science was more difficult than it sounded. All universities have many clubs and societies catering to every interest, but Cambridge University collected them. New students liked to start their own clubs, even if a similar one already existed, and since student lifespans are short (three to four years the norm), there is a rapid turnover. Anywhere else, this would mean that the births and deaths of clubs and societies achieved virtual equilibrium, with the most popular or high profile (like the famous Footlights) hanging around indefinitely. But Cambridge University was defined by its traditions and did not get rid of something just because it had become outmoded, outdated and useless – if they started thinking like that they would have to fire half the faculty. Besides, many students never left, they simply stopped learning. Cambridge University was an institution in which people could make a permanent home, never moving beyond the habits and hang-outs of those halcyon student years. Societies continued to exist with an ever-aging membership, and then existed merely on paper after all their members were dead (or had left the city, which amounted to the same thing).

The University was founded in the 13th century, and while it is unlikely that those earliest students immediately founded a basketball club and a D&D society, there remained a long history that the institution clung to like grim death.

The upshot of which history and tradition was that there were hundreds of University societies still active in some form, and there being only seven days in the week, the chances were that a fair few met on a Thursday.

But it was all Harrigan had.

"I'm going out for a bit," he announced as he strode through the office that morning. No one responded. He wondered if anyone would even notice he was gone, or if they might just assume that Hangdog Harrigan had started his retirement early.

Just around the corner from Market Square, tucked behind a church was St. Edwards passage, home to some of the more interesting second-hand, rare and antiquated bookshops in Cambridge, huddled together as if there were safety in numbers from the encroachment of Kindles and other horsemen of the digital apocalypse. It was to one of these shops that Harrigan now made his way.

"Good morning, Inspector."

Harrigan had worked on a theft at the store some years ago and remained friendly with the owners, who put aside books for him that they thought he might like. Harrigan graciously accepted the gifts, even though he wasn't much of a reader, something he had never had the heart to tell George and Doris.

"Morning George," Harrigan nodded.

"I've got something for you." George Wells always said the words with the same smile. He lived in a world where there was no greater gift that could be bestowed than a book you hadn't read, chosen by a friend. It was a nice world and someone like Amelia Evans would have been very happy there, but Harrigan was just passing through on a tourist visa. He often wished there was something in his life for which he had the same enthusiasm that George had for books.

"I'm actually looking for something specific."

George beamed like an evangelist whose hard work had finally got him a convert. "Really? Well we'll help if we can. What was it

156

you were looking for?"

"Something about Cambridge University clubs and societies?"

George held up a finger. "I have the very thing. Published in the late eighties, if memory serves, but still pretty definitive."

"Sounds ideal." Something told Harrigan that if this club existed, it had been around a while. Secret societies cannot spring up overnight – how would they get members?

"This way." George had an encyclopaedic knowledge of his stock, a walking catalogue of where everything was, when it had been published and who wrote it. "Higgins. Peter. Though I suspect others worked on it too. To my knowledge the only really extensive survey. The University itself has published a few but they're so cagey about the details (not all these societies have the best histories). Ah, here we are."

He drew a book from the shelf. George treated all books, whether a first edition of *David Copperfield* or a second-hand *Where's Wally* with a kind of gentle reverence. His hands always seemed to Harrigan to have the texture of those cotton gloves you wear when handling rare books, as if evolution had produced the perfect bibliophile.

Harrigan took the book, hoping that he held it with sufficient humility; *A Complete Digest of the Social Groups of Cambridge University and Their History – From Antiquity to the Present Day, compiled by Peter Higgins*. "Thanks George, what do I owe you?"

But George waved the question away. "Always a pleasure to unite someone with the book they desire. And we still owe you, Inspector."

Harrigan knew from past experience that there was no sense in arguing with the good-natured man, so thanked him and left. Back in the privacy of his office he began to read. There was a lot to get through but most of the entries eliminated themselves from his enquiries swiftly. He was as sure as he could be that he was not looking for a sporting club, nor an artistic one. He had it in his head that the answer would leap off the page when he saw it.

George had been as good as his word; the book was exactly what Harrigan had been looking for. It was not merely a list of clubs, but included details like club dues; when, where and how often they met; and periods of activity. Most were listed as '*Active but resting*', meaning that the society was defunct but had never been officially dissolved and still had members who perhaps met once year for a glass of wine to chat about the old days.

The diversity was extraordinary. Harrigan had a vague memory of being told in school that animals had evolved to fill every niche, and it seemed that Cambridge University societies operated in the same way. If the Pottery Society seemed too general then you could join the Cup-making and Decorating Club, if it seemed too liberal you could join the Conservative Pottery Society, and so on. There were societies devoted to reading and books in general, to genres or periods of literature, to groups of writers, specific writers and even individual books. (What the hell did The Lord of the Rings Society talk about at their second meeting?) There was Field Hockey, Men's Field Hockey, Women's Field Hockey, Mixed Field Hockey, Gay Men's Field Hockey, The LGBTQ Hockey Society and Indoor Field Hockey which just seemed a misnomer. Science too was well catered for with the Darwin Society, the Anti-Darwin Society (which had presumably been around a while), the Newton Society, the Faraday Society, the Watson and Crick Society (which had 'recently' changed its name to the Watson, Crick and Franklin Society). There were clubs for biochemists, physical chemists, physio-biologists and biophysicists, all of which, Harrigan thought, surely inhabited one big Venn diagram with enough crossover to make all but one unnecessary.

Most fascinating were the ones whose names did not explain them. The Functionary Society, The First of the Month Club, and GROIN (an acronym that even Peter Higgins' exhaustive research had failed to explain) must have had some meaning to those who joined, now lost to the mists of time and disinterest. Another subset was those clubs named after people whose names had, at one time, held such significance that further explanation was considered unnecessary. Perhaps the hallowed names of Bertram Beebe and Ford Millhauser still meant something to those in the know, but to the general populous (or at least that part of it that included Inspector Clive Harrigan) they were meaningless. Harrigan imagined that the only criterion for entry into these societies was knowing who these people were: '*Have you heard of Ford Millhauser? You have? You're in*'. And so the cycle continued, refining the membership of societies to people with extreme knowledge on a single subject but who were unable to tie their own shoelaces without strangling themselves. It is the role of Cambridge University to create such individuals, and then to keep them away from society.

It was into the obscure name category that the R. C. Forrester Endowment Society fitted, and though he could not have picked R. C. Forrester out of a crowd, let alone said what the man had done, it was here that Harrigan paused and read deeper. Founded by pioneering ethologist Donald Drury, the society existed to apportion the titular endowment in generous chunks to scientific projects that struggled to receive funding from mainstream sources.

'*This* raison d'etre,' explained Mr Higgins, '*brought the club more attention than it might have wanted, and into disrepute, when it emerged that funding had been awarded for research into such suspect areas as eugenics, weaponizing space and mind control. Finally, in the early seventies, the society was officially disbanded.*'

Harrigan paused. Hadn't Professor Digges been involved in mind control experiments in the sixties? A flick through his interview notes confirmed it.

The book listed the club as '*Defunct*', but Harrigan found himself whispering the words, "What happened to the money?" before reading on to Higgins' final line, '*The fate of the endowment itself – sustained through the years by alums paying back into it the fruits of their successful research – remains a mystery.*'

All of which was very interesting, but none of it so interesting as the few words in the '*Extraneous Notes*' section: '*Meetings: Weekly. Every Thursday without fail.*'.

Harrigan went online to look up what an ethologist was – something to do with animal behaviour. He did this largely to give himself something to do while his hands shook and his brain fizzed. He still had nothing. He needed to keep reminding himself of that. He had no proof that the three victims belonged to the same club. If they did then he had no proof it was this club. If it was then it still didn't give him a motive, a suspect or any clue as to how the murders were committed. He had nothing.

And yet some instinct told him that he had something. They said that every policeman had them; cop instincts, that feeling in your gut that you were right. It was typical that his would wait right until the end of his career to manifest themselves, but better late than never.

What now?

On the off-chance, he looked up a list of current, university-sanctioned societies online, but the R. C. Forrester Endowment Society was nowhere to be found. A few calls to people in high places – who were willing to be grudgingly helpful because three of their employees were dead – yielded the same response. The Society had been closed after gross misuse of funds and that was an end of it.

What now?

Harrigan leaned back in his chair. He couldn't tell anybody. Certainly not Chief Inspector Lane. Not yet. He couldn't prove any of it, and when you started talking about secret societies then people began giving you funny looks and copies of *The Da Vinci Code* turned up on your desk accompanied by a sarcastic post-it note suggesting that this might be a lead.

Three people didn't seem like a very big society. There had to be more. Were they in danger too? Or were they the killers? He needed names. But a secret society – he hated calling it that, but that was what it was – didn't have an easily available membership list. What about the money? If that was unaccounted for then was it still being awarded to 'deserving projects'? Might bank account details reveal something? If so, whose? He couldn't look up the bank account of a project that didn't exist. Someone in the Cyber division had been through the bank details of all three victims along with their emails and browser histories and had found nothing suspicious – or at least no more suspicious than those searches always turned up (which was horrifying enough as a rule). He would ask them to look again tomorrow but Harrigan had hunch that these people were cleverer than that. They had better be cleverer than that, really. These were supposed to be some of the smartest people in the country, if not the world. If they had not covered their tracks then what did it say about the standard of intellect in Cambridge University? If these brilliant minds could be outwitted by the likes of Harrigan then what hope was there?

No. He'd get no joy that way. What might be their Achilles heel?

Tradition? Harrigan's brows knitted in thought. However super-smart they were, people at Cambridge University would do almost anything if it was traditional. You could get them to hop backwards with a duck on their head singing sea shanties if someone had done it a hundred years ago. And nowhere was that more true than the societies.

A knock at the door roused Harrigan. "Come in."

Stubbs poked his head in. "If you don't need anything else then I'll head home, sir."

"What time is it?"

"Six thirty, sir."

Where had the damn day gone?

"See you tomorrow, Sergeant."

Stubbs nodded. "The CI was asking after you earlier, sir."

Harrigan rubbed his tired eyes. "What did you tell him?"

"That you were hard at it."

"Thanks, Sergeant."

It boded ill that Lane hadn't just called Harrigan or emailed him or... Harrigan frowned. Well that was a point, wasn't it?

As he walked home, Harrigan played the thought over in his mind. They had been through the correspondence, physical and digital, of all three victims thoroughly, and had re-checked it, on Harrigan's instructions, with each new victim, looking for the elusive connection. And yet there had not been a single email between them. Not one text, one phone call, one letter, no hint of a note shoved under a door. Everyone who knew them insisted they had never been in the same room together. So how did they stay in touch?

Of course, people who meet up every Thursday (without fail) may not need to stay in touch that closely but there must have been occasions when it was necessary? What if one was sick and couldn't make a meeting? What if there was an emergency? In fact, they had probably been in touch pretty recently when their members started dying left and right.

There were the secret agent tricks of leaving messages behind bricks or chalk mark codes, but that seemed out of character. Someone would probably have noticed a system of flags hung from their windows. There were some online messaging services that permanently deleted messages after they had been read, making it impossible to trace the sender, but Harrigan found it hard to picture any of the victims, especially Herbert Digges, using something like that. Besides, this was something that had to have worked for decades – longer even.

Harrigan continued to brood on his way home, to no effect. He brooded through dinner and through whatever trash was on TV. The problem was; it wasn't a problem. Although Cambridge was a large town, the majority of the university buildings occupied a small area in the centre, no bigger than a village (albeit a village with very large houses). If these scientists wanted to communicate all they had to do was open a window and shout – though, again, that would probably attract attention. The point was, it was not difficult. And yet, somewhere inside, Harrigan knew that they would have made it difficult. This was Cambridge.

He needed something to take his mind off this damn case and his eyes lit on the photograph that sat on his shelf.

He grabbed the phone hastily and dialled before he could talk himself out of it. Just the sound of it ringing made him nervous, his heart fluttering in his chest.

"Hello?"

The sound of his elder son's voice made Harrigan's words catch in his throat and he felt suddenly as if he might burst into tears. He struggled to speak, the results coming out slightly strangled.

"Hi Will, it's… It's Dad."

There was a pause from the other end of the line that seemed like a few ice ages to the waiting Harrigan.

"Hi. Is everything okay?" That was a fair question; he didn't call often and probably sounded a bit weird.

"Yeah, yeah. Just… Been a while. I thought I'd check in. See how you are."

"Oh." It was hard to say if William was happy, awkward, irritated or just surprised. "Well I haven't got long. I've got to put the kids to bed."

"Sure, sure." Harrigan leapt on the opportunity to find out something about his grandchildren. "How are they?"

"They're good, Dad."

"Make the most of it," Harrigan advised. "They grow up quick."

"Yeah." Maybe it was his guilt talking but Harrigan felt there was reproach in that.

"What are you getting them for Christmas?" Some wildly optimistic part of Harrigan hoped that if he dropped the holiday into the conversation maybe he might get an invite.

"Can't really say with them listening."

162

"They're there now?" The knowledge that his grandchildren were right there by the phone made Harrigan's heart skip a beat.

"Yeah. John's drawing and May's trying to teach her hamster to roll over."

Knowing what they were doing increased the artificial closeness. "I'm not sure you can teach a hamster tricks."

"That's not going to stop her from trying. Are you alright, Dad? Your voice sounds…"

"Yeah, I'm fine." Without realising it he had started to cry.

"Look Dad, unless there's anything specific, I have to get the kids to bed."

At the outside of his hearing, Harrigan caught the whines of children who were definitely not ready for bed yet, and swallowed back fresh tears.

"Of course. Go. Don't know why I called anyway."

"Don't worry about it. You're sure there's nothing wrong?"

"No, no. Having a funny day I guess. Maybe talk properly another time."

A pause. "Sure."

"Have a good Christmas, Will."

"You too, Dad."

Harrigan wiped his eyes as he hung up the phone. He'd wanted to ask about Christmas, but if they didn't offer then… No. He'd lost the right to ask. How many Christmases had he worked when Will and Don were little? Too bloody many. You couldn't replace that. You couldn't turn back the clock.

But at least he had made the call. He had reached out and it hadn't been a train wreck. He should call Don too. But not tonight. That was enough raw emotion for one evening. It was enough to know that his sons were happy and healthy, and that somewhere out there a little girl, who maybe looked a bit like him (God help her), was trying to teach tricks to a hamster.

The flash of inspiration was dulled by regret that it should come from that lovely, and all too rare, moment of connection to his family. Everything led him back to work. But guilty though it made him feel, Harrigan couldn't ignore it. He remembered the crunch under his feet in the office of Evelyn Herrick and put it together with the founder of the R. C. Forrester Endowment Society. What you ended up with was far-fetched, but it was also just the sort of stupid, bloody-minded tradition that Cambridge University cherished.

He would have to thank his granddaughter for that. If he ever met her. At least now he knew her name.

'*Tell John and May I love them.*'

Or better yet, '*Tell John and May that nothing is more important than family.*'.

Not the punchiest last words, but not the worst either.

Chapter 17 – Una Jaffers

Strictly speaking, 'ethology' is the study of animals in their natural habitats behaving as they do naturally, but some of the most renowned ethologists have stretched that rule, notably Konrad Lorenz and his experiments with imprinting in ducks. An interest in animal behaviour is bound to make the researcher at least curious about how that behaviour might be modified.

Unusually, Harrigan rode his bike that morning. Cambridge was a city of cyclists, but Harrigan had come to think of it as a custom more honoured in the breach than in the observance, at least when you were a sixty five year old man straining at the pedals at the speed of an asthmatic tortoise, while everyone else cursed your name and you wondered if that rushing in your ears was a car coming up behind you or an impending coronary. He didn't want his last words to be, '*I should have taken the bus.*'.

Today, however, he would need that blend of speed, manoeuvrability and smug contempt for every other road user, that only the bicycle offered.

Stopping at a pet shop on his way, Harrigan cycled to the Department of Chemistry, this time entering through the back entrance on Union Road, which was quieter and more suitable to his purpose. He had not told anyone else about this experiment, not even Sergeant Stubbs, because he was a bit embarrassed about the whole thing. If he was wrong then he would look like a fool. If he was right then he would probably still look like a fool, but at least he would be right.

The office of Professor Herrick had now been cleared, though it was still cordoned off. Harrigan let himself in, opened the window and looked out over the carpark. A number of doves and pigeons (he couldn't have said which was which) watched him with head-bobbing interest from their perch on a wire.

"Got your attention have I?" Harrigan addressed the birds, idly wondering which of them had crapped on him during his last visit. Perhaps it had been a message. From his pocket, he drew out the paper bag that he had purchased in the pet shop. He took out a handful of bird seed and spread it along the window sill. "I don't know if this is what you're used to but I hope you like it."

Like a scene from an Alfred Hitchcock movie, the pigeons and doves descended on the food, cooing incessantly. Harrigan backed away as the birds jostled, pecked and flapped, shoulder barging each other out of the way, spending more time fighting than feeding.

"Alright stop that, stop that." Harrigan tried to get the birds' attention. "Look I don't know how the system works so one of you is going to have to help me. Raise a wing if you're the bird I'm looking for."

He hadn't really expected that to work.

"None of you look remotely trained." Harrigan took an irritable step forward sending the assembled birds into a frenzy of avian panic. Another step and they took off *en masse* in a cacophony of flapping, dropping off the sill and recovering themselves mid-air to flap awkwardly back to the wire. Not a single bird remained.

That was disappointing. Harrigan waved a fist at the pigeons. "You're all bloody useless."

He turned back to the room and started. Seated on the back of the late Professor's office chair was a single grey pigeon (or possibly dove), calm, apparently quite at home, and watching Harrigan with a beady eye as if to say, '*You're new here, aren't you?*'.

Most surprisingly, it did this while sitting next to the open bag of bird food which Harrigan had left on the desk. It gave the bag a surreptitious look, confirming that it had noticed the food and was just exercising self-control, then turned back to Harrigan. If pigeons (or doves) had eyebrows, then it would have raised one in question.

Very slowly, Harrigan reached into the bag and took out some seed. Holding it in his palm he offered it to the bird, which hopped onto his thumb, making the Inspector jump, and began to peck politely at the food.

This seemed to confirm at least part of Harrigan's theory, that the 'health food' they had found in Professor Herrick's office had been nothing of the kind. (He had always privately considered there to be very little difference between health food and bird food.) The more far-fetched part of his plan was still to prove.

As the bird fed contentedly, oblivious to what Harrigan was up to, the Inspector checked its leg and was pleased to find a red metal ring around it.

"Right," Harrigan found that talking to the bird made him feel more comfortable, although everything he had learned about Evelyn Herrick suggested that she would never have done something so

166

asinine. "If you don't mind holding still, I'm just going to slip something into your ring. So to speak." Rooting about in his pocket with his free hand he located the small cylinder of paper he had furled that morning. "Don't panic."

With delicate fingers he pushed the narrow cylinder into the ring about the bird's leg. There was probably a better way of securing it but that didn't matter for the purposes of this test.

"Right," he continued to speak directly to the docile pigeon, "I know you're probably used to exiting via the window – cos God knows a Professor of Chemistry carrying a pigeon through the building would excite comment – but today you'll have a slightly different start point. I hope this does not throw you off."

Most departmental activities had now closed down for Christmas but Harrigan still got a few intrigued looks as he wove a path through the building back to Union Road with the pigeon perched placidly on his thumb. It had finished eating but seemed to understand that it was still required so waited patiently for further instructions. Outside, Harrigan went to his bike and managed to mount up without disturbing his passenger – he would need a quick start if he was to have any chance at all. He looked around; most of the buildings weren't more than a couple of storeys but it would still be difficult to keep his target in sight.

"Right." Harrigan gently drew back the hand with the pigeon on it, then flung it into the air. "Fly!"

It seemed unlikely that the pigeon needed any such instruction, but it did as it was told. As Harrigan got his feet onto the pedals the bird executed a circle above Union Road to get its bearings, then flew off in the direction of the carpark.

Harrigan bent to his pedals, quickly achieving full speed going the wrong way down the one-way street, his eyes flicking between the road ahead and the pigeon above. The damn thing was travelling as the crow flies (which is also as the pigeon flies) while he was forced to stick to the roads. At the end of Union Road he bore right onto Panton Street – thankfully quiet. But the pigeon had now left Chemistry Department airspace and was headed in the vague direction of the river. Rather than risking Lensfield Road and the morning traffic, Harrigan ripped off a tight left onto the narrow Saxon Street, which he immediately regretted as his bike began to bounce over the cobbles. His skeleton rattled in his body, the breaths were juddered from his chest, and he was forced to stand up on the pedals as the saddle tried to pummel him into soprano. He glanced skywards, scanning for the bird but seeing nothing.

"Come on!" His body was unaccustomed to this sort of sudden physical trial but he willed it into greater effort, sweat pouring from his brow, fires igniting in his calves and thighs, and the need to hurl rising in his stomach.

He careened out of Saxon Street onto the smooth relief of Brookside, and issued a discordant wheeze of gratitude as he sighted the pigeon passing over the yew trees on the corner of Trumpington Street round-about. Feet flying in the pedals, Harrigan tore across Lensfield Road, accompanied by the Cambridge Motorists' Philharmonic playing the '*Get Off the Road You Idiot*' symphony, scored for car horns and casual swearing. He glanced up again. The bird was getting away, passing over the Department of Architecture on the far side of the street. It was now or never. With his heart in his mouth, Harrigan kept going. A screech of brakes told him how close he had come as he wove between moving cars on Trumpington Street. His front wheel hit the culvert by the kerb, nearly throwing him off as he lurched onto the pavement, scattering angry pedestrians.

"Police!" He yelled back, for what it was worth. But he kept pedalling. Something on the bike had clearly been bent, broken or twisted by the cobbles, the kerb or his inexpert cycling, but he managed to drag the unwilling handlebars left into the driveway of the Architecture Department. He kept going furiously. Had he lost the bird? Had he…

Harrigan gripped the brakes to no effect, braced for impact and crashed into a fence.

The pigeon completed its circle and descended on the Department of Engineering, which sat just behind the Architecture building, backing onto Sheep's Green and the river.

Harrigan collapsed off the bike, breathing ragged, chest heaving. He hadn't ridden more than a five minute walk but had done so at speeds at which man was not meant to travel and at risk to life and limb. He clutched the fence for support as the world carouseled around him, and tried to find the damn pigeon. Looking up at the windows, he could see a whole bunch of them dancing before his eyes. He shook his head, trying to dispel the vision –

168

which was a mistake as his brain spun inside his skull. As his eyesight returned to normal, the pigeons stopped dancing, but there remained more than a few of them.

"Bloody things."

Like most tourist-heavy towns, Cambridge had an unhealthily large pigeon population, bullying scraps out of foreigners who didn't know any better. Desperately, Harrigan scanned the verminous rows of feathered pests for the one he had been following, but found they all looked alike and all seemed to favour sitting on window sills.

What now?

The decision was taken out of his hands as a sharp scream erupted from the building in front of him. Pressing his jelly legs back into unwilling service, Harrigan ran through the main entrance and turned right up to haul himself up a flight of stairs. At the top he stopped, gasping like a steam train on an incline as the world spun again. At this rate he wouldn't have enough breath to deliver any memorable last words.

A second scream echoed down the empty corridor. To Harrigan, this one sounded impatient, as if he was supposed to have run in dramatically already. He hurried off again, wending from one side of the corridor to the other while his heart played *Wipeout* in his ears.

Up ahead of him, a woman backed out of one of the rooms, hand over her mouth, eyes wide in shock. Harrigan raced up to her.

"…" he wheezed, unable to get out any comforting or otherwise helpful words.

But the woman made questions unnecessary. Turning to Harrigan, her face ashen, she gasped, "She's dead."

Having despatched the woman to call for the police, Harrigan entered the office, noting the name on the door of '*Professor Una Jaffers*'. The room was still and silent, all except for an insistent tapping. At the window, which overlooked the central courtyard, Harrigan recognised a familiar pigeon, shoulder to shoulder with its feathered brethren, tapping its beak against the glass.

But while all was peaceful in the office, there hung in the air that scent of death that everyone who has worked around homicide comes to know. Not the fruitier odours of the 'five days in the boiler room bloater', but a stale smell that Harrigan had never accurately been able to place. It smelled like the absence of something. Perhaps

169

the absence of life itself.

Professor Una Jaffers lay in a crumpled heap on the floor of her office, her face pointed to the ceiling displaying the started eyes and lolling tongue that had characterised all the victims, and spoke of strangulation. As with Evelyn Herrick, there were signs of a struggle, and the shard of broken glass thrust into her chest seemed to be a weapon of opportunity.

For a moment Harrigan stood back, trying to take in the room, looking for those pesky things that mystery writers call 'clues', which seldom happened in real life (at least not to him) and when they did were more confusing than helpful.

As it stood, this looked like the simplest murder yet, though he was willing to bet that the security cameras would show nothing. But the important thing was that he had been here to share in the moment of discovery, not by chance, but because he had accurately predicted where it would take place. By use of a pigeon. Who would have thought?

The tapping was starting to irritate Harrigan and he crossed the room to shoo the bird away. As he did so, his foot caught in something and he tumbled to the floor, swearing as he went.

Rolling into a sitting position, he reached to free his foot from whatever it was tangled in, and...

Harrigan's heart had still been pounding like the hooves of a racehorse from his recent exertions, but as he laid eyes on what had tripped him, it seemed to freeze in his chest.

Chapter 18 – The Coat

Chief Inspector Lane kept an officious and disapproving eye on Harrigan as the Inspector faced the massed ranks of the press. Because Harrigan had discovered the body (or near as damn it) there had been no keeping him away from reporters, and Lane thought that even Harrigan could not screw it up that badly. His opinion of Clive Harrigan was that the man was a boob – one of a distressing number under his command – and while Lane did not make a habit of exposing his boobs to the press, it was relatively harmless because Harrigan was not, after all, a total incompetent. Lane knew this because, alongside the boobs, he also employed a number of total incompetents, and much of his working life was spent keeping them busy enough that no one found out they existed.

But today, Harrigan seemed to be operating at a level below his usual boobishness. When officers had arrived at the scene, Harrigan had been seated in the office, wide-eyed and slack-jawed, staring at the ground as if this was his first corpse. Lane had given him the benefit of the doubt, and decided that his shock showed a human side to the police that the public liked to see. But now Harrigan was in front of the cameras he no longer seemed shocked, he seemed dopey.

"What will be your next step?"

Harrigan blinked in the bright lights. "I... A link... Between the victims... Find?"

"Are you in charge of this investigation?"

This had gone on long enough. Before the question was even finished, Lane swept in, wrapping an arm around Harrigan and ushering him off while promising "...a more detailed briefing when we know more.".

Once they were safely out of range of reporters he rounded on his subordinate.

"What in the hell is wrong with you today?"

Harrigan shook his head as if the world had suddenly become a baffling and incomprehensible place. "Nothing. I mean... *absolutely nothing.*"

"Well there's something," snapped Lane.

"There's not." Harrigan looked horrified.

Lane made his decision on the instant. "I'm taking over the

171

case."

It wasn't just that the man was a boob who had made a fool of himself in front of the press. It was also the fact that there *was* press. When this affair had started it had seemed like the sort of impossible to solve crime that suited a man like Harrigan. As long as you had a crime that wasn't going to get solved, then you might as well hand it off to someone who wasn't going to solve the ones that could. Why waste a good detective on the impossible?

But then the case had ballooned into the national interest and become more nationally interesting with each fresh corpse. The police had to look like solving it was at least an option. The nation was watching. And if they were going to be watching, then Growley Lane would prefer they were watching him. He was not a media whore *per se*, but he was a man with ambitions that stretched beyond a University town that was only called a city out of courtesy. Even if he could not solve this case, him pitting his brains against it would make for good copy. Everyone would remember the case, and everyone would forget that it had gone unsolved.

Certainly it was too important for a has-been with days left on the force and who was, to be fair to him, a boob.

"What?" Harrigan stirred from the distracted state in which he had spent the last few hours.

"You're off the case," Lane put it bluntly.

"But…" Harrigan looked distraught. "I've been making progress. I found the body. I found the body before we knew there was a body to look for."

Lane pulled a supercilious expression. He had very specifically told Harrigan not to talk to the press about the 'theory' that had led him here. Lane wanted the force to look modern and efficient, and playing Catch the Pigeon in search of the Illuminati did not reinforce that image.

"Harrigan, everyone gets a stroke of luck once in their career. Today was yours. I can't say that you made the best use of it in front of the press, but I'm afraid that's just who you are."

"Luck?" Harrigan's face contorted. "I worked it out, I…"

"Followed a pigeon," emphasised Lane. "Say that over to yourself a few times and tell me you really believe it. You followed a pigeon. We have sniffer dogs; yes. And there are those bugs they use in forensics. But no one follows a pigeon to the body. Look at this place." He swept an arm about the campus. "It's alive with pigeons. You happened to arrive when the secretary screamed, so you got a head-start on the scene. That's all it amounts to. She'd have called us anyway."

"But the pigeon was there," Harrigan insisted.

"There's pigeons everywhere," Lane retorted. "Dead or alive, every professor in this town has probably got a pigeon on their window sill and they all look alike. Besides, does your pigeon explain how the killer walked out through a locked door in the Cranley murder?"

"Well, no…"

"Does it explain how he walked passed cameras in the Digges case?"

"I suppose…"

"No," Lane answered his own question. "You know what does? Science. You've conspicuously neglected the possibility of the cameras being tampered with. I'm sorry to be brutal, Clive, but when a crime involves technology that you don't understand, then you ignore it."

"And *you* ignore the evidence of pigeons!"

It was supposed to be a devastating comeback, but Lane just patted the older man on the shoulder comfortingly. "Yes I do. Now why don't you go home and get some rest. The pigeons won't bother you anymore."

Harrigan left his bicycle where it was. He could pick it up later and right now he didn't trust himself to ride. Perhaps if he had been feeling better, less spacey, then he would have been able to mount more of a defence. His theory had been insane but he had tested it and been proved correct. This was unjust.

But his mind was elsewhere.

He was very aware of the weight in his bag. He had taken evidence from a crime scene instead of handing it in. But what if it was evidence that he was crazy? They thought he was crazy already, he didn't want to remove all doubt.

He plodded home, the weight seeming to grow more with each step he took. He wanted to think about something else, anything else, but his mind only took him back to the contents of the bag, to what it might mean for him. In all his morbid fantasies about last words, he had never considered the possibility of a stream of nonsensical drivel from a man who had lost his marbles.

Back home, Harrigan went to his table and cleared a space in the mess of notes to self, half-empty coffee mugs and bills he hadn't bothered to file. He opened his bag and tipped the contents out onto the table.

Damn it.

He had hoped that in the time it took him to walk home something would have changed. He would still have stolen evidence, which was no small thing, but at least he would have been secure in his mind. As it was…

He picked the item up. It was a coat – he was pretty sure about that. There were the sleeves and the collar, and here a pocket. He could feel them.

But he couldn't see it.

He couldn't see anything. He could feel it in his hands but there was NOTHING in his hands. Either his eyes were lying to him or his hands. One of his senses was on the fritz and in a really specific way that made him either unable to see something that was there or able to feel something that wasn't. Either way, when your brain did that it wasn't good. It was a form of hallucination.

He pinched the cloth of the coat as hard as he could, till his skin turned white. But no matter how hard he pinched there remained a gap between finger and thumb which would not close. It was impossible.

He let the coat drop to the table and heard the sound. It sounded like a coat dropping to a table.

So if he could feel it and hear it then that suggested it was his eyes that were at fault. But why would they choose not to see the coat and work perfectly with everything else?

Maybe they *weren't* working perfectly with everything else?

How would he know?

Maybe this was all a fever dream.

His stomach rumbled. The practicalities of life did not go away just because you were beginning a precipitous descent into derangement. He made himself a bacon sandwich. It wasn't good for him but that barely seemed to matter now. He had better enjoy things like bacon while his mind still allowed him to do so. He also had an ice cream, because Harrigan was one of those who can enjoy an ice cream in the depths of winter as easily as in summer. He had a beer too. Why the hell not?

He sat at his table, eating his unhealthy lunch, his eyes trained on the empty space where the coat lay. Every minute or so he poked at it and was depressed to find that it was still there.

It would have to be the doctor next. And he would refer Harrigan to a psychiatrist (or psychologist; Harrigan had never been clear which was which). And then? Harrigan didn't know a lot about dementia, but he was aware that there wasn't much you could do about it.

He was glumly draining the last of his beer when the doorbell rang. He thought about not answering it – he certainly didn't want to speak to anyone – but Harrigan had been raised to good manners and they had not abandoned him yet.

Outside stood two women, one short, the other shorter; one with long dark hair, the other a tangle of red hair tied up on top of her head. He wondered briefly if they were real.

"Are you Inspector Harrigan?" asked the redhead.

"I think so."

The red head frowned. "You look like the Inspector Harrigan who was on the news, so I'm going to take that as a yes. You found the body of Professor Una Jaffers this morning, didn't you?"

"I'm not allowed to talk to reporters."

Harrigan went to close the door but the redhead stuck a booted foot in it. "We're not reporters, we are…"

"Investigators?" suggested the other woman.

"That'll do. We are investigators looking into these crimes, and based on what we saw on the news, you've actually made some headway. Unlike the tall one with the face you want to slap."

"Chief Inspector Lane?" suggested Harrigan, recognising the description.

"Yeah," replied the redhead. "He was a moron."

Though he did not know who these people were, and although they seemed very much like reporters fishing for an exclusive, Harrigan could not help warming to their fair and honest appraisal of his boss. "What do you mean, I've made some headway?"

"You were there before the body was found," the redhead replied. "You knew where the next killing was going to be. Which

175

means you've figured out the connection between the victims. Something we've had no luck doing."

It was nice to be appreciated but Harrigan remained cautious. "What's your interest in this?"

"You wouldn't believe us if we told you."

"Try me." Harrigan was currently ready to believe anything.

The two women looked at each other before the dark-haired one spoke. "We're looking for an invisible man."

Harrigan tried not to let his reaction show in his face. Was it possible he wasn't crazy? Or were these people further symptoms? Right now he preferred the former option. "Come in. I'd like to show you something."

A minute later they were standing in the dining area of Harrigan's bachelor flat, staring at the table.

"There's nothing there," said the dark-haired girl, who had introduced herself as Amelia.

The redhead (Elsa), reached for the space on the table and smiled as her hand closed. "Oh yes there damn well is."

"You can feel it?" Desperation made Harrigan's voice tremble.

"Oh yes." Elsa pushed the invisible coat towards her colleague, who prodded at it, goggling in wonder as she nodded.

"It's there alright."

Harrigan tried to moderate his sigh of relief but Elsa still noticed.

"Thought you were losing your marbles, huh? Been there. This one time in Greece I was chasing a half-man, half… You know what? Not the time. Now…" She turned the coat in her hands, getting it the right way up. "You know, this is the sort of thing you'd think you could do by feel. I mean how many times a day do you pick up a coat? You use your eyes more than you know. Even when you're not looking directly at something they're still taking it all in, helping you out. Brilliant thing, vision. Hold this." She thrust the invisible jacket toward Amelia who took it by the shoulders and held it as Elsa made a series of wavy motions with her hands where the coat hung.

"What are you doing?" asked Harrigan.

"Frisking it," replied Elsa, amiably. "Aha."

With triumph she plunged her hand into a bit of empty air where a pocket might be and drew nothing out of it.

"You got something?" asked Amelia.

"A piece of paper," replied Elsa, somewhat irritably. "On which, I imagine, is the killer's current whereabouts and a signed confession, for all the good it does us."

"Add paper to the list of things that can be made invisible," said Amelia.

"So it would seem. Why carry it with you? It's not like the Invisible Man can read it either."

"Must have been in his pocket when he became invisible."

Elsa stared at where the paper ought to be between her finger and thumb. "Harrigan, you got any fingerprint powder?"

Harrigan shook his head. "They don't let us take it home anymore."

Elsa rolled her eyes. "How about a pencil? You got a pencil?"

"One of those propelling ones?"

"Perfect."

When Harrigan returned with the propelling pencil, Elsa carefully passed the paper to Amelia. She then took the pencil from Harrigan and extracted the lead.

"Do you have a pestle and mortar?"

"No." Harrigan shook his head. A man who lives on ready-meals has little use for a pestle and mortar.

"How about a bowl and a spoon?"

With her improvised pestle and mortar, Elsa ground the pencil lead into a powder.

"Right. Hold the paper at both ends."

Amelia held the invisible paper horizontally in front of her, stretched between her hands, and Elsa sprinkled the ground-up graphite onto it. Harrigan shook his head in disbelief as the powder hung in the air in a perfect plane.

"Give the paper a bit of a side to side shimmy," instructed Elsa. "Just enough to move the lead about, let it get into every crease. Get me a sheet of plain paper, Harrigan."

177

Harrigan followed her instructions. "I don't know if I'm crazy or not, but an invisible man would really explain how the murders were committed. Even Cranley. There we were, wondering how the killer got out; all he had to do was wait till we turned up. We let him out."

"Easy when you know how it's done," murmured Elsa. "Now…" She took the invisible paper from Amelia, held it out in front of her, and blew the excess graphite dust away. "Put the paper on the table, Harrigan."

Harrigan did so, then he and Amelia watched in rapt attention as Elsa laid the invisible sheet on top of the plain paper.

"Get in, you beauty," muttered Elsa.

"It's incredible," breathed Harrigan.

There were the words written on the invisible paper, delineated in graphite dust that had found the creases where the pen had scored it. Hanging in the air they had been unreadable, but against the stark, white paper they stood out as clearly as if they had just been written.

It was a list of names: Herbert Digges, Evelyn Herrick, Sampson Cranley, Una Jaffers, and…

"We need to find this guy. Vincent Radcliffe," said Harrigan, firmly. Suddenly he was feeling like a new man.

Chapter 19 – Vincent Radcliffe

It didn't take long to find the name 'Vincent Radcliffe' in the Cambridge University Directory; a professor of high energy physics currently residing just outside Cambridge in the village of Madingley, and Harrigan called him straight away. Amelia noticed how the man seemed to have come back to life from the dazed figure they had seen on the news and the downtrodden one who had answered his door. This Harrigan was alert and eager; he knew they were onto something. He reminded her of an old bloodhound scenting its prey.

Radcliffe's office said that the Professor was working from home today so Harrigan tried his home and mobile numbers.

"Not answering."

"Oh great," muttered Elsa. "Daft sod's probably already got himself killed."

"Why wouldn't he go to the police?" The question had been bothering Amelia for a while.

"I think that's over to you, Inspector," said Elsa. "You're the one who knows the connection between these people."

"I'll explain as we go." Harrigan led the way out of the flat with the confident strides of a man inches away from yelling, '*The game is afoot!*'.

In the car, driving out to Radcliffe's, Harrigan outlined the connection between the dead scientists; a tale of secret societies, forbidden experiments and pigeons that sounded straight out of cheap fiction. Elsa then shared what she and Amelia had found out about Stuart Price, the Invisible Man.

Harrigan shook his head. "If I hadn't seen the coat. Or not seen it. Or whatever. Even now I still don't think I really believe it."

"Which is why we came to you direct rather than going through official channels," explained Elsa.

Harrigan nodded. Chief Inspector Lane would never have believed such a thing. Even if Harrigan had beat him about the head with the invisible coat, Lane would probably have said it was just the wind or something. The man had a mind like an old deck chair; once it was closed, it was impossible to open again.

"So we don't think Price himself is a scientist?" Harrigan attempted to sum up.

"Doesn't seem to be," Elsa nodded. "And we can't find any ties between him and the university. (We did a bit of digging and he seems to have worked part-time in a coffee shop.)"

"But the scientists of the R. C. Forrester Endowment Society tried out their invisibility experiment on him," Harrigan went on, "and now he's out for revenge, killing them one by one."

"While forging a successful media career," muttered Amelia from the back seat.

"Not saying we have all the answers," Elsa admitted.

"Isn't it odd that he announced himself to the world as the Invisible Man and then committed murders only an invisible man could commit?" wondered Harrigan. "Wouldn't he be afraid the police would twig?"

"You didn't though, did you?" pointed out Elsa. "Not until he left his coat behind. And I doubt that was intentional. Probably came off in the struggle and he didn't have time to look for it. An invisible coat is a hard thing to find."

Amelia just listened as the two actual investigators talked. She was not sure if she had any role left to play here, but if she did then that role was her knowledge of Stuart Price, and something about this did not add up. *The Life of an Invisible Man* had no story as such, it was a series of events that described an arc of self-discovery for its protagonist, from the chaos of its opening to the almost zen-like calm of its final sentence; '*I have discovered who I am; I am the Invisible Man.*'. There was no anger or lust for vengeance; it was the story of a simple soul.

Maybe she had read the book once too often but Amelia struggled to put the writer's hands around her throat or anyone else's. It was contrary to all the facts, but she did not think Stuart Price was guilty. Or perhaps she just didn't want him to be.

The late afternoon dusk was gathering as the car pulled up outside the handsome abode of Vincent Radcliffe, and the three of them hurried out and up to the door. Harrigan rang the bell.

Nothing. He tried again, but Elsa was already on the move.

"Where are you going?"

"I'm going to find a window that can't be seen from the street."

"Why?"

The sound of breaking glass answered Harrigan's question.

"I've found a way in," Elsa called, and Amelia and Harrigan followed her around the corner of the house.

"I'm really not sure I should be doing this," muttered Harrigan. "I am a policeman."

"If you prefer, you can stand outside and pretend it's not happening," suggested Elsa. "But I'm going in. A man's life is at stake." She reached through the broken pane to unfasten the window. "Probably."

"If no one's home, then this is just breaking and entering," pointed out Harrigan. "There were days between the other killings – two weeks between Digges and Herrick. We've no reason to assume he's in a hurry."

"Except that you knew where to find the body," said Elsa, as she slid the window open. "It was all over the news. This morning you told Mr Price that you had made the connection. That put a clock on it. Professor Radcliffe is in danger now."

The house was silent as they climbed in. Even the bickering of her colleagues could not penetrate the thick, claggy quiet that pressed in around Amelia like cotton wool, making each breath seem to stick in her throat. She saw no movement in the shadows that surrounded them and yet each shadow seemed pregnant with the possibility of movement, as if someone or something was standing very still, waiting to leap out at her. But of course, an invisible man had no need of shadows.

As Elsa and Harrigan stopped in a doorway – Harrigan insisting that he was going no further without a warrant, and Elsa helping herself to an apple from a fruit bowl just to be contrary – Amelia ventured closer to the stairs. At the top of the first flight, a large window allowed a gloomy light down into the stairwell. From outside, a tree cast skeletal shadows of outstretched twigs across the

181

glass, moving in the wind. At moments like this Amelia always expected her sister to leap out from somewhere yelling 'Boo!', because, when they were kids, it had amused Zita no end to make Amelia pee herself. As it was, even the sound of a text alert from her phone made her jump.

It was Jack, asking why she had not answered his last message.

Amelia pocketed the phone again and peered up the stairs.

A loud thump came from the floor above, and with it the faint sounds of what might have been someone in distress. It might also have been a cat startled by its own reflection or a creaky door that had chosen an inopportune time to swing, but Amelia didn't wait to find out, she ran up the stairs in the direction of the sound, with Elsa and Harrigan following.

Why was she leading the way? This was not her job. But whether it was her job or not, Amelia realised she was smiling

Rounding the corner on the little landing and running up the next flight, she saw a door up ahead with a sliver of light shining from under it. Shadows moved sharply in that bar of light and sounds came from behind the door. Amelia didn't hesitate, throwing the door open.

The sumptuous living room beyond had only one occupant.

And yet he very clearly was not alone.

Professor Vincent Radcliffe was a tall, bearded man in his middle-fifties, sporting a natty silk dressing gown with monogrammed initials on the breast. He was currently sprawled back on his sofa, clutching at his throat, kicking his legs. The way he moved suggested that someone, perhaps as a prank, had superglued the back of his neck to the sofa. His head twisted and his torso convulsed but his neck remained where it was as if pinned there.

That neck…

Amelia could see white bands of pressure on the flesh of his neck, thin red lines of skin between them. Like fingers. At his Adam's apple, she could see the compression, could see the frantic movements of his throat as he fought for air and none came. His eyes started, goggling from his head then rolling back up into his skull till they were all whites, tinged pink with blood. His tongue protruded from his gaping mouth as his red face began to turn purple.

"Hey!" It was all that Amelia could think to do.

For a fraction of a second the pressure on Radcliffe's throat seemed to lessen and he gulped in a frantic, stolen breath. Then suddenly he was being strangled again, the unseen hands returning to their task, apparently finding Amelia no threat.

Amelia started forwards just as Elsa and Harrigan entered. Elsa didn't even slow down, charging the sofa as she had charged in to save Amelia on Tennis Court Road a few days ago. Harrigan faltered on the threshold, staring in disbelief, his legs rendered useless in astonishment. It is one thing knowing that there is an invisible murderer out there, but it's something else to see him in action.

Amelia rounded the sofa as Elsa vaulted over it, swinging blindly at where the Invisible Man ought to be. Radcliffe gasped suddenly and deeply – he could breathe again, the hands around his throat were gone. Amelia flung her arms out wide as she approached, trying to block the killer's exit, but the Invisible Man had gone the other way.

Harrigan cried out in shock, lurching backwards, pushed by unseen hands.

"Get out of the way!"

The inspector was thrust aside and a moment later there was a thundering of footsteps running down the stairs. In a heartbeat, Elsa was back over the sofa, through the door, past Harrigan and down the stairs in pursuit.

Harrigan still stood, staring out in front of him; embarrassed, guilty, frozen in shock. Vincent Radcliffe moaned as he lolled, limply on his sofa, dragging weak, raw breaths through his bruised throat. Amelia stared after Elsa and the departing invisible man.

Invisible Man.

But no. She had heard – they had all heard – the voice of the 'Invisible Man' pushing Harrigan out of the way. There was no question; it had been the voice of a woman.

Chapter 20 – The Invisible Woman

Elsa returned, scowling. "Don't know why I bothered. How do you catch someone who only has to stand still to hide?"

"Invisible," murmured Harrigan, still standing by the door. "I mean… actually invisible."

Elsa patted the inspector on the shoulder. "We were there."

"But," Harrigan kept shaking his head. "She was *invisible*. Don't you understand?"

Elsa clicked her tongue. "There's a whole bunch of things I don't understand, Harrigan, one of which you just touched on. Everyone heard that, yeah? That was no one called Stuart Price. Which means we've got things wrong."

"Some things." Amelia was simultaneously sure that Stuart Price was the Invisible Man and that he was not.

"And I think," Elsa turned to the man on the sofa who had remained quiet, "there is one person here who can explain all this. Over to you Vince."

Vincent Radcliffe looked up sharply, fearing that his saviours had become his captors.

"Might I have a glass of water?"

Elsa shrugged. "I daresay you know where it's kept."

"Actually invisible," Harrigan kept repeating as Vincent Radcliffe helped himself to a glass of water from a jug (that he would probably have called a 'carafe') on a side table.

"Now," Elsa patted the sofa, "take a seat, and tell us who attacked you."

Radcliffe gave a nervous smile and made a vague gesture with his hands. "How would I know? As your friend keeps pointing out; she was invisible. It's simply too fantastic."

Elsa's face remained unchanged but there crept into her tone a note of threat. "I probably should have made some introductions. Over there in the doorway, doubting the evidence of his own senses, is Inspector Harrigan of Cambridge City Police. He is the only one here working in, shall we say, an official capacity. The only one who might feel constrained by the rule of law. My name is Elsa. It's me you have to worry about. Something about this doesn't add up and I am not leaving until it does. You've had one brush with death tonight and unless you want another then I suggest you stop lying to me."

Boris, Amelia considered, would probably not have taken such a line. Presumably there was some code of conduct for Universal agents, but they also seemed to work each in his or her own way. Elsa was more direct.

"No." In the doorway, Harrigan had shaken his head clear, adjusted his view of reality and come back to his senses. "You're not going to hurt this man."

"Of course not," smiled Elsa, still eyeballing the terrified Radcliffe. "Because he's going to tell me everything he knows, starting with the name of the woman who tried to kill him tonight and who succeeded in killing all his mates."

"What mates?" A career as an actor did not beckon for Vincent Radcliffe.

Harrigan rolled his eyes. "Good grief, man, I'm trying to help you and you're making it very difficult. This whole good cop, bad cop thing only works if both players are in fact cops."

"But I really don't know what you're..."

"She's talking about the R. C. Forrester Endowment Society."

Once again Vincent Radcliffe's acting skills singularly failed to cover his shock as he quavered, "I've never heard of it."

"Inspector, I'm going to need you to step outside," said Elsa.

"Not a chance."

Amelia watched the scene. Unlike Radcliffe, Elsa and Harrigan both seemed excellent actors. Or possibly no acting was going on.

"Her name is Dr Carol Griffin." Act or not, the tactic seemed to have worked.

"Carol Griffin?" Harrigan reached into his pocket and brought out a tatty notebook. "I interviewed her." He flicked through the pages. "She worked with Professor Digges."

"Not exactly with," Radcliffe went on. "They were part of the same faculty. Perhaps he told her about the society – Digges was

185

getting on and could be a bit careless about who he spoke to. Or maybe he genuinely thought her research deserved a chance."

"Seems to have been a roaring success," said Elsa.

Radcliffe smacked a frustrated fist into the arm of his sofa. "It didn't work! We didn't even know what she was... If we'd..." He took a sip of water to calm himself. "One of the requirements of the endowment is that it have clear and immediate commercial potential that can be demonstrated to a panel. We are not allowed to know what the applicant is presenting (to protect their research, you understand). Dr Griffin came in and... blew up a dead rat."

"And you didn't know why?" asked Elsa. "You didn't know what she was trying to do?"

Radcliffe shrugged. "All we knew was that she had some theory about the electrical agitation of cells. We all thought it was something to do with resurrecting the dead."

"Resurrecting the dead?" Harrigan pulled a face.

"It's not that uncommon as a research subject," Radcliffe explained airily.

"Sounds pretty uncommon."

"In my experience," put in Elsa, "getting the dead to stay that way is the difficult bit."

"Yours is a pretty unusual experience," Amelia pointed out. "What happened next?"

A faint smile crossed Radcliffe's lips. "Well, you have to understand, it was a train wreck. She was mid-explanation – all confidence – and the thing went off. There she was, covered in rodent guts, *begging* to be given another chance. There was a string of intestine hanging off her ear that kept swinging and the more upset she got the more it swung."

"I bet you all laughed at that," said Elsa, quietly.

The smile vanished from Radcliffe's lips. "Not very professional in hindsight. But it was very funny."

Elsa shrugged. "Yes, well, seeing someone's life's work blow up in their face in a cascade of rodent entrails is an acquired sense of humour. It's all fun and games until four people get strangled. When did this happen?"

"Her trial? Six months ago, or thereabouts."

"When did you find out that she was invisible?" asked Harrigan.

"Tonight." And the tone of Radcliffe's voice made it obvious that this time he was telling the truth. "That came as a total shock. I mean, obviously I wondered how she'd killed the others, how she'd got past security cameras and so on, but… Never in my wildest dreams…" He shook his head. "If only it had worked that day. It would all have been so different."

"How many more members of the society are there?"

Radcliffe slumped. "I am the last one."

Harrigan pinched the bridge of his nose. "You were the last one left alive, you knew she'd be coming for you, and you still didn't go to the police?"

Radcliffe looked shocked. "The Society has been a secret for over a hundred years. It's tradition."

Elsa turned to Amelia. "I hate this damn city of yours."

"How do we find her?" asked Harrigan.

"I can give you all the details I have," replied Radcliffe. "In return for protection."

Elsa half-smiled. "You know, if we'd turned up a bit later tonight the problem would have gone away by itself. You're the last one. That would have been that. Frankly it might have been a whole lot easier."

"Or she might have kept killing," put in Harrigan. "People get a taste for it sometimes."

Elsa nodded. "Ain't that the truth."

"What about Stuart Price?" Amelia had been genuinely relieved that it hadn't been the Invisible Man who had killed the scientists and tried to kill her, but now everyone seemed to have forgotten that he existed.

Radcliffe's brow furrowed. "Who?"

Elsa sighed. "I don't know what to make of Mr Price. If he's not involved then it's a hell of a coincidence, but if he is… maybe an early test subject?"

"She must have tested on humans before trying it on herself,"

Radcliffe said, firmly. "Given how unstable the experiment was."

"Unstable!" Harrigan pummelled the back of the sofa and returned to his notebook, riffling through the pages. "Damn it she actually *told* me. If you needed a better stabilising agent and you'd tried everything else." He found what he was looking for. "Monocaine."

Radcliffe looked up sharply. "Are you sure?"

"It was written in Professor Digges' notebook and Dr Griffin told me about it."

"In *Digges'* notebook?" asked Elsa.

Harrigan nodded. "Maybe the rest of your society didn't know what Griffin's experiment was about, but my guess is that Professor Digges did. Maybe he saw an opportunity."

Radcliffe sighed. "His career was on the rocks, he'd have given anything for a discovery like this. But still; monocaine?" He shook his head. "Dangerous. And it might explain the murders. It affects the mind."

"It could explain *Wake Up!* too," Amelia hastily put in. "Why he suddenly became violent."

"Any long-term side effects?" asked Elsa.

Radcliffe shrugged. "This is all uncharted waters. But if you're saying that this man Stuart Price has been invisible for; what? Months? You can't do that to the human body. Cellular flux will result in cellular degeneration."

"And?"

"Death."

Chapter 21 – The Scapegoat

It began with a phone call.

"Hello. Is that Mr Price?"

Back in his other life, the Invisible Man had always had a bit of a cash flow problem because there was no job he would not abandon on the instant if it conflicted with the many extracurricular interests that would one day make him a star. He therefore preferred part-time jobs augmented with casual work. One particularly lucrative source of income was medical testing. He had been nervous at first of being pumped full of something and then stared at by people waiting for him to grow extra ears, turn green and explode, but it had all proved pretty standard. Such testing is stringently regulated and over a few years of doing it he had suffered only the mildest of side-effects.

"I wondered if you would be interested in taking part in a new drug trial?"

"Sure. You guys usually just email the details."

"This is a little different," the unidentified woman had continued. "Off the books if you like."

"Oh. Then maybe…"

"But we would be willing to pay more than usual for the inconvenience."

The not yet Invisible Man had swallowed cautiously and asked, "How much?"

Then the woman had told him.

Dr Carol Griffin flipped a switch and felt the familiar tremors overtake her body. Holding her hands up in front of her face she watched the bones, blood vessels, muscles and skin vibrate into existence as she became visible once more. She cut the current and laughed to herself. She didn't know why she was laughing; tonight had been a failure in every respect. She had failed to kill Vincent Radcliffe, her existence had been confirmed to those people who had already been creeping around the fringes, and Radcliffe had doubtless filled in the details. She couldn't even go home now, they were bound to come for her. All her meticulous preparation had been for nothing.

After that encounter on Tennis Court Road when she had tried to kill the Evans woman (whose connection to this she still could not fathom), and had been stopped by the other woman (who remained unidentified), Dr Griffin had realised that she needed a scapegoat. Fortunately she had already been grooming one.

It had been a shock to discover that Stuart Price was still alive. Only one of the her test animals had continued to live in a stable invisible state, a rabbit (named Flopsykins) who was currently nibbling on a carrot in his pen and wondering why the other rabbits had been so stand-offish of late. When Price had vanished from her lab that fateful day…

But it had started before then. It had started with the R. C. Forrester Endowment Society. Just the thought of them sent a flash of hatred searing through Dr Griffin, swiftly followed by delicious memories of choking the life from those men and women who had laughed at her, mocked her and rejected her. Stabbing Evelyn Herrick had been so satisfying that she had briefly toyed with the idea of stabbing the others. But so far she had been unable to make metal reliably invisible (it came and went). Besides, knives were sharp and it was easy to be careless when you couldn't see your own hands – a woman could get hurt that way. The important thing was that they were dead. Although their deaths had done nothing to silence the laughter in her head.

After their cruel rejection, Dr Griffin had continued with her work. The unfortunate accident of blowing up the rat had pushed her to try a different stabilising agent. Switching to monocaine had been risky, but it had paid off. The hairs on the back of her neck still raised as she recalled that first success, watching the wave of invisibility flicker along the rat's body, briefly revealing blood, bone and guts. She adjusted the current, the body fluxing before her eyes then vanishing completely. Then it exploded again.

Through trial and error she learnt what current was necessary but not too much; what materials it worked on and which just caught fire; the specific amounts of monocaine required. Only when these questions had been answered did she move onto living creatures.

In hindsight, she had probably jumped the gun on a human subject, but The Plan had already formed in her mind and she needed to know the process was safe before she tried it on herself.

She had found Stuart Price's name on a list of people who volunteered as subjects for paid experiments. He had been a willing participant, showing little to no interest in what all this was for, and the experiment had gone well. Until she tried to make him visible again. Then something had gone wrong; one of those freaks that even the best of scientists cannot plan for. Possibly there had been a power surge, perhaps in her excitement she had got the settings wrong. From the pitch and volume of Price's screams it had hurt quite a lot. Looking back, she was still surprised that the pain itself had not killed him.

Once she had put out the fire, Dr Griffin had spent some time searching for the body, or what was left of it. That had been another error. The length of time she had spent determining that there was no body had allowed Price to get away.

For days afterwards, Dr Griffin waited for the inevitable news. It was inconceivable that an invisible man could go unnoticed – however incongruous that sounded – he was bound to talk to a friend, some family member or the papers, and then Carol Griffin's career would be over. But nothing happened, and Dr Griffin came to the happy conclusion that Price had done the decent thing and died, hopefully someplace where no one would trip over him.

'My body still shaking, my heart trying to tear itself apart, I broke through the undergrowth and stumbled blindly onto the path, and into the light of a new world.'.

On auto-pilot, the Invisible Man staggered home through Cambridge, away from the House of Pain, his mind a barely conscious chaos. The pain itself had stopped, but it had scrambled his brain, rendering him an insensible wreck, shaking from the force of it, from the memory, from fear. In his head he still heard his own shrieks. He knew that he could not see his hands and feet. He knew that his reflection no longer appeared in the windows of buildings that he passed. He knew that others seemed unable to see him (people had always looked through him as if he wasn't there, but now a woman jumped in surprise when he opened a gate). But none of it mattered, he just wanted to get home. It would all be better after a good night's sleep.

Back at his flat, he found himself locked out – he had had to remove all metal items such as keys before undergoing the experiment. So he broke a window. He could deal with the consequences tomorrow; he *had* to sleep.

He collapsed onto his bed and recalled no more until the following morning.

It was then that he had to face the reality of his condition.

It was shocking, of course, and yet… After an initial bout of screaming, the Invisible Man found that he wasn't as surprised as he ought to have been. He had always known that he was special in some way that he had yet to discover and the world yet to recognise. He had imagined that he would take the world by storm as an actor, writer, singer, director, or comedian, as a street artist in the Banksy mould or cultural commentator. He had spent years trying to find that skill which would elevate him above the ordinary, the talent that would make him famous. Now it had finally happened.

He went out to face the world. Nothing had changed; and yet it was all different.

On his return, the opening sentence of what would, in surprisingly short order, become *The Life of an Invisible Man,* sprang fully formed into his mind and he dashed it out onto a notepad, followed by more furiously scribbled lines until he had almost a full chapter. He then switched to his laptop, but always kept the notepad there on his desk beside him as he worked; a self-mythologizing reminder of how it had started. One day TV interviewers would be fascinated by titbits like that.

He was supposed to be at work that day, at the coffee shop where he held down a part-time job, and he wondered momentarily if he should call in sick. He decided not. No one would miss him. No one ever did.

More tests on animals convinced Dr Griffin that she had made an elementary error with Stuart Price.

"My bad," she muttered to herself.

Still, human subjects came with an inherent problem; they could talk. After the fiasco with Price there was only one human she wanted to try to the experiment on; The Plan had waited long enough.

It would be a lie to say that she did not tremble as she added monocaine to the chemical cocktails that she injected into her arm and sprayed over her clothing, but it was partly from excitement. She set the equipment up in front of a mirror. It was a mistake she would not make again. Watching the living organs of a test subject revealed before her, peeling out of existence, was one thing; watching her own was nasty.

But it worked. Immediately she tried to reverse the process and found that that worked too; switching from visible to invisible and back again as easily and painlessly as changing clothes. Hastily she made herself invisible once more and went out to walk through the city. She stole a chocolate bar, because she could.

The next step of The Plan would be plain sailing. The R. C. Forrester Endowment Society would not meet her again – the rules of the society were clear on this – but if she went to Professor Digges in person whilst invisible then he could hardly deny what she had achieved. The thought of seeing that old goat after how she had been treated made her sick, but it was the only way.

Entering the faculty party was easy, but when she arrived there was no sign of Digges. The old fool had already retreated to his office to tank up from his secret stash of best brandy. Dr Griffin waited impatiently for someone else to approach the door.

"Not through here, if you please, sir."

"I was just looking for the toilet."

As the conversation between guest and Porter continued, Dr Griffin walked straight past them and down the corridor, the security camera staring straight through her. She crept up the stairs but faced another obstacle as the door to Digges' office was closed.

"Hah!" Digges threw the door open to confront whoever was

creeping up on him and Dr Griffin clamped a hand over her mouth to stop herself from crying out in shock.

The professor frowned at the empty stairway then hurried down to check the corridor. Griffin flattened herself against the wall to let him pass, then entered his office. She wasn't really interested in what the washed-up old has-been was working on but there was a notebook open on his desk and a word caught her eye because it had been circled in red. *'Monocaine???'*. A cold, clutching sensation seized Dr Griffin as she read on. The notes were deliberately vague, almost cryptic – a good theory was like gold dust and you didn't want anyone else seeing it – but there was no question what Digges was working on. He had guessed the purpose of her experiment and come to the same conclusion about where she had gone wrong. Directly after the word, Digges had written another: *'Dangerous.'*.

Naturally Dr Griffin had heard the stories about monocaine; about psychosis, violent rage, emotional instability. Nothing had been substantiated, but…

The sound of the door closing heralded the return of Professor Digges. Dr Griffin looked up.

And her blood boiled.

As the old man went back to his seat, Dr Griffin heard his laughter in her mind, she saw his guffawing face and heard the sarcastic comments. And now he was stealing her work?

"Good evening, Professor Digges."

This wasn't the effect of some drug. It was justice.

Professor Digges had deserved to die, but what Dr Griffin had not considered, had not even imagined, was how wonderful it would feel. It was not just righteous vengeance satisfied, it was the lush, velvet sensation of taking a life with her own hands. The Plan now changed. Though the others had only laughed at her, from that moment, their fate was sealed.

This would of course deny her the R. C. Forrester Endowment, but money was not a problem to an invisible woman. Nor, she thought, was being found out.

To preserve his anonymity, the Invisible Man used the address of one of the colleges when he started sending his manuscript out, and checked their mail every day as he waited for a response. Such things were easy for an invisible man and he had become adept at them. He had retrieved his spare key from his neighbour's flat by knocking at their door, then stepping in when they answered to take it from the hook in the hall. He kept the key hidden in a gap in the brickwork above his door so he did not have to carry it. Being an invisible man required some very specific life hacks.

It was inconvenient having only one set of invisible clothes but he discovered that they could be washed without losing their invisibility. He tied coloured wool to the clothing when he undressed to make it easy to find.

Sometimes he thought of the woman who had done this to him; Dr Carol Griffin. He didn't know whether to hate her or to thank her. But when the publisher's acceptance came and he felt that thrilling tingle of long-dreamed of success, he certainly warmed to her. Even now he shuddered at the memory of that pain, but perhaps it had been worth it.

After the book launch, and the extraordinary weeks that followed, he could have kissed her.

The Life of an Invisible Man came out only days after Dr Griffin had killed Professor Digges, and had roughly the same effect on her as a lightning bolt has on an English muffin.

Stuart Price was alive.

What if he named her? It was a narrow gap between that and a murder charge.

The police investigation had not worried Carol Griffin; no one had seen her and any DNA or fingerprints were easily explained as she worked in the same department as Professor Digges. It had been a surprise when the policeman asked about monocaine but of course it had been in Digges' notebook; no reason to panic. Price was another matter. She visited his flat, but found no sign of him. She read his book, and while she was pleased to find it scant on detail (he never addressed how this had happened to him), she remained uneasy.

195

But the days turned into weeks and it became clear that Stuart Price had some bizarre agenda of his own. Dr Griffin watched in fascination as her test subject embarked on his celebrity dream. The legend he was writing for himself did not include her, and on this occasion, she was quite happy to remain unidentified.

The next murder was thought out in advance. She killed Evelyn Herrick (who admittedly put up a fight), then waited patiently for the caretaker to open the door. The one mistake she made was the threatening letter, which had seemed like fun but which she didn't want the police to find. It had been a nightmare to locate in the post-fight chaos of Herrick's office. She wouldn't do that again. Murder was a learning curve.

Discovery was the furthest thing from Dr Griffin's mind. She was invisible; she could be neither followed nor identified. So it had been a shock when she returned to her secret lab, after doing some invisible reconnaissance work prior to the killing of Sampson Cranley, to find a trespasser. Fortunately, the woman (whom she later identified as Amelia Evans) did not find the basement and was not connected to the police, but it was still a jolt. Obviously the woman would have to die (*after Cranley, don't get side-tracked*), but if she could find the lab then others might.

It was then that the idea of using Stuart Price as a patsy first occurred to Dr Griffin. The good news was that while she had used invisibility to remain in the shadows, Price had used it to make himself very visible indeed. If people were hunting an invisible killer, they would look no further. The bad news was that everyone loved him and no one would believe anything ill of him.

The *Wake Up* affair had scarred the Invisible Man and left his burgeoning media career in tatters. If only he could get his hands on Oskar Cole, Oskar the Omnipotent, then he would...

But that was where he had gone wrong. In one rash act he had torched his dreams. All that he had gone through, all that he had suffered, was now all for nothing. That bright, gleaming star of celebrity had been cruelly wrenched from his grasp.

Some days he did not get out of bed at all, but lay there,

shivering, moaning and crying. Others, he would trash the house he was currently living in, tearing the place apart in an uncontrollable fury. Sometimes he would just feel blank, empty, meaningless.

While he had been happy and busy it had not seemed to matter, but now his isolation weighed on him. He started sitting with people in pubs or on buses, listening to them talk, just to feel part of their group. He was used to being alone, but the total absence of human interaction was something else. He wondered what affect it might be having on his mind.

Even Dr Griffin was prepared to admit that she had gotten lucky. The *Wake Up!* interview had revealed a side to Price she had never anticipated. Could this violent temper be a side-effect of the experiment? That would tally with the behaviour of some her test subjects (Flopsykins could be a total bastard).

She smiled to herself. "Thank God it hasn't done that to me."

Whatever the reason, Price was now the perfect scapegoat, and Griffin set about strengthening the case against him. After killing Sampson Cranley, she left her old base of operations, relocating her lab equipment and clearing the basement. The bag of rubbish containing an envelope addressed to Price, she was particularly pleased with. It was subtle enough to be believable but also gave any potential investigators the address of a genuine invisible man; *The Invisible Man* in fact. A search of his home would surely yield some evidence identifying Stuart Price as the elusive author, and everyone now knew that he was dangerously violent.

But was it enough? Price's behaviour suggested a mind at the end of its tether. Such a mind might well be pliant; suggestible.

Una Jaffers.

The Invisible Man had not recognised the name when he saw it written on the map he found on his kitchen island, but he soon found out who she was when he turned on the news. She had been killed the night before in the same building that was circled on the map in front of him. *His* map. Apparently.

He stared at the TV in a mixture of incomprehension and

horror. He had no memory of owning the map let alone annotating it. He could have sworn he hadn't gone out last night. But he had woken up covered in blood that was not his own. And his memory had not been working perfectly of late. In fact, nothing had.

For some time he had suffered from a periodic tingling in his limbs. Three days ago that tingling had ended with him losing all feeling in his left hand. It had slowly numbed from existence, flopping uselessly from his wrist. It had only lasted half an hour but the following day one of his legs did the same. It had become a daily occurrence, and he had started to wonder; if this was happening to his body, what might be happening to his brain?

Since he had struck the child in Market Square, the Invisible Man had known that his behaviour was changing. He was also aware that, try as he might, he could not bring himself to care about it. Even given the shocking possibility that he might have killed this Una Jaffers – a person he had never even heard of – he was still more intrigued than concerned.

He should have been horrified. Shouldn't he? If only there was someone he could talk to about this.

As parts of his body randomly shut down, so parts of his brain seemed to do the same. Some flickered on and off, while others vanished, perhaps never to return.

And the problem seemed to be getting worse. Which suggested that parts of his body would continue to shut down, until something vital failed him.

The Invisible Man realised he was dying.

Tracking Price down had been more time-consuming than difficult. Dr Griffin had staked out his flat for days before seeing the door open of its own accord.

That was the easy bit. Following him, listening for the sound of the hemp slip-ons they both wore (the only shoes she had found that could reliably be made invisible) was incredibly difficult, and might have been impossible had the streets been busier.

She was startled, and a little impressed, on seeing the home her subject had appropriated for himself, showing more initiative than

198

she would have granted him. Now she knew where to find him, the rest was easy. Every day she stopped in to move things around, steal his shopping, turn appliances on or off, and do everything she could to make him think he was losing his mind. About the house, Price wore visible clothes so Griffin could easily observe his movements. Sometimes she was bold enough to stand in the room with him, waiting for his back to turn before moving something, then smiling at his terrified confusion.

The night before she killed Una Jaffers, she drugged his food and stole into his bedroom as he slept. The blood on his hands (pig's blood) might have been a step too far, but it had a shocking immediacy to it. Along with the map with the victim's name on it, it would make Price question his innocence as well as his sanity. If he was ever arrested then he would be unable to mount an adequate defence, because he would never be sure himself.

The blood meant that she had to stab Una Jaffers *post mortem*, but that had been a pleasure. Jaffers had put up a fight and stabbing her with a broken bottle, even after death, was very satisfying. During the fight, Dr Griffin had lost her coat, and was forced to leave without it when she heard the Professor's secretary arriving. It was a serious loss; what if someone found it? And yet she didn't really care. Was that odd?

The reaction of the Invisible Man to the likelihood of his impending death was an oddly dispassionate one. He recognised it, but could find no emotional response.

The only thing that unfailingly stimulated his numbed emotions was his lost celebrity. That still tore at soul. Before all this started he had been worse than invisible; he had been unseen, and now he had gone back there, hurled into anonymity and destined to be forgotten.

No.

He would *not* be forgotten. Whatever else happened, he would not suffer that. If he could not be famous, then he would be infamous. Perhaps he had already written his legacy in blood (he could not be sure), but that was not BIG enough.

In the privacy of his empty house, the Invisible Man laughed wildly to himself. They would all pay. They had made him a celebrity then torn him down. They would all pay. Not one individual in a bookshop, not the city of Cambridge, nor even the country. But the world. They would learn that the Invisible Man was not so easily forgotten. They would pay.

All of them.

Because, when you got right down to it, however responsible the Herbert Digges and Vincent Radcliffes of the world were, they were part of a larger machine, of Cambridge University and of Cambridge itself.

She had failed to kill Radcliffe. Did they think that was that?

Dr Griffin laughed wildly to herself. If she could not have the individual, then she would have the institution. And more.

She would make everyone pay.

Chapter 22 – The Winter Festival

"But…" Amelia looked crestfallen. "Boris let me help."

Elsa shrugged. "And look how that went. Or nearly went. Anyway, as I understand it, he needed your skills in ancient Egyptian languages. Unless this affair takes a very weird tangent, I do not. I'm not involving a civilian. Me and Harrigan can handle it. Have you got a place to stay?"

"I can't stay at mine?"

"We'd prefer you not to," Harrigan interjected. He was back to being professional and confident. "Chances are Dr Griffin is on the run and has better things to do than kill you, but we'd rather not take the chance."

"I can find somewhere."

"Good," Elsa nodded firmly. "I'll let you know how it ends."

Amelia felt disconnected and aimless as she took a taxi home to pack an overnight bag. On the way she called her friend Izzy.

"Amelia!" Izzy's excitable voice rang down the phone. "How's things? I have so many questions."

"Any chance they could keep? I'm feeling a bit…"

"What's up? Talk to me."

"Are you still in town? I know it's short notice but I need a place to crash tonight. And for the next few nights."

"Okay, first; you're back in Cam and you didn't tell me? What the hell? Second; no. Back with the folks for Christmas. But you're still good to crash. Kay's there – you know Kay – I'll tell her you're coming. Take my room."

"Thanks Izzy."

"Are you really not going to tell me what's going on?"

"Maybe after Christmas."

"Are you hanging with Boris again?"

"No," said Amelia, grateful she could mislead her friend without actually lying.

"In that case it's got to be guy trouble. But at least that means you have a guy. Am I right?"

"Maybe," hedged Amelia.

"Tell me all or I will pester you incessantly."

It being a safer topic than that of invisible men and women, Amelia told her friend about Jack and the two dates they had been on, while Izzy rattled off questions like a verbal machine gun.

"I'm back at mine now Izzy, I've got to go."

"Okay. To be continued. When are you seeing him again?"

It took all the time she spent packing, walking to Izzy's – where she was let in by Kay – and unpacking again, for Amelia to come to a decision and pick up the phone.

"Hi, it's Amelia."

"Hey." Jack sounded pleased to hear from her, which hadn't been a given. "You called me."

"Did you think I wouldn't?"

"I absolutely thought that. You're a very hard woman to persuade to pick up the phone."

"Well, you're very persuasive."

"How are you?"

Not knowing how she could even begin to answer that question, Amelia side-stepped, moving straight to her reason for calling. "You invited me to the Winter Festival to see your jolly chair and maybe other stuff, if I was free, and as it turns out; I am. I didn't think I was going to be or I'd have answered sooner but… I am. Are you?"

"Well obviously I will have to oversee some chair-related issues."

"Obviously."

"But I think I could make time."

Amelia beamed involuntarily, and then wondered when a man had last brought a smile to her face so readily. "Great. How about lunch and a stroll around?"

"Perfect."

"Maybe we could stretch it to dinner as well?" Amelia's heart nervously fluttered in her chest. "Make a night of it. Maybe at your place? I'd say mine, but there are issues at mine. Another reason I haven't called."

"We can do that. For sure."

They agreed time and place, exchanged a few awkward pleasantries and 'looking forward to its' then hung up.

Amelia let out a long, slow breath. She had not said anything specific, she had not guaranteed anything; Jack had no reason to think that he was on a promise. But he was definitely on an implication. And she was okay with that. Maybe she was falling into the American sitcom version of the third date, but it felt right. She'd been feeling pretty low after Elsa and Harrigan had side-lined her (when *she* was the one who had linked the Invisible Man to the killings), but now she was feeling good again. Maybe she didn't need these little adventures in her life as much as she needed *a life*.

Getting a life didn't necessarily mean getting a man, but it did mean exploring all possibilities to the fullest, and Jack was a possibility worth exploring.

Oddly, the decision made her think of Stuart Price. Whoever he was and whatever he had done, he seemed to have spent much of his life watching quietly from the side-lines. But when an opportunity to get in the game had come, he had taken it. Amelia determined to do the same, and hope she got better results.

She spent the evening looking through her notes on the Carpathian pictograms. Work was suddenly feeling good again.

The weatherman had apologetically reported a slim but insignificant chance of snow for the Winter Festival, or Christmas Eve Eve, but the sharp bite of frost in the air made it seasonal enough for the many already enjoying it.

"What are you doing for Christmas?" asked Jack. They had enjoyed a light lunch at a nice, if crowded, place off King's Parade and were now strolling through the stalls and entertainments set up to delight children of all ages.

"Heading home tomorrow," Amelia replied. "Home home, that is. Family Christmas."

"You and Zita under one roof?"

"We get on best at Christmas," said Amelia. "Plus I've got a her dress she will love."

"You sure? The two of you have different fashion senses."

"I'm sure. She sent me very specific instructions."

Jack laughed, and Amelia took a moment to consider what a lovely sound it was. Zita had already given her a pretty great present.

"Would you like me to win you a bear?" asked Jack, as they passed a generic throwing balls at targets stall.

"I get the feeling you'd like to try."

"No, I'd like to succeed," replied Jack. "Nobody admits it, but these games are secret tests of masculinity."

"With a cuddly toy as a prize?"

"There's nothing manlier than a bear."

"Even the one with hearts for eyes?"

"Get that bear in a corner and it'll tear you to shreds."

Amelia laughed. "Fine. Win me a unicorn and I promise to swoon in a girlish fashion and call you my hero."

"Right." Jack turned to the stall, then stopped. "I'm now feeling a lot of pressure."

Amelia nodded. "You should. I saw man winning a giraffe earlier and I don't think he had a wedding ring."

Jack slumped. "I shouldn't have built this up. I'll come back with a unicorn or not at all."

As Jack made his way to the stall, Amelia soaked in the Festival atmosphere. Although there were a lot of people, King's Parade was long enough to contain them without it being too crowded, especially as the Festival spilled into adjoining streets and as far as Market Square. The stalls were brightly coloured, strung with tinsel and fairy lights augmented with occasional bunches of mistletoe, one of which Jack and Amelia had taken advantage of. The usual fairground games had been given a festive spin by the more enterprising store-holders, so Whack-a-mole had become the equally brutal Whack-an-Elf, the Ring Toss now involved tossing rings over reindeer antlers, and the Test Your Strength Machine had the head of Rudolph at the top whose nose flashed red if you hit the bell. The smell of snack food filled the air; roasted chestnuts, caramel-coated peanuts, hot mince pies, candy canes, turkey burgers, spicy potatoes and more, to keep you fortified for the long trek though the stalls. Complimenting the food, and to keep the adults from going insane, was the heady scent of mulled wine, an array of craft ales, hot chocolate and fruit-infused teas. For sale was an even split between brightly coloured tat designed to catch the eyes of children, and general stalls cornering the 'last person you haven't bought a present for' market. The former boasted a gaudy collection of plastic things that spun, whirred, screamed, whistled and lit up, alongside furry creatures with glitter, sequins and enormous staring eyes. It looked as if someone had collected the waste from a Christmas decoration factory and said, '*I can make something out of that*'. The latter stalls could be summarised as 'what to get the person who has everything', or more accurately 'what to get the person for whom you forgot to get anything'. They featured candles heavily, but also driftwood 'sculpture', Cambridge souvenirs, personalised bookmarks, mugs, and anything else that shop-owners had over-ordered for the summer tourist trade and now wanted to get shot of.

It was loud, crass and commercial and yet there was a conviviality about it. People always ranted on the over-commercialisation of the season, and they had a point, but Amelia liked to think that, rather than commercialisation dragging Christmas down, Christmas managed to make it almost cosy. Say what you liked about the naked materialism of the Festival, it had brought families together for a day out and everyone seemed to be having a good time. Why not look at the positive side? It only came once a year, and if there was nothing else to be done about capitalism, you might as well stick a bow on it.

"Unicorn." Jack proudly presented Amelia with a fluffy toy, dusted with glitter, its mane studded with plastic jewels and its wide eyes making it look as if it had just snorted a line of sparkly cocaine.

"My hero!" She threw her arms around Jack and kissed him.

They strolled on together, the unicorn's head sticking out of the top of Amelia's bag, eyeballing anyone who looked their way. They stopped at a few stalls and Amelia bought some noisy presents for young cousins and a woolly hat for her namesake, Great Aunt Amelia.

"You were going to show me your jolly chair."

"Oh. Good point." Jack checked his watch. "We've still got time, the grotto opens at three."

Holding Amelia's hand, Jack led the way towards the St. Mary's end of King's Parade. This grotto was even more impressive than the one in the Grafton Centre; a fibreglass log cabin that dominated the street, flanked by animatronic dancing snowmen, with reindeer grazing outside and Rudolph standing on the roof. A queue had already formed, and children wolfed down sticky, sweet treats while waiting for Santa to take a break from his busy toy-making schedule to open his doors for last minute petitions.

"We'll go round the back," said Jack.

"Friends of Mr Claus," Amelia explained to a little girl who had been eavesdropping and who now looked suitably impressed.

A barrier had been erected at the back of the grotto to stop the curious and Jack made his way through the gate using a card key.

"You didn't design the grotto itself?"

Jack shook his head. "I don't work in fibreglass."

"Looks good."

"Wait till you see the chair."

"I'm sure that will be its crowning glory."

"Watch what you say or I might not make dinner for you."

Amelia moved closer to him. "But if you don't make dinner, then I might not come to dinner."

"You make a good point."

They kissed.

"How do you feel about an early dinner?" suggested Jack.

"We just had lunch, I'm not hungry."

"Nor am I."

"Show me the chair, you idiot." Amelia was enjoying today a lot, and she had a feeling that she was going to enjoy this evening too.

They pushed through the staff entrance into a decidedly unfestive storeroom where 'Santa' kept his street clothes, packed lunch and cigarettes, then through a rich, velvet curtain into the grotto itself. The room was lit by hundreds of multicoloured fairy lights twinkling from the walls and ceiling, keeping the atmosphere festive but also dark enough that older, more astute children didn't start making comments about false beards. In one corner, beside a window that was covered in spray-on snow, was a scarred and paint-spattered wooden table, on which lay some unfinished toy soldiers, a doll with one leg and a teddy bear lacking eyes – Santa's workbench. Opposite the main door, beside the curtain through which they had entered, was a rough-hewn oaken chair, friezes of holly carved into its panels. It was grand enough to be a throne and yet humble enough to be a fireside rocker. Its bubbled varnish and the rubbed smoothness of its arms spoke to centuries of long-use, even though Amelia knew it had only been finished this week.

"Jack, it's great."

"Yeah," Jack nodded, without any false modesty. "I'm actually really pleased with it. Feels like a pretty cool thing to have done."

"And Santa's chair looks good on the CV."

"Do you think it's jolly?"

"Jolliest chair I ever saw. Where's Santa?"

"Probably in position already," replied Jack.

"In position?"

Jack grinned. "He starts out on King's College roof then ziplines down here."

"Just like the real thing."

As Amelia spoke, a sound came from the behind the curtain on the other side of the chair. It sounded like a moan of pain.

Jack strode around and pulled the curtain back. "Charlie?... Charlie!"

On the ground behind the curtain lay a heavy-set man in his underwear. His feet and hands had been tied, there was a gag over his mouth and a bloody mark on the back of his bald head. Beside him was a wooden toy train, stained with blood.

Jack dropped to his knees, hastily untying the ropes and removing the gag. "Charlie? Are you alright? What happened?"

Amelia was still stood back, staring. This couldn't be connected. Could it? Dr Griffin had a grudge against University scientists, not Santa. But there was a maniac on the loose, and the evidence suggested that she was becoming more maniacal all the time.

Charlie groaned something unintelligible.

"I'm going to get help," said Jack. "Can you stay with him?"

"Of course."

Amelia stooped to lay a comforting hand on the injured Charlie's shoulder, as Jack ran from the room.

"How you doing, Charlie?"

The big man's mouth opened and he murmured something that Amelia could not catch, but sounded like, "…venge…"

"Sorry, Charlie?"

"…said… 'revenge'…"

Clearly what Charlie needed was to be allowed to rest, but Amelia had to know; lives might depend on it.

"Charlie? Did you get a look at who attacked you?"

Charlie's vague eyes rolled upwards and managed to focus on Amelia as his forehead creased into a frown. "No one… there was… no one there. Watched… *no one* take my clothes…"

Moments later, having placed a fluffy unicorn under Charlie's head as a pillow, Amelia was sprinting towards King's College as fast as the crowds would allow.

"Sorry!" She bumped into a family while trying to find Elsa's number on her phone as she ran.

"Hello?" The familiar, sharp voice answered.

"Elsa, I think she's here."

"That's no use to me, Amelia, I don't know where you are."

"The Winter Festival, damn it! King's Parade."

"We'll be there as quickly as we can."

"She's already attacked someone. I think she's making for King's College." Given her chosen disguise, that would make sense.

"Hang tight," Elsa replied. "I'm calling home for back-up."

"Okay. I'll see you soon."

"Amelia."

"What?"

Elsa spoke with deliberate emphasis, "Don't do anything."

"I won't," replied Amelia, as she passed through the gates of King's College and hung up the phone.

Chapter 23 – The Library

Amelia could never walk through the 19th century gatehouse of King's College without thinking about the history of the place and the wealth of fascinating people who had walked through those gates before her, but if she did it this time then it was only in passing. On the far side she hung a left towards the Wilkins' Building. Dr Griffin would not have dressed as Santa on a whim, it would be part of a larger and presumably murderous plan, and though Amelia could only guess at what that plan might be, Santa's zipline led from the roof of the Wilkins' building, so that was the place to start.

It was this south side of the college that Amelia was most familiar with thanks to the presence of the King's College Library, sandwiched between the Wilkins' Building and the Old Provost's Lodge. There was not a library in the city that Amelia had not visited for either pleasure or practical purpose. In fact, she and Izzy had once gone on a 'library crawl', visiting every library in the city in one day and reading the first page of one book before moving onto the next. It was exhausting and somewhat pointless, but they'd both agreed that it was time well-spent and that they would do it again one day. The King's Library was, naturally, beautiful and historically significant, but it was also useful to Amelia, who had spent much time there, studying the rare and ancient manuscripts within the collection. Since graduating, her visits to King's had been exclusively to use the library, and she could not help glancing towards it now.

She frowned.

Though she could not see the library building clearly from here, there seemed to be a light in one of its latticed windows. At this time of year there was no reason for anyone to be in there.

Changing course, and ignoring the strict notices telling her to keep off the grass, Amelia ran towards the gap between the Wilkins' and Gibbs' buildings that led to the library. As she got closer, the knot that had started to form in her stomach tightened. The light in the window was not the warm, yellow light she knew from past visits, it flickered and changed colour. Amelia ran faster.

Inside, her shoes echoed loudly against the cold stone as she ran up the familiar staircase. As she went, she did still have just enough self-possession to wonder what she was doing. What was her plan? What did she think was going on and how did she imagine she was going to stop it? If she found the invisible Dr Griffin – and there was one very obvious reason why she might not – what would she do next? And yet on she ran.

Amelia was not an adrenalin junkie. She did not get her kicks from rock climbing, bungee jumping, or swimming with sharks. She got her kicks from a good book and a properly brewed cup of tea. Why then did she keep chasing this particular dragon?

These were questions and general musings on her life that could probably wait for a better time.

Reaching the library doors, Amelia paused, partly to get her breath back, partly because she did not know what might lie within, but also because this was a library and one did not just go barging in, one showed respect. Pushing open the door, she entered quietly, tip-toeing into the gloom and breathing in the comforting smell of books that went some way to settling her rattled nerves. The stacks of shelves stretched away into the darkness. Libraries were sacred places to Amelia, but that didn't stop them from being spooky. She wondered what the books got up to when there was no one around to watch them, and if one night she might catch them at it.

The library was set far enough back from King's Parade that it caught none of the lights of the festival, but up ahead of her, coming from between the shelves, was an altogether eerier light. It dappled the floor in shifting patterns of bright white, dull red and vivid green, throwing distorted moving shadows like a horror film carnival.

Something was wrong here. Beyond the busy hum from outside, she heard subtle but closer sounds; metallic clicking, tapping, hissing, humming.

Though she kept her steps to the cushioning rugs that ran down the central aisle, the wooden floorboards still creaked noisily as Amelia crept forward – she had always found that charming in the past. To either side of her the books seemed to whisper, perhaps telling her how stupid she was being. Elsa had made a point of telling her not to do anything, but if she did nothing then… what? Griffin had already proved herself capable of murder; whatever she was doing now she had to be stopped. Elsa and Inspector Harrigan were on their way, but Amelia was *here*. Right now, there was no one but her.

The weird lights and sounds were coming from one of the four book-lined alcoves that flanked the central aisle. Amelia tried to hold her breath as she approached, her heart thumping in her ears. Cautiously she peered in, and could not suppress a gasp.

On the wooden floor, near the window, was a strange device, not much smaller than a banana box. It was from this that the lights and sounds were coming. As Amelia stared, the metal casing of the device rippled before her eyes, affording glimpses of the circuitry within. The plastic coating of wires peeled back then zipped up again; circuit boards blinked in and out of existence; the LEDs on a display hovered in mid-air as the display itself vanished, leaving them stranded there. At one point, Amelia could see straight through to the floor beneath. This state of permanent flux was the source of the flickering lights, as the lights within the machine were covered and uncovered or temporarily disappeared. A word came to Amelia's mind as she looked at the device, and the word was 'unstable'.

But it was not the device itself that had made Amelia catch her breath, it was its operator. Finding a picture of Dr Carol Griffin had not been difficult, and Elsa and Harrigan had located one quickly so they would know who they were looking for – assuming she was visible at the time. But they would have struggled to identify the creature hunched over the device in King's College Library. A brain hovered in mid-air, pulsing gently, a few inches above a disembodied lower jaw with tongue in place, moving slightly like a fish in a small tank. The figure's clothes were as erratic in their existence as the casing on the machine, ebbing and flowing to reveal the body beneath doing the same thing. Skin receded and returned like a tide over striated muscles, which then disappeared to show blood and bone, pulsing viscera and streaming fluids. The blood vessels themselves vanished while the blood remained, pounding through unseen veins and arteries. A pair of lips swiped across the unseen face to mutter swear words as the figure clumsily tried to operate the device with fingers that kept fluctuating in and out of sight; disembodied nails pecking at buttons, strings of nerves and capillaries wandering homeless through the air. Before Amelia's horrified gaze, optic nerves juddered uncertainly back into visibility, tracing the route to a pair of eyeballs that hung horribly in the air before the brain.

Amelia had gasped before she could check herself, and the eyeballs instantly twitched in her direction. No doubt the eyes would have widened if they had possessed lids with which to do so, but they locked on Amelia and even without a facial expression, Amelia could feel the white hot hatred directed at her.

Dr Griffin leapt up, lunging towards Amelia with a sharp hiss of anger. As she moved away from the machine, out into the central aisle, the fluctuations of invisibility across and through her body ceased, as if Harry Potter's cloak had been flung over her, and she became completely invisible.

The shock of seeing her attacker vanish before her eyes made Amelia slow and stupid, and in the next instant she felt a hand at her throat driving her back against the shelves.

"You spoiled everything." The voice grated from the emptiness in front of her in a tone of focussed rage, and Amelia could feel that rage as fingers dug into her neck, choking her. Desperately she clawed at the shelf behind her, finally grabbing hold of a book. This was not how one was supposed to treat books, but desperate times called for desperate measures and Amelia brought the sturdy hardback around in a wheeling arc, aiming for where her attacker's head ought to be.

The action brought a satisfying 'whap!', and a cry from Dr Griffin, whose grip loosened enough for Amelia to tear herself free and run for the door.

"NO!" It was practically a shriek.

The rug beneath Amelia's fleeing feet was given a hard yank and Amelia went flying, landing hard on the floor, catching one arm beneath her at a bad angle that made her howl in pain.

"Yeeessss!" Dr Griffin hissed in manic delight.

Amelia struggled to get back up but her arm was kicked out from under her. Blows began to rain down on her from above. She tried to fend them off and got lucky with a flailed kick that knocked the mad scientist back.

Scrabbling to her feet, Amelia again fled for the door, but was dragged back, turning her ankle as she went. She tried to run the other way but found herself in a hail of books, flung at her from behind, forcing her to duck between the shelves to hide. She was a mass of bruises, her arm was badly wrenched and her left ankle was too painful to put much weight on. What now?

Silence.

Now the cat had its mouse cornered, it wanted to play.

Amelia wondered how long it would take Elsa to get here. But all Elsa knew was King's College, there was no guarantee she would start in the library. Limping forward, Amelia peered out past the end of the shelves into the library beyond.

"Boo."

The word was whispered into her ear, close enough to feel the breath, and Amelia started backwards, crying out and tripping over a chair behind her, while Dr Griffin's laughter echoed about the room.

Clumsily, Amelia fumbled her phone into her hands. Maybe she could…

But the phone was snatched away and hurled across the room, clattering to the floor.

Silence again.

A floorboard creaked, making Amelia jump. Where had that come from? From a shelf she grabbed a heavy hardback as a potential weapon, turning this way and that, wheeling the book around her, trying to stop Griffin from getting near.

"I'm here."

This time the Doctor just pinched her arm, gone by the time Amelia lashed out.

More horrible silence.

From nowhere, a foot stamped on Amelia's. She cried out, going onto one leg, and was instantly shoved to the floor.

Scrambling back up, Amelia made another rush for the door,

but an invisible leg tripped her, sending her tumbling floorwards once more, adding bruises to her bruises. She rolled over in time to see a stack of books awkwardly extracting itself from a shelf. It hovered briefly in mid-air before the books began to fly at her one by one, accompanied by the high-pitched laughter of her tormentor. The hard spines smacked against her raised arms, always seemed to strike with sharp corners foremost. Splayed pages crashed into her face, lacerating her skin with dozens of tiny papercuts.

The one positive thing was that Dr Griffin seemed to enjoy this torture too much to actually finish Amelia off – which she could probably do any time she chose. If Amelia could get through this then her moment might yet come.

At the other end of the room, a short flight of wooden steps led to the landing where there was an emergency exit. If she could just reach that…

The pile of books was exhausted, and Amelia saw one of the wooden library ladders rise into the air. It was now or never. She ran.

The ladder flew through the air, crashing into the shelves where Amelia had been standing a moment ago. She heard the roar of fury as she dashed for the stairs, ignoring the pain in her ankle. She made it up the steps to the landing, but as her hand closed on the door handle, Dr Griffin grabbed her by the shoulders, yanking her back and pushing her away. Before Amelia could recover herself, the doctor was on her again, driving her victim back, hard and fast, hitting the big, floor to ceiling library window. The glass shattered.

As she went through the window, Amelia flailed out, reaching for something, anything, to stop her from falling and finding the cold stonework. She tightened her grip and pulled herself away from the broken window, perched precariously on the sill, clinging on like a living gargoyle. She made the mistake of looking down to the solid paving slabs below. Falling was not an option.

Now what? If she went back inside then nothing had changed. Down was an easy climb, but Dr Griffin might even now be clambering out to follow, and if she stamped on Amelia's fingers then it was game over. Up was the safest route.

The carved stone was weathered smooth by the decades but

was still ornate enough to present plentiful handholds, and Amelia made quick progress. Her fingers found the balustraded edge of the roof and she started to pull herself up.

A hand closed around her ankle and tugged.

Losing her grip with one hand, Amelia slid back, the bottom of her stomach seeming to drop out as she went. She clutched tighter with her remaining hand, desperately kicking down at her unseen attacker.

"Let… me… GO!" With a lashing kick, Amelia broke free. She listened for the sound of an invisible body thudding to the ground, but no such luck.

With urgent, scrabbling movements, like a cat climbing the curtains, she managed to crawl up onto the roof, skidding on the slippery slates, still frosty from the previous night. She rolled over into a sitting position to stare at the edge of the roof, then gave it a vicious kicking, pounding her feet on the bare stonework, hoping to take out any fingers that might be gripping it. She heard no cries of pain or of someone falling. Had Dr Griffin given up?

Amelia did not wait around to find out, but ran (or limped as fast as she was able) towards the metal ladder that led up to the higher roof of the Wilkins' Building. Higher was not ideal, but the only way down from here was through the library, and she was not going back in there.

On the roof of the Wilkins' Building she hurried on. There *were* steps down, she knew there were, she just didn't know where. She clambered up onto the steeper roof of the building's mid-section.

But before she could take another step, her legs were kicked out from under her and she fell, hitting her head as she went down. A hand grabbed her collar from behind.

"Got you." You couldn't beat an invisible adversary; they would always have the drop on you.

Dr Griffin began to drag Amelia bodily along the icy rooftop, past the ornamental chimneys, towards the Parade end of the college building.

"You've only yourself to blame," growled the disembodied

voice of Carol Griffin "There was no reason for you to get involved in the first place."

And Amelia had to admit that this was quite true. She'd been having a lovely day; how the hell had it ended here?

"Maybe the people of Cambridge would like to see their hero kill," Griffin snarled.

She was going to throw Amelia off the roof, down into King's Parade. Up ahead, Amelia could hear the noise of the crowd. It sounded as if they were cheering something.

Exhausted as she was, her head still spinning, Amelia started to struggle again. She wasn't going down without a fight. Being invisible didn't make a person super strong.

But it did mean that you didn't see the blows coming, and the element of shock made them seem so much harder. The backhand slap spun Amelia around, sprawling face-down on the freezing surface of the roof. She looked up… And wondered if she was suffering from concussion. There, standing at the far end of the roof that overlooked the street, was Santa Claus. He was looking right at her.

But past the beard, the hat and the little round glasses, the multi-coloured Christmas lights of the Festival illuminated an empty space. Amelia shivered, as she realised that Santa had no face.

Chapter 24 – The Vengeance of the Invisible Man

How did you go about punishing the world?

In his angrier moments – and those moments were increasingly frequent – the Invisible Man *did* consider acts of horrific terrorism. What could stop him? There was no security he could not bypass, no public figure who was safe from him. He could kill individuals or *en masse* with total impunity. Then they would remember the Invisible Man forever.

There were three reasons that he did not got through with this. Firstly; though his morality had gone walkabout of late, something inside him told him that this was not the thing to do. It just didn't feel like the correct course of action. After all, there were lots of terrorists – he needed to do something special. Secondly; the bomb, or whatever weapon he used, would be visible, which would be a bit of a faff. Thirdly; it just wasn't big enough.

The Invisible Man was not angry at Cambridge or London or even the United Kingdom. Well... he was, but not *solely* at them. He was angry at the whole world. How many people did you have to kill to punish the whole world? However many it was, it was probably not realistic. Besides, if you killed that many people, would the survivors remember you or the event? He didn't want the memory of himself, the individual, to be dwarfed by that of his actions.

And again; it did feel somehow not right.

He wanted to take something from them. To take something precious and irreplaceable from the world as they had taken it from him. For two weeks he had been their darling, the most famous unknown person on the face of the globe, and they had retracted their approval and damned him back to the ranks of the nobodies, all the worse for having had that one brief sip from the heady cup of fame.

What could he take from them that would equal that loss?

Christmas.

Obviously Christmas wasn't celebrated everywhere but you had to stick to achievable goals and it would still affect a large portion of the world.

He knew he could not 'take' Christmas. He was not the Sherriff of Nottingham barking orders in the sharply recognisable tones of the late, great Alan Rickman. But he could ruin it for people. Most importantly, he could ruin it for children. If you made children miserable then generally everyone else would follow.

By this point, the Invisible Man knew that something was wrong with his mind, so he did stop to examine the plan for signs of insanity. It didn't look good when you tried to explain it to another person (if he had only had another person to explain it to) and yet it felt right, because he would be using the instrument of his own destruction. The media would take this, his final stunt – The Last Trick of the Invisible Man – and broadcast it all over the world. They would do his job for him. He could do something small in Cambridge and it would resonate globally. He had done it before. The camera phones would again be the eyes of the world, and through them he would show a Santa Claus that nothing would ever erase. He would take away the childhoods of a generation. The Vengeance of the Invisible Man.

He would be remembered.

He would not be loved. He would not be remembered as a hero, or a glittering personality. But he would be remembered, and that was all that mattered. People would be talking about the Invisible Man decades and centuries after his death.

On the day of the Festival, the Invisible Man made his way to King's Parade, walked past the queue of children and parents that was already starting to form, and let himself into the grotto. He had learnt a number of things since becoming invisible and one of the main ones was that people never questioned a door opening and closing of its own accord. They wrote it off as something to do with the springs or some wind tunnel effect. The world was how it was, and people would come up with any amount of crap to justify it.

Inside the grotto, 'Santa'; was already in full uniform. It was important to the plan that this person be out of the way; there could not be two Santas or it would undercut his appearance.

Truthfully, he probably had not needed to hit Charlie as hard as he did. But the sound of the wooden train cracking against the

218

man's skull had sent a flicker of electric pleasure shooting through the Invisible Man. While Charlie lay groaning on the floor, eyes rolling, the Invisible Man undressed him and tied him up. He donned the red suit, put on the beard, the wig, the hat, the little round glasses (conveniently hiding most of his invisible face) then he snuck out the back way to avoid the queue.

At this time of year, a man dressed as Santa excited little comment, but the Invisible St Nick still stuck to the shadows, away from the crowd. By going down Senate House Passage, turning left and hopping the fence, he could approach King's College from another angle, avoiding the Festival-goers filling King's Parade.

On the way, he retrieved the sack that he had secreted the night before. A disadvantage of being invisible was that it made carrying things almost impossible, so he had snuck out last night, bundled up in coat, hat and scarf, to position his sack in advance.

No one attempted to stop him as he made his way through the college grounds and into the Wilkins' building. In some ways, being Santa was a lot like being invisible; you could go where you pleased. It would only work at this time of year, and of course it was a lot less surreptitious, but still; interesting.

People even helped him.

"It's that way, Charlie." A man on the door of the Wilkins' building pointed to the stairs then offered a cheery thumbs up. "Good luck. Try not to kill yourself."

The Invisible Man nodded his thanks and went on his way.

At the top of the stairs he encountered a problem.

"Damn it."

As he stepped, his left foot twisted floppily under him and he fell heavily to the floor.

"You alright, mate?" came the call from below.

"Fine," the Invisible Man called back, hoping his voice, when muffled by a beard, was not too dissimilar to Charlie's. "Just tripped."

"Be careful. Santa doesn't limp."

The Invisible Man sat on the floor with his back to the wall and lifted his left leg. The foot at the end of it drooped. He had lost all control of it and feeling in it; one of the increasingly frequent 'outages' in various parts of his body.

Yesterday he had woken up blind. That one had scared him. But his sight had returned within the hour and he was sure his foot would come back too.

Was that how it might be in the end? Parts of his body switching off one at a time until there was not enough left to hold him up? So he would lie in a heap somewhere, unnoticed by passers-by, dying by degrees, his brain trapped by a body in which the lights were being turned off one by one, until that final light too went out.

He could not help thinking that the prospect ought to scare him, or at least get some emotional reaction. But that light had been turned off long ago. Perhaps for the best. Besides, he had already decided that things would not reach that point.

As the feeling began to flicker back into his foot one tendon at a time, he settled down to wait. This was the worst part. He knew what time Santa was scheduled to go on and he did not want to pre-empt that big entrance because he wanted everyone's attention, but he had become fearful of being left alone with his own thoughts.

The problem was that he no longer felt 'alone'.

Two sides of his nature seemed to slug it out in his head, as his thoughts turned to the contents of his sack.

It's too mean, one side insisted, *too cruel to take something like gift-giving and turn it into a bloody horror show.*

No, the other side chipped in, *too easy. Letting them off too lightly after what they did to me. Remember the online abuse. Remember the marked-down books. Remember the cheers when I turned on the Christmas tree lights, and remember that I'll never hear those again. They deserve worse, so much worse. I'm not actually hurting anyone.*

Why would I want to hurt anyone?

Because they deserve it. All of them.

But to hurt? To kill?

I've done it before.

Have I?

Had he? Memory was going the way of emotion. He had no

memory of things that he seemed to have done. What remained, unaffected through it all, was that fiercest of desires; the desire to be seen, for better or worse. To be seen, and remembered.

They will remember.

What will they remember?

The conversation went back and forth with the ebb and flow of the different parts of his personality, as if, in that particular room of his mind, someone was flicking the light on and off.

In the sack were bones scoured from butchers' shops, bottles of blood, dead animals to be hurled from the rooftop into the crowd. But first he would pour the blood over himself. Then they would see Santa's invisible face appear before them, picked out in blood, and that memory would live in their nightmares their whole lives through. He would show them the gruesome face of Santa, and he would laugh at their screams.

Then he would jump to his death, and they would see Santa's broken body, made stark by the trails of blood seeping from it. They would never see the man in the red coat in the same way again.

It was an ideal vengeance.

As the clock ticked closer to the appointed hour, the Invisible Man stood up, shouldered his sack and made for the ladder which led up to the roof, from where Santa was supposed to zipline. Charlie had gone through the health and safety training yesterday, but for the Invisible Man it probably wasn't necessary.

The cold wind bit at him as he emerged out onto the rooftop. From below he heard the sound of excited children and parents, chattering and squealing. He hated every one of them. They had all abandoned him, they had all robbed him of his celebrity status. At that moment, with his anger peaking – that anger over which he had lost all control – the plan seemed like the best he could have imagined. They would regret what they had done.

The Invisible Man smiled to himself, though no one could see it, and opened his sack.

"Maybe the people of Cambridge would like to see their hero kill."

It was not the words themselves that arrested the attention of the Invisible Man, but the voice. He knew that voice. He had heard it at his birth. It was the voice that had brought him into this new world and stranded him in it. It was a voice that had inflicted unspeakable agony upon him. It had given him chances. But had left him without choices. For a long time he had not known how he felt about the owner of that voice; she had lied to him and made no reparation when her experiment went wrong. On the other hand, for a while, it had worked out well for him.

But when he looked back towards the voice now, and saw a woman being dragged along the roof by an invisible hand, he felt only rage. Not because he had lost his celebrity or because he was losing his mind or even because he was dying. It certainly wasn't anything to do with the helping the woman. He was angry because she had done it too. He had been a guinea pig. Now she was the invisible one, taking from him that claim to fame that was the one thing he had left. She profited on his suffering and then took his reward.

The Invisible Man saw red.

Chapter 25 – A Christmas Miracle

When Harrigan reached King's Parade, the festival-goers were just starting to turn their gaze towards the roof in anticipation of Santa's arrival. He followed Elsa as she forged a path through the crowd as if she had a cowcatcher out in front of her.

"How's he going to get to his grotto?"

"Zipline," said Harrigan, who had sat through the official briefing wondering if the Festival organisers would be doing the clean-up if Santa proved too festively plump for the wire.

"You don't think Santa could be a target, do you?"

"I can't see why he would be," Harrigan replied. But there was a lot about this case that confused him. An assassination attempt on Father Christmas seemed about average in the weirdness stakes. "Where's Amelia?"

"No idea. I told her to wait."

"Excuse me." Harrigan flashed his ID to a porter on King's College gate. "Did you see a woman come this way? Long dark hair, kinda short…"

"Not that short," corrected Elsa.

"…slim…" Harrigan floundered. He'd never been very good at describing women and these days found himself increasingly unsure what adjectives he was permitted to use.

"You mean Amelia?" the porter suggested. "Sure. She was heading for the library in a hurry." He shook his head. "Which is how she always heads to the library."

"Thanks."

Elsa and Harrigan ran on.

"I told her to wait!"

"Did you expect her to?"

"No, but that's hardly the point."

Inside, they ran up the stairs and into the library.

"There's a broken window up here," Harrigan called from the landing. "And I think something's happening outside." He could hear the crowds on King's Parade and the noise they were making had definitely changed in the last few minutes.

"We may have other issues."

Harrigan found Elsa in the main library, staring at a mass of circuits, wires and flashing lights that hovered just above the floor. As he watched, a metal case appeared around the electronics, its surface rippling, waves of invisibility passing over it, back and forth.

"Doesn't work so well on metal," mused Elsa.

"What is it?" asked Harrigan.

Elsa's eyes never left the offending box. "Could be a time machine for all I know. But if I was a pessimist I'd say it was a bomb of some sort. Though what sort, I am at a loss to say."

"Are you a pessimist?"

"No, I'm an optimist, but that's not going to stop it from being a bloody bomb. An invisibility bomb perhaps."

"So; what? Cambridge is going to vanish?"

"Maybe just King's Parade or…" Elsa stopped mid-sentence, her face blanching.

"What?"

"I just remembered; invisibility doesn't work on bricks, it…" She turned to Harrigan, her green eyes hard and serious. "You need to evacuate the Festival. I don't know what's going to happen if this thing goes off, but I don't think it will be pretty."

"What about you?"

"I'm going to try to defuse it."

"Do you have any idea how?"

Elsa shrugged. "At least I don't have to open the case to see how it works."

"But…"

"We don't have time to discuss this. You're police, so you do the evacuation. I'm technical support, so this little bastard is my area. I don't know how much time we have, but let's not waste any more of it."

Enough has probably not been made, thus far, of the genuine brilliance of Dr Carol Griffin. Though biochemistry was her chosen specialty, she was also well-credentialled as a physicist and engineer. The bomb (and Elsa was quite correct, it was a bomb) had required all of that know-how.

It went without saying that the invisibility process worked in different ways on different materials. Its effect on living tissue was conveniently similar to its effect on certain types of clothing (natural fibres, etc), which meant that she and Stuart Price had been able to remain clothed. But nothing with zippers. Not only was the effect on metal erratic and unstable, but it radiated that instability to other invisible items around it. On stone the effect was different again; it fluctuated wildly, then crumbled.

If Dr Griffin had done her sums correctly (and Dr Griffin *always* did her sums correctly – she was psychotic, not sloppy), then the bomb would effect most of the city centre; buildings and roads crumbling as they were hit by a wave front of invisibility fall-out. Some people would be crushed or suffocated, as for the rest... If they were pre-treated with monocaine then they would be made invisible and some might even be lucky enough to survive. But without a stabilising agent the process would shred them inside out, as it had a disgusting number of rats.

It is possible that, as she was setting the bomb, Dr Griffin wondered if she was taking her revenge too far. But unlikely. It was not just the R. C. Forrester Endowment Society who had laughed at her, it was the institution that had produced them and the city that had fostered that institution. They were all culpable. They would all suffer. Besides, it would be fun.

She had a car parked nearby and had already intended to be in it, speeding away from the bomb site, terrifying anyone who looked into the car as she drove past.

But things had gone awry, and the timer was ticking down.

Amelia had the breath knocked out of her as Santa attacked. She rolled down the slope of the roof, grateful for the little crenelated wall around the edge that stopped her from falling.

Looking back, she saw Santa locked in combat with the invisible Dr Griffin, his big boots finding more purchase on the slippery roof than whatever invisible shoes Griffin was wearing. It was a bizarre sight; Santa's weight thrown forward, leaning against apparently nothing. What the people down below thought was happening, Amelia could only guess. And they did not yet know that inside that suit, Santa was invisible too.

Who was this invisible Santa?

Stuart Price. It had to be. And Amelia was overcome with the desire to call to him, to let him know that she knew who he was and was on his side.

But as she thought this, Santa/Stuart flew forwards, tripping and falling flat. Dr Griffin had suddenly pulled away from him and his own momentum had taken him down.

A sharp 'Oh' of in-taken breath came from the crowd below.

As he tried to get back up, Santa's left arm gave under him, perhaps slipping on the roof, and Amelia scrambled back to her feet to go to his aid.

She barely got two steps before a blow from nowhere sent her reeling. Dr Griffin hadn't gone far. Again, Amelia felt fingers close around her throat, dragging her painfully up from the cold slates. It was then that the people of Cambridge realised, not wholly accurately, what they were looking at; the return of their fallen hero. The Invisible Man.

Something was happening outside but it did not intrude into Elsa's world. Her intent focus had erected a soundproof barrier around her, inside of which nothing existed but her and the bomb.

Peering through the casing, she could more or less follow the basics of how the detonation system worked, although the fact that random bits of it kept winking out of existence was unhelpful. The 'sciencey' bit in the middle, where a normal bomb would have explosives, meant nothing to her, but stopping the detonation was all she needed to worry about.

Now she had to open the case and, in the grand old tradition of bomb disposal cliché, cut the right wire.

Though Elsa invariably carried a pocket tool kit in her voluminous coat, she did not need it as whoever set the bomb had very decently left their tools behind. The case did not seem to have any anti-tamper precautions, all she had to do was carefully unscrew it. For a moment the side of the box disappeared while the screw remained, rotating in mid-air.

"You're just doing this to mess with me, aren't you?"

The love that the city had once had for its strange celebrity had long since gone, and they now booed the unseen figure on the rooftop. Which, Amelia considered, was nice, but not immediately helpful. They thought this was another stunt. They thought that some clever promoter had staged a mock battle between Santa and the Invisible Man, good vs evil. And she was the helpless damsel in distress to be menaced by one and saved by the other.

Did that mean no one was coming to help? She was aware of the sound of sirens somewhere behind the jeers of the crowd, but they were not going to get here in time.

"You did this to me!" It was the first time that Amelia had heard the voice of Stuart Price, coming to her rescue just when she needed him.

The fingers left her throat, and Amelia dropped again, too weak to stand. The Invisible Santa swiped a fist through mid-air and swore. He had once again lost his adversary.

"Go on Santa!"

"Get him!"

The cheers from below underscored the misunderstanding, and Amelia wondered if she should explain. Then wondered if she could explain.

The audience gasped as Santa's head jolted backwards as if he had been grabbed from behind. With his right hand – he seemed to have a problem with the left – he tugged at where an arm might be around his throat. With an effort, Santa tore himself free and a cry of shock exploded from the crowd.

As he had pulled away, the grasping hands of his attacker had torn off the hat, the beard and the glasses, revealing… Nothing. Every audience loves a twist, and no one had dreamed that Santa too might be invisible. Some people weren't sure this was a good idea from a narrative standpoint - it detracted from the drama having *two* invisible men. After all; which was the real one?

The Invisible Santa whirled about, desperately feeling for his opponent. He cried out in pain, going down on one knee as an unseen foot stamped at the back of his leg.

Amelia was on her feet again now, eager to help but not knowing what she could do.

"Uhhh!" The Invisible Santa folded in half as he was punched in the stomach, then jerked back up from a blow to the face. He was getting beaten.

The crowd were not engaged anymore; this had gone too far. They all knew – they all *knew* – that Santa would win in the end, but no one wanted to see him get beaten up first. That was supposed to be a light-hearted Christmas show.

Amelia rushed forward, flailing ineffectually. She was shoved back for her trouble, skidding on the rooftop and teetering for a moment at the edge, her heart in her mouth, before regaining her balance.

Santa stood straight again, ready to fight, tugging off his gloves with his teeth (what was wrong with that left hand?). But what chance did he have against an enemy he could not see? And then…

…it started to snow.

With a clunk that sounded ominously loud in the still silence of the library, the side of the case came off. The bomb looked pretty much the same; there was just one less bit of it to be irregularly invisible.

Elsa examined the workings one more time. That had to be the timer. Although it lacked anything helpful like a dial or numbers, Elsa had been able to ascertain from the flashing LEDs that 'very soon' was a good estimate of when it was due to go off. This, beside it, was the detonator, and these wires…

She took the bundle of six, or possibly seven or eight, in her hand and looked at them. One of these had to be cut. She really wished that they would all stay visible long enough for her to decide which.

Dr Griffin raised her hands. They made voids in the falling snow.

She could see the individual flakes settling and melting on the heat of her invisible skin, each one leaving a shiny spot of water.

The forecast had said snow was highly unlikely. It was a Christmas Miracle.

She looked up just in time to see the empty sleeve of the Invisible Santa driving towards her face.

The cheer that erupted from the crowd was like nothing Amelia had ever heard. Invisible or not, Santa or not, this unknown figure had been established as the good guy. He had taken appalling punishment as he tried to save the girl, and now he had landed his first blow. Catharsis was not the word.

The Invisible Man stopped as he heard the cheer. He looked down at the people below, and Amelia was sure she saw the ghost of a smile on his face, picked out by the whirling snowflakes.

He stood like a hero now and pointed a hand at the outline of Dr Griffin, shimmering in the snow.

"Give up. You're beaten."

As he spoke, the bell of King's College clock began to toll the hour. The outline of Dr Griffin threw back its head and laughed. It was a horrible sound, and Amelia's stomach tightened.

This one.

This wire.

This was the one she had to cut.

Elsa looked down to pick up the wire-cutters from the floor then turned back. Where had the wire gone? In the split-second she had turned away it had vanished. And not just that one; three or four had gone, and while she could find them with her fingers she could not tell which was which.

"Come back, you bastards."

Feverishly she tried to trace the path of each wire by touch, if she could do that she could find out which was the...

The sound of the clock bell from outside shattered the privacy of her sealed-in world and a cold sensation seized Elsa. She had no proof that was it, but somehow she knew that was it.

There was a wire between her fingers. Well, this one was as

good as any.

As the bell tolled, Elsa cut the wire.

At the last strike of the bell, time seemed to stand still. The chime hung in the snowy air, as if reverberating in the flakes themselves. Slowly it died away and the next second landed.

Amelia looked around. Maybe she had been wrong. But if she had been wrong then so had Dr Griffin, whose whole posture, as much as it could be determined, was one of; what the hell?

For a moment longer, the trio on the roof – the invisible scientist, the headless Santa, and the Egyptologist way out of her depth – stood, uncertain of what was supposed to happen next. Maybe the college clock was fast.

Dr Griffin moved first, making a dash for the stairs. Instantly, Amelia made to stop her. But her feet were uncertain on the smooth and increasingly snowy rooftop, and as she stepped forward she tottered. Griffin saw the imbalance, and shoved.

Amelia's feet seemed to go five different ways at once as she skidded backwards, her arms windmilling in the snowy air. She felt the back of her heel hit the little wall at the edge of the roof and she desperately tried to keep herself there.

But not this time. This time Amelia fell back into space and a scream went up from the crowd below.

Pawing the air as she fell, Amelia groped wildly for anything to cling onto. There was a flash of red before her eyes, her hand gripped something warm and the something gripped back. With a smack she fell against the wall and heard a grunt of effort from above.

Looking up from her position, suspended against the wall, her feet hanging not far from the statue of Henry VIII but not near enough to stand on his head, Amelia found herself holding onto nothing, just below an empty sleeve. Further up, she looked into the hollow interior of the Santa suit, peering over the edge of the roof.

"Thanks Stuart."

He didn't seem to hear her. As the snow continued to fall, Amelia could make out some semblance of his features as he stared into the crowd that was currently whooping and applauding.

"They're cheering for me."

Amelia nodded. "You're a hero, Stuart."

"Wow." The indistinct face looked down at Amelia. "You should know; I have no feeling in my left arm and the right may go at any moment."

Chapter 26 – Last Words

You couldn't help some people. Or at least not in Harrigan's estimation. Since his earliest days on the force he had found the same problem with crowds; the more you told them to disperse, the less likely they were to do so. Tell them they were in danger and they pressed forward to see what all this 'danger' was about.

It seemed to take forever for the vans to arrive, and all efforts he made in the meantime to get people out of the danger zone were futile. At least none of his kids were in Cambridge; they were safe. He should have called.

When more officers did arrive, the crowd began to realise that this was not just a show, it was real and it was life or death. They definitely weren't going to leave that.

"What is all this about, Harrigan?" snapped Lane.

"There's a bomb in the library," said Harrigan, bluntly.

"A bomb?" Chief Inspector Lane arched an eyebrow. "In Cambridge?"

"Yes." And to his irritation, Harrigan realised that his voice was getting defensive rather than angry. He was in the right and yet still backing down to his asinine superior. He should have been telling the man off while he had the chance.

Lane looked up at the rooftop. "Well, whatever else is going on, they certainly didn't get a permit for that." He pointed at Harrigan. "You stay here. You are no longer a part of this force, *Mr* Harrigan."

A better man would have said something pithy along the 'screw you' lines. Hangdog Harrigan just stayed where he was, watching dumbly as the police moved in.

Which was why he was only one who saw the window open. Taking a step back into the shadow of a building, Harrigan watched. He saw the Christmas lights reflecting off nothing, then a shimmering shape (like an energy alien from *Star Trek: The Original Series*) dropped from the window to the ground. Amongst the snowflakes, he saw the outline of Dr Carol Griffin, as she took to her heels, turning right down King's Lane.

Harrigan knew that it was a stupid thing to do, but his feet had already made the decision for him. He had spent a lifetime chasing bad guys, and if this was his last then he wasn't about to let her get away without a fight.

"Stop in the name of the law!" All those years on the force and he'd never said those words. Better late than never.

He saw the snowy outline before him look back and run faster. Maybe yelling had not been the smart thing to do, but smart had never been Harrigan's wheelhouse. He was dogged.

Careening through the metal bollards, he turned left onto Queen's Lane, imperious college buildings looming to either side. As he raced along, Harrigan was aware of an almost lightness within him, buoying him up. He would miss this.

"Get her down!"

Hearing Elsa yelling instructions gave Amelia some comfort, but she could feel the Invisible Man's grip loosening.

"What do you mean you have no feeling?"

"Legs going too," the Invisible Man murmured. "Everything going. Maybe adrenalin speeds it up. Sorry."

His fingers relaxed and Amelia clung onto the dead limb like a squirrel that has just noticed the cat in the garden below. But that would not be enough; the Invisible Man was losing whatever purchase he had on the roof, his body sliding forwards.

"There's no time! Just get something out there to catch them!" For a small person, Elsa's voice carried like a megaphone.

"You said hero?" The Invisible Man asked. "Did you mean that?"

"You saved my life," replied Amelia, unable to stop her eyes from flicking downwards. "Potentially."

"A hero." His voice was becoming slurred. "Do you think they'll build a statue to me?"

"Sure. I don't how, but I'm sure they will."

"That should get my book off the marked-down shelves."

The Invisible Man lost his grip.

It wasn't the longest drop – King's College is only three

storeys – but it felt a very long way, and Amelia gasped in a breath of hysterical relief as she landed in a tarpaulin that had been hastily stretched out beneath them.

"Amelia!" Jostling through the crowd, Jack seemed to come to her out of another world and another time. It was years ago she had last seen him, wasn't it?

He caught her up in his arms and held her. "Are you alright? What the hell happened?"

"That's a very big question."

Gently extracting herself from Jack's embrace, Amelia turned to see the man who had fallen with her.

The crowd had formed a nervous arc about Stuart Price, afraid to come too close, staring in wonder. Amelia scuttled over, scooping her hand under where his head ought to be and feeling the weight as she lifted it. The snow settled on his face, slowly revealing more of his features in icy pointillism. He looked up at Amelia.

"Was anyone filming that?"

"I think about half a hundred camera phones and at least one news outlet."

The snow twitched as The Invisible Man smiled.

"That's not celebrity. That's immortality."

The weight remained the same in Amelia's arms but she felt it shift as his body fell limp. The snowflakes showed the sag of his face, and yet the smile remained. No one here today would forget what they had seen, and they would not be shy about sharing it. Stuart Price was right; The Invisible Man would live forever.

"But we caught him," said a voice from the crowd – they might not be able to see him but they could tell what had happened.

"It wasn't the fall that killed him," said Amelia. "It was someone else."

By the time he reached the end of Queen's Lane, Harrigan had established that, invisible or not, Carol Griffin was in better shape than he was. He might be running on adrenalin and the thrill of the chase, he might be feeling younger now than he had in years, but he was still sixty five year-old Clive Harrigan, and adrenalin would only take you so far.

Not that he was giving up. He swerved right onto Silver Street, almost losing his footing in the snow, and ran on towards the bridge, scanning the road up ahead. Damn it; he had lost her, and in this old part of town every building seemed to have been designed to create alcoves for people to hide in.

He ran on. She had been running scared even before she saw him so the chances were she would just keep running, and as long as there was a chance he would keep going too. Reaching Silver Street Bridge, he glanced out across the water, still enough here to have frozen. He turned around…

From nowhere, Harrigan was body-checked against the low wall of the bridge. He cried out at the sharp pain in his back and tried to fight his attacker off, but he was already at a disadvantage, taken by surprise and bent backwards over the frozen water. Dr Griffin drove him back with frenzied violence, a woman possessed. Harrigan could feel himself sliding over the parapet, and with a cold sensation he realised that he had passed the point at which he could do something to stop this.

For a split-second there was nothing as he fell, then he hit the ice, smashing through into the freezing water beneath. Harrigan's breath instantly fled his body, the shock of the cold driving every nerve to panic stations. His thick clothes, soaked in water, dragged him down, his numb limbs like lead. With a last desperate effort he struck for the surface, but found only ice above him.

Couldn't he at least have caught his last killer? Couldn't he have died doing that? But that summed up the life and career of Clive 'Hangdog' Harrigan; so close, but ultimately disappointing. Nothing to write about.

In the event, the water silenced any last words Harrigan might have had, which, he thought as the void beckoned, might be just as well. '*Bugger*' wasn't really much of an epitaph.

Chapter 27 – The Statue

New Year's Day dawned bright and clear, only a scudding of grey cloud marring the ice blue sky.

Opening the window of her flat, Amelia shivered and her breath showed in clouds. Cold, inevitably, but at least the rain had held off. She showered, breakfasted and dressed smartly. She wanted to look her best for the memorial, which started at eleven.

The only place was Market Square, and that morning it filled with conscientious citizens, keen to pay their respects. At the Guild Hall end of the square, a dais had been roped off, and Amelia made sure she had a good spot in the front row. The crowd stood silent as the King's College clock struck eleven, then the Mayor made a brief speech, speaking of uncommon heroism and a figure who would be greatly missed. He then turned to the shrouded object beside the dais and pulled back the sheet.

Beneath was a pair of trousers, rendered in cast metal. They were a little larger than life-size and were caught in the act of skipping, one knee raised. No feet protruded from the bottoms but if you looked closely you could see the cunningly disguised support bearing the weight of the trousers on their low plinth. They were hollow all the way through, of course. On the plinth was a plaque that said simply, 'The Invisible Man – Here we go gathering nuts in May.'.

Amelia had been asked if she wanted to speak, but she had decided that everything she knew about Stuart Price – and everything that she might have wanted to say about him – was aside from that media persona he had worked so hard to cultivate. That was what made this memorial so appropriate. It did not commemorate the man, but what he had wanted to be; what he had made himself. It celebrated perhaps his greatest public appearance, one that had gone around the world and won him fans wherever it was seen. Stuart Price hadn't wanted people to know the details of his life before he became the Invisible Man, he wanted people to remember the celebrity who took the world by storm.

He would live on here in Cambridge's busiest thoroughfare, a place where people would pass him every day and remember.

Now he would always be seen.

What was not mentioned at the memorial, the subject that had in fact been studiously avoided by all, was the nature of the Invisible Man. Had he really been invisible? Everyone who was there that night said so. But, once again, as the pictures spread around the world the theories spread with them, of computer-generated trickery and of good old-fashioned stage magic. It should have been an easy question to settle, but Stuart Price's body had gone missing in a way that no one could account for. And so, with time, even the people who were there began to doubt the evidence of their senses, because; what was the alternative? He couldn't actually have been invisible. Could he? Was he? No. That was impossible.

In the end it didn't matter. Everyone prefers a mystery to the tedium of a cold, hard fact. The Invisible Man had thrived on that sort of divisive mystery throughout his brief but wildly successful career. Why should anything be different now?

In total, when everyone was done speaking, listening, looking and dispersing, the memorial took about an hour. Which was the only reason Amelia was not in Addenbrookes Hospital that morning, and so the first thing Clive Harrigan saw when he opened his eyes was Elsa.

He tried to speak, but all that came out was a sound like gravel in a cement mixer.

Elsa offered a sippy cup of water and the former-inspector took a pull on it then painfully cleared his throat.

"Am I dead?"

"Good question. No."

Harrigan pulled a face. "Dumb question. If I was dead I wouldn't be able to ask."

Elsa shrugged. "In my experience, it's actually more of a grey area than you might think."

"You must have an interesting experience."

"Oh I do, Mr Harrigan. I do."

"Okay." Harrigan looked about enough to establish that he was in a hospital room. "Next question; why am I not dead?"

"Another good question," nodded Elsa. "Especially since you did your damnedest to die by pursuing an invisible psychopath without telling anyone. You deserve to be dead really. But you got lucky. Someone was passing and saw you go in. They jumped in and dragged you out."

It was possible that, in the course of a patchily successful career, Harrigan never had a more insightful moment than he did right then. "Was that person you?"

Elsa's expression did not change.

"Thank you." It came out as a whisper, as tears threatened to choke him.

Elsa shrugged.

"I need to…" Harrigan sat up, suddenly aware of the various tubes and wires that were attached and inserted about his body. "I need to go. I should spend Christmas with my family. My sons."

Elsa pressed him back to the bed. "Small problem. Christmas was a week ago."

"I've been out for a week?"

"Well you did insist on swallowing a lot of water. And the Cam is not a clean river, by all accounts. The cold didn't do you much good either. Frankly," Elsa's gaze flicked away from him for a moment, "the doctors were making some pretty pessimistic noises about you ever waking up."

Harrigan lay back on his bed and stared at the ceiling. As his police career had ended, his life had damn near done the same. And now… it felt like a second chance. A second life that he was starting anew. It all seemed so clear now.

"I still need to see my sons."

"They've both been here," said Elsa, reassuringly. "Once you're done asking questions, I'll give them a call and let them know you're back with us."

"They came?"

"Of course they did," snapped Elsa. "In fact, if it matters to you, you *did* spend Christmas with them."

"First in a while," mumbled Harrigan.

Elsa leaned in. "Don't let it be the last."

Harrigan nodded firmly. Come hell or high water he would be there next year. He shivered; high water was not a subject he cared think about right now.

"Did we get her? Griffin?"

Elsa barked a humourless laugh. "Typical police." She got up and headed for the door.

"Elsa?"

Elsa stopped and turned back.

"I'm…" Harrigan groped for words. "I'm not sure I'm in a position to take you anyplace but… I wondered if you had dinner plans for New Year's Day?"

Elsa spent so long with her hand on the door looking at him that Harrigan wondered if she had frozen.

Finally she spoke. "Spend it with your family, Harrigan."

"Right."

"But I'm free tomorrow night, if the offer still stands."

Epilogue

Christmas Eve Eve.

Dr Griffin ran down the slope of Silver Street Bridge, slipping and sliding in the snow, her mind fizzing happily as she listened to the helpless thrashing of the drowning policeman. How had she gone this far through life without learning what fun it was to kill people? Whatever the reason, now she had tried it, she intended to keep going. It was a hobby that offered great variety, as well as getting you out of the house and meeting new people. It was so obvious that she again wondered how she had never thought of it before.

A flicker of doubt entered her mind. Could it be a side-effect of invisibility? The monocaine? No. After all, Price hadn't killed anyone and he had been invisible far longer than she had.

Then again, he *had* started to lose his mind. And while it was true that he had been invisible longer than her, he had only undergone the process once, while she had made herself invisible repeatedly over the last month. That was a lot of monocaine.

Perhaps she should take a break from it. Just to be on the safe side. There would still be people to kill after she had taken a month off.

The snow continued to fall. That was a problem, not only did it make her steps very uncertain (she had to find a way to make sturdy boots invisible), but she was leaving clear tracks behind her. The snow had not yet had a chance to be macerated by the passage of feet and bike wheels and was not falling fast enough to hide her tracks. She needed to keep moving.

As she turned right, following the line of Queen's Road but sticking to the grass in the hope of hiding her prints, her foot skidded out from under her and she landed on her hands. She swore under her breath; the last thing she needed was to leave more signs in the snow. She got back up but her foot skidded away again. Next time she was more careful, but as she put weight on her left leg it buckled beneath her.

In the cold she had not noticed the ebbing of sensation, but now, in a wave of frigid horror, she realised that she could not feel that leg at all.

With numbing fingers she groped for a stick to support her as the snow continued to fall, harder now, blowing into her. She tried to shrug it off. Was her arm merely frozen or was she losing the use of that as well? She tried to massage feeling back into her hands, then, with no other option left to her, began to drag herself along the ground, tugging her dead leg behind.

The unforgiving snow fell, burying her even as she dragged herself on. She had never felt so cold in her life. Her breaths shivered from her shrinking lungs, she felt the tears freezing on her eyelashes. This wasn't fair, this wasn't how it was supposed to end.

"Dr Griffin?"

With an effort, Dr Griffin turned her head to see a woman standing nearby. She looked almost as cold as Dr Griffin felt. She was shivering uncontrollably, her face almost blue, and Carol Griffin realised that the woman was soaking wet.

"Heh…" Dr Griffin tried to form the word 'help' but her lips and tongue were too cold to respond.

"The good news is," the woman spoke conversationally, "I am not the police. The bad news is you tried to kill a friend of mine. He may still die. So I am not well-disposed toward you. In fact, right now, I'm happy enough to stand here and watch you slowly freeze to death."

"…" Dr Griffin tried to protest but not even a sound emerged from her cracked lips.

"Your case couldn't go to trial anyway," the woman went on. "That would make the whole invisibility thing public, and my colleagues and I think it better to just let your experiment die. Perhaps you could die with it."

Dr Griffin resumed her efforts to crawl forward. Every movement it felt as if her brittle joints would snap with cold. The pain was unbearable.

The woman sighed irritably. "I hate being the good guy."

Dr Griffin barely had the sensation left to feel the woman's fist as it connected with her jaw, knocking her over into merciful unconsciousness.

Elsa stepped back, sucking her knuckles. "Well that was bloody stupid."

She stripped off her great coat and laid it over the prone, and still invisible, form of Dr Carol Griffin, then stood beside her, waiting.

A minute or so later a black van bearing the words 'Universal Exports' on its side pulled up, and two men got out. They carried Dr Griffin into the van, where Elsa joined her.

"One more stop to make. There's a body we have to collect."

The van drove off.

Having spent the Christmas and New Year's period bouncing between family and the hospital, watching over Harrigan, Amelia finally managed to catch up with Jack.

"Do you want to talk about it?"

"I sort of don't."

"Then we won't."

Who knew what Jack thought of her after the Winter Festival? He must have gleaned that she was more involved than she had let on. Perhaps he thought that Amelia was a member of an organisation like Universal. Perhaps he just thought she was someone who rushed in feet first without thinking.

Amelia had never thought of herself as one of those people. She was ill-suited to being one because anything that did not involve books, tea or Egyptology left her woefully out of her depth, and emergencies seldom involved those three in any great measure. By nature, Amelia was a housecat (or maybe house-rabbit; she didn't like cats), and yet something kept pulling her out into the big wide world to be an unadventurous adventurer.

Maybe she would be happier as a housecat (or rabbit) if she had more to come home to. Like Jack perhaps.

"I told you," Zita had said, when they met at Christmas.

"It's still early days," Amelia had hedged. "But thanks."

And Zita had beamed, knowing that she'd done good. "You're welcome. Now what the hell was the deal with you and my author?"

Whatever Jack thought of Amelia after the events of last

month, he kept to himself. As far as Amelia could see, his opinion of her was of a bookish Egyptologist and tea enthusiast whom he was getting to know in an openly romantic milieu.

Put it another way; he was more interested in her than what had been happening to her. And given all that had happened, that was pretty damn flattering.

She was in the mood to be flattered. Flattered in the truest and nicest sense; by someone taking an interest in her.

They went out to dinner and talked about anything but. They swapped family Christmas stories; Jack had visited his parents in the country; Amelia had loved the box of second-hand books her parents had bought her with the caveat '*We don't know what else to get you*'; Zita had adored her new dress (and had reluctantly accepted Amelia's refusal to answer the many questions she had).

"When are you going back to Romania?" Jack asked.

"Once the snow clears in the mountains," Amelia replied. "Till then I can work on deciphering the pictograms." She was looking forward to it, both the work and returning to the dig. For whatever reason, her uncertainties about what she was doing in life had resolved themselves. She was once again enthused by her work and keen to back to the exciting new discoveries they were making.

Ironically though, now she was eager to get back to work, she had something to keep her in Cambridge.

They stayed late at the restaurant, and as they left Amelia saw Jack open his mouth to ask if he could walk her home. She decided to take the initiative.

"Would you like to come back to mine?" She was kind of glad that it had worked out to be their fourth date rather than third; buck the trend!

Arm in arm, they walked back, Amelia very conscious of Jack's strong presence beside her. There was a warmth and simplicity to him which she found both comforting and homely.

When they entered the flat, Amelia closed the door behind her and turned to find herself in Jack's arms. They kissed. Tonight suddenly felt as if it had been a very long time coming.

"Make yourself comfortable, I'll get us a drink to warm up," said Amelia as they broke.

The light on her phone was blinking, telling her that she had a message. It could probably wait, but when you had family living so far away, then you listened to messages as soon as you got them; just in case. She picked up the phone, scrolled through the menu, and selected playback.

"Amelia? Maggie. Back at the site. Look... I..." The uncertainty in her voice was quite out of character for Maggie Moran. "Something's happened. In the tomb. Something's wrong."

The End

About the Author

Robin Bailes lives in Cambridge and has been writing in one capacity or another for the last twenty years. Outside of these books his fondest achievement is the 6-part comedy/drama web-series Coping, which you can find on YouTube (if you look hard enough). Robin's interest in old films began with a book about Lon Chaney that belonged to his Grandpa, resulting in a lifelong passion for cinema, particularly the horror movies of the 1920s and 30s. That passion has also led Robin to volunteer at London's Cinema Museum (where he can be found serving coffee at most silent film screenings) and to the creation of weekly web-series Dark Corners...
@robinbailes

Dark Corners

Co-created by Robin Bailes and Graham Trelfer, Dark Corners Reviews began as a bad movie review show on YouTube and has grown into sprawling collection of videos celebrating the best and worst of cult cinema. With new bad movie reviews every Tuesday and monthly specials about classic films, franchises or biographies, the show has a loyal following of movie fans from all over the world, pcople who share a love of cinema and a sense of humour. The success of Dark Corners directly gave rise to The Universal Library...
@DarkCorners3

The Universal Library

The idea of a series of books featuring classic characters from horror's golden age initially came when the movies themselves were being re-booted. There didn't seem to be a lot of optimism from the online horror film community about the studio's treatment of these much-loved stories and the idea was to do my own take, something that was tongue-in-cheek but also respectful. Hopefully the series meets with the approval of horror fans, film fans and neophytes alike.

Facebook – The Universal Library

Printed in Great Britain
by Amazon